**This Large Print Book carries the
Seal of Approval of N.A.V.H.**

WAYNE OF THE FLYING W

Ce

La

WAYNE OF THE FLYING W

Arthur Henry Gooden

CENTER POINT LARGE PRINT
THORNDIKE, MAINE

This Center Point Large Print edition
is published in the year 2013 by arrangement with
Golden West Literary Agency.

The text of this Large Print edition is unabridged.
In other aspects, this book may vary
from the original edition.
Printed in the United States of America
on permanent paper.
Set in 16-point Times New Roman type.

ISBN: 978-1-61173-869-8

Library of Congress Cataloging-in-Publication Data

Gooden, Arthur Henry, 1879–1971.
Wayne of the flying W / Arthur Henry Gooden. — Large print edition.
pages ; cm.
ISBN 978-1-61173-869-8 (library binding : alk. paper)
1. Large type books. I. Title.
PS3513.O4767W39 2013
813′.52—dc23
                                                    2013012360

TO

MAHLON F. PERKINS, JR.

CONTENTS

CHAPTER I
DRUMS OF WAR

THE big wolf trotted warily through the sparse clumps of bunch-grass that had found root in the sandy slopes of the arroyo scorching under the hot New Mexico sun. It was clear that some living prey lured the sinister skulker.

Stealthily the grey killer floated up the slope to a strip of bench-land, where a lone cow browsed on the yellowing buffalo-grass. Midway between the cow and the prowling wolf was a new-born calf, curled like a furry red ball under a juniper-bush.

The lobo had pulled down many a calf, and knew from experience the savage ferocity with which a range longhorn defended its young. Gnawing hunger pains rendered the wolf reckless; ignoring caution, the would-be assassin trotted boldly towards its intended little victim.

Perhaps a shifting vagrant breeze carried the killer's scent to her, or it may have been the watchfulness of a nervously apprehensive young mother that discovered the danger threatening her precious offspring. With a prolonged bellow of fright and rage the cow charged. Warned by the anguished call, the calf rose and scampered to meet its frantic parent. Scarcely three yards

9

behind sped the wolf, only to swerve as the charging longhorn intervened with lowered lance-sharp horns.

Foiled for the moment, the marauder circled, to be met with the threat of those rapier horns as the cow swung with him, turn for turn, the calf pressing close to the maternal side.

Like the great buffalo wolf, the cow was representative of a vanishing breed, a leggy longhorn, such as in countless thousands had come up the historic old cattle-trails out of Texas—that tremendous saga of cattle following the Civil War. The little new-born calf crowding to her protective side showed by white head and sturdy shoulders that imported Hereford sires had replaced the old-time KC-Bar longhorn bulls, for so the Hereford inevitably and surely marks his progeny.

Relentlessly the giant wolf continued his wary manoeuvring for the chance to leap in and slash a tendon. Thus crippled, the cow's defence would be ended—the calf won to his snarling jaws.

Rush after rush he made, only to be confronted with the long, spearing horns of the brave little range mother. From the distance suddenly broke a shrill cry—the crack of a six-gun. The dis-appointed wolf whirled, and streaked for cover. Gun spurting flame and lead, the newcomer tore past in hot chase.

The rider held no hope that a bullet would reach

the fleeing lobo. The distance was too great for a six-shooter; pursuit and bullets were merely grim warning to the marauder to seek distant hunting-grounds.

The appearance of a second rider from the mouth of a high-walled canyon sent the hastening wolf scrambling up the arroyo slope; a rifle leaped to the man's shoulder, and the first rider's trained ear knew that slugs from a Winchester .44 were screaming destruction at the disappearing grey killer. Still the beast ran—a thousand yards; again the Winchester spoke, and the wolf hurtled into the air—to lie limp and shuddering against a clump of yellowing bunch-grass.

Sheathing his smoking rifle, the man remained motionless in his saddle, steady blue-grey eyes gravely intent on the other rider, now leisurely loping towards him. He was long and lean, keen hawk's face darkly weathered by sun and wind, and, despite a somewhat harsh and forbidding expression as he watched the other's approach, was decidedly good-looking, with his high-bridged nose and firm, finely chiselled lips. A dusty black Stetson rakishly adorned dark reddish hair, and worn leather chaps encased black-garbed and booted legs. Blue flannel shirt and the inevitable bandana knotted loosely round bronzed throat completed his attire; and augmenting the rifle were two formidable six-guns in low-swung holsters.

High-heeled boots, chaps, wide-brimmed hat, gay neckerchief, the low-hanging colts, were not worn for embellishment. They were necessary equipment for the man who rode the vast wild cattle ranges of the West. The cowboy's work called upon him to face all kinds of weather, scorching sun and wind, rain and sleet and snow —the suffocating dust of the great herd trails. The wide hat-brim shielded his face from the sun and the back of his neck from dripping rain or snow, and the big bandana, with its wide folds hanging loosely under his throat, could be quickly grasped to wipe sweat and dust from face and eyes, or when the herd was churning great clouds of choking dust could be pushed up over mouth and nose. The leather chaps protected his legs from inclement weather and from the sharp thorns and spines of brush and cactus, that would otherwise rip trousers to shreds and tear the flesh. The high heels of his boots prevented his feet from slipping from the stirrups when he leaned back to hold a thousand pounds of wild-eyed steer plunging at the end of his lariat. And last, but not least, was the six-gun a necessity. Judge Colt was often the final arbiter in this remote land, where the law was still a feeble gesture. A man's lack of ability to use a six-shooter was likely to speed him to some nameless Boot Hill cemetery.

A startled expression fleetingly broke the Indian-like immobility of the man's countenance as he saw that the nearing rider was not, as he had thought, a half-grown boy, but a girl—a grown young woman—a slimly lissom figure in trig black chaps decorated with silver conchas, boy-like enough in the distance, before one could clearly see the lovely face under the wide-brimmed Stetson. That she straddled a saddle man-fashion in no way disturbed the serenity of her poise. The fair sex was still enslaved to the side-saddle and clumsy riding-habit decreed as the proper and modest garb for the horsewoman of the late eighties. Despite the bifurcated cow-girl of the cinema, young women of the Western cattle ranges had not yet adopted the masculine style of sitting a horse. Such defiance of modesty would likely have marked her for ribald jest.

The man's face darkened, perhaps with displeasure at the girl's costume, or perhaps some inward turmoil was roused by the glimpse of the brand carried by the sleek bay mare she bestrode. Whatever the reason, a chill expression crept into the watchful grey eyes.

"That was right smart shooting," she greeted. "Glad you happened along, mister." Dark-fringed golden-brown eyes coolly appraised him. "That lobo would have done some killing on this range if he'd got away."

He nodded. "Heard your gun. . . . Thought maybe it was worse than a wolf needed killing." His voice was unfriendly.

The girl's eyes widened, lost their friendly look. "Why—what do you mean?" she asked, startled. Then, curiously, "I don't think I've seen you before. . . . Thought I knew all our KC-Bar boys—"

His smile was bleak. "No—you don't know me." He shrugged. "You see—I'm not a KC-Bar man."

She flushed, eyed him doubtfully. "In that case what is your business on KC-Bar range?" she asked pointedly.

The grey eyes in the dark hawk's face held a hauteur that matched her own, and, sitting there, lance-straight in his saddle, he seemed in complete harmony with the wildness about them. The girl sensed it—was inwardly disturbed, troubled, as she waited for his answer.

"KC-Bar range?" His tone was bitter. "Yes— title vested in old King Cole by right of his hand-picked bunch of gun-fighters."

"I'll have you know that King Cole is my father!" cried the girl furiously.

He pulled the dusty Stetson from his head. "I'm humbled to the ground," he apologized, with an ironical smile. "So I'm talking to King Cole's daughter?"

She crimsoned from throat to brow, intuitively sensing that he was well aware of her identity from the first. "You knew the moment I rode up," she accused. "I saw you reading brand."

The young man shrugged his shoulders. "Yes—I knew you could be none other than Lylah Cole," he admitted coolly. A whimsical smile suddenly warmed his sombre face. "You see, I've heard plenty about King Cole's daughter—"

"And just what have you heard about King Cole's daughter?" asked the girl icily.

"For one thing, that her hair is the colour of a raven's wing—"

"I didn't ask for nonsense," she interrupted unsmilingly.

"For another thing, since you insist upon knowing what I've heard about you," he continued, with a frown, "I've heard that you're the only young lady in this part of New Mexico who dares to sit a saddle man-fashion—and get away with it." He chuckled. "Wasn't hard to guess who you were—black hair, like they said, bronc wearin' the KC-Bar iron, young lady forkin' saddle like a top-hand puncher."

"Why shouldn't I ride this way?" she defended. "King Cole is the law in this cow country, and King Cole's daughter can dress as she pleases and ride as she pleases. I'd rather lead fashions than follow senseless customs like a silly sheep—and you needn't sneer!" she finished hotly.

"No call to get on the prod with me about it," said the tall stranger good-naturedly. "Myself—I plumb admire the idea. Never could see the sense in ladies ridin' side-saddle." He nodded at her. "Reckon it

15

won't be so long till the only place you'll ever see a side-saddle will be in some museum."

The girl coloured under the approval in his eyes, curved red lips returned his disarming smile.

"Well," she said, mollified, "thank you for dropping that lobo, Mister Stranger." She studied him with a pretty frown. "And speaking of strangers—unless you have honest business in these parts take a tip from me and say *adios* to this range pronto." A note of warning was in the sweet-toned, friendly voice. "King Cole's outfit has no use for strangers roaming the KC-Bar."

His gaze was again forbidding and bitter. "My plans will keep me on this range for a long time, thank you just the same," he told her coldly. "Furthermore, I'm not quite the stranger to King Cole that you think."

Lylah stared at him, surprised, indignant; then, succumbing to overpowering curiosity: "Who are you, anyway, and what plans can you possibly have that keep you on my father's cattle range?" she asked him.

"My name," said the young man quietly, "happens to be Jeff Wayne—and this land you claim for the KC-Bar happens to be part of the Flying W Ranch—"

King Cole's daughter stared at him aghast, sudden fear in her lovely eyes. "Jeff Wayne?" she faltered. "*Jeff Wayne?* Why, Jeff Wayne is dead—long years ago!"

"Yes," agreed the young man bitterly, "long years ago—killed—defending what was his—here on the Flying W." He paused, added in a low voice: "But he left a son—"

"You mean—"

He nodded, a hint of regret shadowing his face as he saw the fear in her eyes. "You may as well know now as later," he told her; "there's a trail herd coming up from the Pecos country—three thousand head—wearing the Flying W brand—coming back to the range that King Cole took from my father twenty years ago, before you were born, I reckon."

"I was a baby," Lylah Cole said sadly, "but, of course, I've heard the story." Her face was as pale as the linen blouse she wore. "My father never intended the men to—to do what they did. But I am sure my father was in the right!" she added passionately. "Jefferson Wayne tried to bully him—defied him! KC-Bar cattle were on this range years before your father came to the Don Carlos Hills."

"Well," said the young cattleman, "Jefferson Wayne's son aims to defy him plenty more." There was grim finality in his voice.

"It will mean trouble," she protested, in a faint voice. "You must be mad! Go—before it is too late! Turn your cattle back. You do not know my father. . . . He brooks no opposition."

"There is range enough for both," argued Jeff

Wayne, unmoved by her frantic warning. "I've worked for this end for years . . . ever since the day my father was shot down on his own doorstep. I was nine then," he added, "and I promised myself that some day I would be back . . . that some day Flying W cattle would cover these hills and valleys."

"You don't know King Cole," she repeated. "Once his mind is made up he is as immovable as—those mountains." She gestured at the crags of the distant Sangre de Cristo. "He is the law in this country—men do his bidding, whatever that may be. His cattle range clear to the Lava Hills, seventy miles to the west, and east across the border into No Man's Land—all the country lying between the Cimarron and the North Fork of the Canadian." Her voice was suddenly scornful, her golden eyes blazed defiance. "Do you think for a moment that the great King Cole will permit this thing? Others have tried—have failed—as your own father failed twenty years ago."

For answer he gestured to the south. The girl looked, saw the lifting yellow haze low on the horizon, and knew that low-lying haze was the dusty banner raised by an approaching trail herd—Flying W cattle from the distant Pecos, in South-western Texas. She stared with stricken eyes.

"Reckon they'll be in by noon to-morrow," Jeff said placidly. Lylah felt that she hated him.

"Never saw buffalo-grass so good as this," went on the young cattleman. "Aim to range 'em from No Man's Land clear back to the Don Carlos Hills west, and south of the Rio Lobo here to Hondo Creek. Plenty of streams and plenty good bluestem in the bottoms."

"You're crazy," the girl told him seriously. "Do you think my father will let you coolly help yourself to nearly half a million acres of his best range?"

"He'll still have close to a million acres left," Jeff pointed out. "He can hog all the range he wants over in No Man's Land. . . . Not aimin' to run my brand east of the border."

"Rio Lobo!" sniffed the girl. "There is no such river—unless you mean the Rio Carrampao—" She gestured at the swift stream flowing from the mouth of the high-walled canyon above them.

"It's the Rio Lobo from now on," he assured her firmly. "Now it sort of commemorates the day we first met."

"I hate you!" she said viciously, the colour high in her cheeks.

"Couldn't expect much else of King Cole's daughter," drawled Jeff. "Just the same, Rio Lobo she is from this day on. Kind of like namin' streams and things," he added musingly. "Reckon there's a heap of canyons and streams an' all I'll be putting new names to."

She was silent, her gaze following the longhorn

cow walking briskly down the strip of bench-land, evidently seeking to rejoin the family herd. Close on her heels trotted the white-faced calf. She was a staunch fighter too, that little longhorn range mother, thought Lylah. Courage was a fine thing, and courage was something possessed to the full by this imperturbable, cool-eyed young man sitting there on his tall roan horse and telling her his wild plans to beard the formidable old man who was her father. Or else he was completely a fool, which she instinctively knew he was not. She had spent all her days among hard and tried fighting men, and knew courage when she saw it. Lylah fully recognized the utter fearlessness that looked out of those clear grey eyes—the sheer indifference to personal danger. She sensed in him, too, the same iron-willed determination so characteristic of her dominating cattle-baron father. The thought of these two coming into conflict left her limp with sickening apprehension.

Again her troubled gaze sought that distant horizon to the south, lingered on that trailing banner of dust that marked the approach of the Flying W herd. The sky had darkened, she noticed, and the dust haze was no longer yellow, but hung dark and menacing.

Startled, she turned her gaze towards bristling Saw Tooth Mountain; black thunder-clouds were enveloping the craggy peaks—sure sign of a late summer thunderstorm. Cloud scud was spreading across the sky, slowly obscuring the sun. She glanced at Jeff Wayne. He was rolling a cigarette, relaxed easily in his saddle and watching her reflectively, and not without regret, she sensed. She flushed, her pride touched that he should be analysing her chaotic emotions.

"You are determined, then, to go through with this?" She spoke quietly, her gaze squarely meeting his.

"I don't change my mind about things easily," he answered. His eyes saddened. "I'm sorry—"

Her slim figure tensed in the saddle. "It means—*war!*" she warned him unhappily. "I'm sorry too—"

The sun was gone, blotted out by the massing black clouds; they became aware of a curious stillness, an ominous hush. Lylah glanced apprehensively at the cloud-draped pinnacles of Saw Tooth; the black void above the mountain seemed to split asunder with myriad stabbing spears of flame—thunder rolled like drums of war across the storm-racked sky.

CHAPTER II
TWO BLACK BEARS

BLACK thunder-clouds pushed towards them from the south-west; big drops of rain spatted into the sand of the arroyo-bed. The girl looked ruefully at her companion.

"It's going to be a young cloudburst," she prophesied, "and home a good fifteen miles away. These midsummer storms come up so quickly," she complained.

Another terrific thunder-clap went reverberating from mountain wall to mountain wall. The bay mare pawed the sand nervously, laid her ears back. The girl tightened rein.

"Nothing to do but ride for it," she said worriedly.

Jeff shook his head, his frowning gaze on the embattled peaks of Saw Tooth, that of a sudden disappeared behind a solid sheet of water loosed from the lightning-riven clouds. "You'll never make it," he told the girl. There will be a world of water in the streams between here and the KC-Bar ranch-house before you're five miles on your way."

Lylah eyed the approaching deluge dubiously. None knew better than she the devastating power of those flood-swollen canyon streams. She had seen trees torn from their tough roots and great boulders ripped from their beds, and she knew, too, that more than one hardy KC-Bar rider had been swept to his death in the turbulent waters of ordinarily placid creeks. Her gaze went helplessly to the tall Flying W man.

"What else can I do?" she asked, in a plaintive voice. "No sense staying here to drown—" She glanced apprehensively up the arroyo, towards the narrow, high-walled canyon from which the newly named Rio Lobo forked round the upper side of the bench-land. "The spill-over from the Lobo will run this arroyo bank full as soon as the storm hits the upper canyon—" She broke off, annoyed at using his new name for the river. The big drops of rain were coming thicker and faster, hissing into the sand.

Jeff swung from his saddle and hurriedly tore at the thongs that bound his oilskin overcoat. "Put it on," he ordered curtly. Before she could protest he flung the oilskin round her shoulders, and reached up to button the throat-tab under her chin. Her brown eyes sparkled resentment.

"I'm not accepting favours from you!" she exclaimed. She jerked at the fastening, and found her fumbling hand imprisoned in his hard brown palm, his face close to hers, grey eyes stormy.

"Don't be a little fool," he said harshly. "We've got about ten minutes to make it to my place before the storm hits us in earnest." He released her hand and swung into his saddle.

She flung him an indignant look. His face hardened. "Are you coming, or must I drag you there?"

"I'm not coming!" she cried, furious at his masterful insistence, his amazing effrontery in thinking for one moment that King Cole's daughter would accept shelter and protection from this avowed enemy of the KC-Bar. She swung round the fidgeting bay mare; again his capable brown hand reached out—clutched her bridle-rein.

"Let's call a truce," he begged. "An hour or two of my company won't be as bad as getting all wet and cold—and maybe worse—"

The last vestige of blue sky vanished under the storm's dark mantle, which suddenly took on a ghastly green look. Hard on the lightning's flare followed a terrific clap of thunder that seemed to jar the earth to its foundations. The mare plunged frantically, and would have bolted but for the clasp of Jeff's hand on the bridle-rein. Lylah's face was pale.

"That was the worst I ever heard!" she gasped.

"Struck mighty close," declared Jeff. He spoke soothingly to his powerful roan. The well-trained animal was trembling, ears laid back.

The titanic assault of the elements had shattered Lylah's opposition. Stark primitive fear was the compelling force now, and drove her mutely to obey his gesture. Side by side they raced their horses up the hard wet sand of the arroyo towards the narrow portal of the canyon.

Towering cliffs shut out what little light there was, making the gorge a nightmare of darkness through which the rain fell with a weird hissing sound. Jeff took the lead, the big roan moving with quick, sure feet along a rough trail that followed the windings of the river. The bay mare pressed closely on his heels, as though fearful of losing the companionship of comforting friends. Even had she so desired Lylah could not have prevented the mare from following the roan horse and its rider.

The sound of the rain increased to a roar, a monotonous *crescendo* of fury that drowned out the clatter of their horses' shod hoofs. Above the ceaseless drumming of the rain rose the thunderous musketry of the stormgods—titanic salvos flung against the mountain-tops. Rivulets of water streamed down the oilskin coat that hugged the girl's slim form. Except for her rain-lashed face she was still comfortably dry. The oilskin, the protecting chaps that covered her legs, shed the rain perfectly. Lylah was grateful for the former. She knew that its rightful owner was in sad plight by now. His flannel shirt might turn an ordinary drizzle, but not this father of all rains.

He glanced back at her, smiled reassuringly under streaming hat-brim, and called out something or other, but the words were lost in the avalanche of rushing waters and rumbling thunder. She gathered from his gesture, however, that they were nearing their destination, though for the life of her she could see no sign of an opening in the sheer cliffs that formed the walls of the canyon.

A new note suddenly forced itself into the mighty cataclysm of sound, a deep-toned, thunderous roar that filled her with dread. Jeff was calling back to her, was urging his horse to a trot up the slippery trail, and the meaning of that deep-throated rumble was clear. The inevitable cloudburst had struck the higher reaches of the canyon up which they were labouring—was already hurling its turbulent flood downstream with the speed of a racing horse.

The thought of that irresistible avalanche of descending flood-waters was enough to chill the heart of the bravest. Lylah was frightened utterly. She knew that never in her nineteen years of life had she been so completely terrified. Frantically she urged on the mare, reckless now of the slippery footing.

The appalling uproar drove down on them with incredible swiftness. Lylah's heart sank. They would never make it—would never gain the safety of Wayne's haven from the storm. And then, to her vast relief, came a break in the towering cliff to the left, a gap scarce ten yards wide. Vaguely she glimpsed a man crouched high above them in a crevice of the cliff's portal. A rifle was in his hands; the barrel glistened wetly. An armed look-out, guarding this secret pass. Jeff called to him, made violent gestures. The man disappeared, and Jeff swung the roan to her side.

The roar of the approaching flood drove against their ears with the stunning impact of colliding worlds. Lylah needed no warning to make haste. That hole in the wall was the most welcome sight she had ever set eyes on. Smiling happily at her companion, she sent the mare flying up the steep ascent to the small clearing in front of the funnel-like opening in the cliff. Vague shapes came crashing from the bushes on the right, and two black bears, fleeing from the death awaiting all life in the canyon, headed for the gap at a clumsy gallop.

The sight and smell of the brutes drove the already overwrought mare into a frenzy of ungovernable terror. With a shrill squeal she plunged from the clearing and fled down the slippery canyon trail.

Lylah felt that her last moment had come. She was sure that nothing less than a miracle could save her—was sure that the mare could not hope to outrace that roaring wall of water dropping down the canyon with thunderbolt velocity. She was doomed.

CHAPTER III
MYSTERY VALLEY

FOR all that Death rode at her heels Lylah kept her head; there was nothing she could do, except pray that the runaway mare would not stumble—pray for that miracle. Suddenly a roan nose forged alongside, the powerful neck and shoulders of Jeff's big horse, the most beautiful thing in the world at that moment to Lylah. She heard Jeff's voice, ordering her to free feet from stirrups; she had already done so. The gallant roan drew closer, she felt Jeff's arm go round her waist, and the next instant he was holding her across his saddle and the roan horse was heading back for the safety of that narrow gateway between the towering cliffs.

The affair had been a matter of moments; the rescue effected within a hundred yards of the gap. Perfect coordination of mind and body, of horse and rider, coupled with flawless nerve, had performed the seemingly impossible. Lylah knew that she was always going to believe in miracles from now on, for a miracle had saved her. Her chaotic, racing thoughts went to the doomed bay mare. Poor scared Conchita—perhaps a miracle would save her too. She prayed it might be so.

She lay very still inside the encircling arm,

fearing to disturb balance and delay that race with Death. Cheek pressed against the sopping flannel shirt, she could feel the steady throb of this man's heart. Nothing panicky about the beat of that heart, just the strong, steady beat of courage, the heart-beat of a *man*. Lylah was sure of that, and her own heart was perturbed. This man was likely to prove her father's most dangerous enemy, and she had been taught to hate her father's enemies; and she knew that she never could hate this man. She had gone a hundred yards down the trail with Death at her heels—was returning over that same hundred yards with Life beating a new and wonderful song. So much can happen in Time's fleeting moments.

Jeff's voice reached her consciousness, his lips close to her ear. "Hold tight," he warned.

The roan horse went plunging up the swift ascent; powerful pistoning legs carried them swiftly across the little clearing towards the mysterious cleft in the granite cliffs. Behind them roared the turgid flood, wave upon wave, bearing on its crest the wreck and ruin of its violent passing. Horror seized the girl as she saw what they had escaped by mere fleeting seconds—and then the dreadful scene was gone from her eyes and they were riding swiftly across the rolling land of a long, narrow valley.

Rain still fell in torrents, although a clearing of the sky beyond the eastern wall of the encircling mountains presaged the storm's early passing. Lylah heard the hoofbeats of a second horse surging up on the farther side. A voice addressed the roan's rider in the soft drawl of a Texan.

"Gosh! Thought yuh was a gone coon, boss! Had me holdin' my breath." The speaker's voice grew curious. "Who's the kid? . . . Reckon he's fainted, way he lays there so still."

"It's a young lady," answered Jeff's voice.

"Yuh're outer your haid, boss. . . . Fee-males— they don't fork a bronc like this kid was doin' fore yuh picked him outer that saddle!"

Lylah lifted her head; twisted round for a look at the speaker, a gaunt, middle-aged man with drooping, grizzled moustaches and weather-bitten face. He stared with bulging light blue eyes at the lovely face under the damp dark curls.

"Well—brand me for a maverick!" he gasped.

The girl smiled at him; he grinned back, frowned thoughtfully.

"Say, boss," he offered gallantly, "reckon the little lady'll be more comfortable settin' my saddle. Ain't hurtin' me none to hoof it from here."

"Don't say I made you, Brazos," chuckled the young boss of the Flying W. He reined in the roan horse, and gently eased the girl from the saddle.

"Ain't a better-sensed bronc 'tween here an' the Pecos, ma'am," assured the grizzled Brazos, swinging from his saddle. "Ol' Rock-me-to-Sleep

I calls him, an' he'll ride yuh gentle as a lamb."

Those who know the Simon Pure cowboy will recognize and salute the chivalry of this bow-legged veteran of the range. A cowboy does not walk when he can ride a horse. The mere thought of walking is abhorrent to his nature. Also his high-heeled boots are not for that purpose. Lylah, knowing these peculiarities, was reluctant to allow this self-sacrifice on the part of the gallant Brazos. Furthermore, she was the least bit dubious of the honest character ascribed to the vicious-eyed, hammer-headed animal so affectionately known as "Ol' Rock-me-to-Sleep." She knew a bad actor in the horseflesh line as well as the next man; instinct warned her against Ol' Rock-me-to-Sleep. Not that she feared her own ability; she just was not in the mood.

She glanced at Jeff; his expression was non-committal.

"How much farther?" she asked.

"Less than a mile," he informed her. He gestured at a large clump of trees down the valley.

Lylah looked, and realized that those clustering trees would easily conceal the secret abode so cunningly established in this hidden valley. From where she stood she could see no sign of habitation.

"I think," she said, smiling at the grinning Flying W rider, "I think it will be a shame to make Brazos walk. . . . I don't in the least mind riding double with Mr Wayne—if Mr Wayne does not object."

For answer Jeff reached down a hand; she clasped it, slipped a foot into the stirrup he freed for her, and in a moment was up behind him.

"She ain't likin' your looks, ol' pizen-face," chuckled Brazos, resuming his own saddle. He was secretly vastly relieved at this solution of the matter.

Patches of blue sky peeped through the cloud-drift; the thunderstorm's fury was spent. With the lifting of the curtain of rain Lylah's interested gaze absorbed further details.

Sheer, towering cliffs, running from five hundred to fifteen hundred feet in height, formed a solid wall from end to end of the valley, which she estimated was four or five miles across at its widest, and some ten or twelve miles long. It was heavily grassed, and wooded with scattered groves of trees. Cottonwoods and willows marked the meanderings of small creeks, which probably emptied through underground channels into the Rio Lobo, flowing on the other side of the northern wall. An ideal location for a home ranch, she realized immediately.

The condition of the grass told her experienced eyes that the valley had not been pastured in years. She was completely mystified, and found herself wondering why her father's herds were not grazing on the lush grass of this lovely valley.

Surely he was aware of its existence! Some amazing explanation lay behind the mystery. Lylah was sure of that. King Cole always had a reason for what he did—or did not.

Lylah was destined to know the solution to the puzzle before many hours had passed, a solution that was to leave her breathless with amazement.

They were nearing the thick fringe of trees. Jeff, silent, apparently immersed in his thoughts, abruptly addressed the grizzled cowboy.

"Seen anything, Brazos?"

"Nope." Brazos chuckled. "Nothin' 'cept plenty dust comin' up from the south. Reckon Buck Saunders an' the outfit'll be ridin' in come sundown to-morry." He grinned. "Them cows'll sure be leg-weary time they hit the valley."

"We'll give 'em a week to rest up, then shove 'em through West Pass into the Don Carlos Hills," said Jeff. He frowned thoughtfully. "Got to get word to Buck to shove 'em up through Ute Canyon, and head in by way of West Pass. No chance makin' it up Lobo Canyon. . . . That cloudburst will have done plenty to Lobo Canyon."

Lylah listened, interested to learn that the valley had another entrance. The information might prove of value. There was, she told herself with feigned indignation, a bare possibility that this bold young invader from the Pecos would seek to hold her a prisoner in this valley. He might not be ready for King Cole to learn of the Flying W's invasion of the KC-Bar.

"What yuh mean—Lobo Canyon?" Brazos desired to know. "Figgered the name was Carrampao—"

"She's Lobo—from now on," drawled the boss of the Flying W.

"Well," chuckled the cowboy, "she was sure one mean, onery ol' wolf when yuh come high-tailin' through the Gap . . . sure was on the howl."

Widening vistas of blue sky opened above them; sunshine drenched the sodden landscape. And suddenly they were riding into a large clearing in the heart of the grove. Lylah saw a long adobe building, with side-wings enclosing a *patio*—an ancient structure, from its weather-beaten look, and obviously very recently repaired. She knew without being told that she was looking at the old ranch-house built by the slain Jefferson Wayne, the birthplace of the tall young man sharing his horse with her. There were other buildings, also showing signs of recent repair: a bunkhouse, a barn, corrals, in which idled some score of horses. The place had a settled air that told her Jeff Wayne and his outfit had been in possession many weeks. She marvelled at the secrecy with which they had carried on operations. King Cole was due for the surprise of his eventful life.

A wisp of blue smoke lifting above the kitchen quarters, the damp horses drooping in the corral, were the only visible signs of life. Lylah sensed that Jeff was displeased, felt a tensing of the hard-muscled shoulders as he reined in the roan horse.

Brazos drew a formidable six-shooter from his holster. "We'll give them cowboys one everlastin' scare," he announced grimly. "Sure will teach 'em to set round in the bunkhouse playin' poker an' leavin' the place wide open like they done."

Lylah could hear the murmur of voices percolating from the men's quarters, the gibes and jests of absorbed card-players.

Jeff nodded, drew his own gun. A startled yell arose above the uproar of crashing .45's, then a dead silence as the surprised Flying W men made cautious reconnaissance through window and loophole. Too wise, these experienced range veterans, to rush pell-mell into the open. Jeff and Brazos grinned at each other, pleased that though the boys had been caught napping they had also proved they were not to be easily stampeded.

Muttered exclamations from the bunkhouse, and presently a quartette of sheepishly grinning cowboys emerged from the door, followed by a short, rubicund individual wearing a soiled apron.

"A fine bunch you are!" rasped the outfit's young boss. "All hands and the cook loafing on the job. Might just as well have been KC-Bar gun-fighters shooting the place up for all you poker-playin' cow-nurses would have known what was going on."

"Shucks, Jeff," drawled one of the shamefaced

culprits, "not even them KC-Bar skunks would be out in a storm like that one we just had. An' at that we figgered Brazos was on post at the Gap and that Chuck Wallis was watchin' things at West Pass. . . . And there ain't no way in or out of this valley 'cept through them two holes in the wall."

"Talking fast don't get you anything, Curly," retorted Jeff. "You'll be looking for a new outfit to tie to if you don't mind orders better than you did to-day. Didn't I tell you to keep your eye peeled?"

"Reckon so," mumbled the crest-fallen Curly contritely. He was a short, stumpy, bow-legged man, with thick, long arms that hung ape-like from massive shoulders. He fixed pale, hard blue eyes on Lylah as the latter slid from the roan horse. Amazement filled his face when he saw that the slim young stranger wearing the garb of a cowboy was a girl. She met his incredulous stare resentfully.

"And you listen to me, Mister Curly," she warned him indignantly; "don't you call KC-Bar men skunks when I'm around!" Her sparkling gaze went to the others, eyeing her in silent wonder. "And that goes for the rest of you Flying W cow-wallopers," she flared.

Jeff slid easily from his saddle, his glance warning the startled men to keep silence.

"Boys," he introduced, "the young lady is King Cole's daughter. . . . Lost her bronc in the storm. You'll find her plumb peaceful if you don't go

36

stepping on her toes." He smiled down at the girl, conscious of surprise to find that the top of her head scarcely came up to his shoulder. She was smaller than he had realized, not more than a couple of inches over five feet. "Reading left to right, Miss Cole, you're looking at Curly Stivens, Ace Peters, Long Tom Jones, and Slim Dally—all of 'em top-hand riders, or they wouldn't be drawing Flying W pay."

Lylah's good sense told her that she had no grudge against these men. She knew the breed. Loyal to the last breath of life to the man he served. Rough and over-boisterous, perhaps, in his scant moments of relaxation, but ready at all times to make the boss's quarrel his quarrel too. His outfit's enemies were his enemies, as proved by many a bitter range war. His pay was small, his job man-size, and calling for that fine courage and devotion to duty required of every good soldier. Long days and nights in the saddle, in all the varying assortment of weather brought by the cycle of the seasons, with often his saddle for pillow, his groundsheet both bed and blanket. He might complain at times, but he never gave up a job. The blistering heat of summer or the fierce tempests of winter, the long, soul-galling months on the trail, with the great herds bound for distant Northern markets, the perils of the dread stampede, of dangerous river-crossings, the ever-present menace of marauding Indian and rustler—

these things were all cheerfully accepted as part of the day's work. As in all walks of life, there was an occasional bad man mixed with the good, but the average cowboy was well up to the average standard of manhood. He was loyal to his trust and chivalry itself to all good women. He worked hard, and played hard when he had the chance. And that chance was often only to be found in the saloons and dance-halls of the frontier cow-towns.

Knowing these things, Lylah's sense of fair play forbade any personal resentment against the Flying W's hardy riders. The code of the range demanded loyalty to their boss, and it was that individual who alone was entitled to her resentment for this amazing invasion of territory sacred to the KC-Bar. Her smile swept the group of punchers, who reddened with pleasure and embarrassment. Smiles from such a girl as this cool-eyed young beauty did not often come their way.

"Ain't yuh forgettin' me, Jeff?" asked a reproachful voice.

"Just saving the best for the last, Barbecue." Jeff grinned at the fat cook. "Miss Cole, behold Mister Barbecue Thompson, who put the cook in cooking."

"I hope Mister Barbecue Thompson will prove his fame to me very soon," laughed the girl. She looked at Jeff coolly. "A sandwich will help me on the ride home," she added. "And please have one of the boys saddle a horse for me. I really must be on my way if I'm to make it before dark."

A frown chased across his face. He avoided her gaze. "Curly," he said curtly, "you and Slim Dally get your horses and head for the Gap pronto. . . . It's your turn for night-shift as look-out. Long Tom and Ace will relieve Chuck Wallis at West Pass—" He hesitated. "I forgot—reckon Ace must get word to Buck I said for him to swing the herd up Ute Canyon, and come in by way of West Pass."

Obediently the men hastened away to make ready for their departure, and at a nod from Jeff old Brazos started for the barn with the tired roan and Ol' Rock-me-to-Sleep. Pink with indignation, Lylah flung Jeff a scornful look.

"Is it your intention to keep me a prisoner, Mr Wayne?" she asked, in an icy voice. "I observe that you ignore my request for a horse."

"You'd never make it the way things are," he told her. "Best for you to wait till morning. The creeks will have run off the storm-water by then. . . . No sense you taking risks—"

"I'm the judge of that," she declared. "I can ride with those two you are sending to West Pass. Won't be hard to find my way home from there."

"You are not riding anywhere till morning," he said bluntly. "Better get into the house and let Barbecue fix you up with some nice warm food."

"I know well enough why you wish to keep me here," she charged. "You fear that I will carry the news of this outrageous invasion to my father! You are not fooling me, Jeff Wayne!"

He gave her a thin smile. "Maybe you are right," he admitted. "You see, I've some three thousand head of cows due to come through West Pass to-morrow. Don't aim to have KC-Bar men interfering with my plans. Can't blame me for not caring to take chances, can you?"

"I'm going!" she stormed at him. "You know perfectly well that I can't stay here alone at this hateful place."

"You'll be as safe here as in your own home," he said.

A statement that Lylah knew in her heart was the truth. It was not fear of being alone with these men that really troubled her. Rather was it inborn loyalty to her father. It was his right to know what was taking place on his range. She was aware, too, that it was Jeff Wayne's right to do all in his power to keep the news from reaching King Cole until such time as he had strengthened his position.

"I didn't think you would bully a defenceless girl," she taunted.

He paled with anger, and, remembering those moments in Lobo Canyon, Lylah was stricken with remorse.

"Aside from any other consideration, I still think it would be madness for you to risk it so soon after the storm," he said quietly. "However, if the risk means nothing to you—and I let you go—have I your sacred promise to say nothing to your father of what you've learned?"

"You know I can't make any such promise!" she wailed. "It's his right to know anything I know about your plans."

"Don't you see what will happen if I let you get word to King Cole?" he asked gravely. "You know well enough that your father would make every effort to turn my herd back. . . . It will mean a fight . . . men killed—"

CHAPTER IV
KING COLE'S MEN

LYLAH'S good sense told her that what Jeff said was tragically true. To warn her father could only precipitate a bloody conflict. The thought was intolerable. It was best for her to remain powerless to carry the news to the KC-Bar. . . . Jeff Wayne had won the first trick.

Sadly she turned away, and seated herself on a bench placed against the adobe wall of the ranch-house. Savoury odours, the smell of hot coffee, came to her from the kitchen, where Barbecue was busy with pots and pans. Jeff followed her.

"I'm sorry," he said awkwardly.

She shrugged slim shoulders, removed her damp Stetson, and placed it to dry in the sunshine on the bench. Her thick black curls shone with a soft lustre in the bright sunlight; she fluffed the shining mass, thoughtful gaze on the tall young owner of the Flying W.

"You have been here for weeks—to have done so much."

"Since last June," admitted Jeff. "Was here last summer, looking the ground over." He smiled. "Yes, we've been right busy since I got in with Brazos and the boys. Lot of repair work. . . . Had things lined up the first trip in, so we knew just what to do and how to do it." He gazed round contentedly at the several buildings and at the newly erected corrals of split rails.

The men were riding away from the corral, two of them heading for West Pass and the others turning towards Lobo Canyon Gap. Brazos watched from the barn door, arms akimbo, thumbs hooked in cartridge-belt. Jeff called to him, and the cowboy hurried across the yard.

"Grab some food," ordered Jeff, "and then go post yourself at Lone Butte. . . . Not worrying right now about Lobo Gap, but can never tell what may happen over at West Pass. When Buck gets here we'll keep two of the boys on look-out there day and night. If we ever have trouble it will be at West Pass."

Brazos grinned at the girl, hitched up sagging gun-belt, and clattered into the kitchen.

"What's the Lone Butte?" queried Lylah curiously.

Jeff indicated a columnar mass rising sheer from the floor of the valley some three miles from the ranch-house. She saw that its lofty summit commanded a view down the valley to the Pass, and north of Lobo Gap.

"Keep a telescope there," Jeff informed her. "Can catch signals from the Pass or the Gap in case of trouble."

The girl smiled derisively. "Lot of good signals will do you once KC-Bar men come riding into the valley," she scoffed. "You'd be outnumbered."

"Well," drawled the young cattleman, "Buck has a dozen mighty good boys with him, and counting Barbecue there are eight of us here. Yes, ma'am—reckon the Flying W can muster some twenty top-hand riders and fighters, all told. Hand-picked 'em my own self, and shouldn't be surprised if your KC-Bar fellers will think they've got a mighty mean bull by the tail if they start an argument with us." He moved towards the door. "I'll tell Barbecue to fix something for you to eat out here in the sunshine. . . . Be with you soon as I've changed into some dry clothes."

She called him back. "It was nice of you to let me wear your slicker." Her smile lingered on him, warm and friendly. "And I—I haven't thanked you for what you did. I—I wouldn't be alive—but for—you—"

He flushed, and disappeared quickly through the door, and presently the jovial Barbecue came out

43

to her with a box which he turned over and covered with a piece of what suspiciously resembled a well-washed flour-sack. He caught her amused glance, and grinned complacently.

"Ain't often we have wimminfolk visitin' the Flying W," he chuckled. "But, ma'am, we sure knows our manners when a lady *does* drop in. Now, ma'am, the beef herd ain't arrived yet, but I can serve yuh as tasty a cut of fried deer meat as yuh ever et—an' hot biscuits right outer the oven, sopped in gravy, and a cup of good ol' Arbuckle—"

A tin plate of sizzling venison was soon placed before her, and a large tin cup of steaming coffee, not to speak of the biscuits sopping in their rich brown gravy. Lylah discovered that she was ravenous, and hugely delighted the attentive Barbecue by demanding a second cup of his coffee. Brazos sauntered out of the kitchen, wiping drooping moustaches on shirt-sleeve.

"Well, ma'am," he drawled, in a satisfied voice, "mebbe there are better cooks than ol' Barbecue— but I ain't met up with none of 'em." He jingled on his way to the corral, duty bound for the look-out station at Lone Butte.

Lylah's spirits, temporarily cheered by hot food and drink, began to droop. She was more worried than she cared to admit. What would her father think upon discovering her absence from the KC-Bar ranch-house? He had ridden off early that morning accompanied by Steve, her elder step-brother, and Bart Sladen, the KC-Bar foreman. She had supposed they were planning to inspect one of the line-camps north of Carrampao Canyon, and later had ridden in that direction, thinking to spend the day with them, only to learn from the camp-tender that King Cole had not ridden that way. Returning by a seldom-used short cut, she had chanced to glimpse the sorely pressed mother cow making her plucky fight to save her bald-faced progeny from the big wolf. And then this startling affair with Jeff Wayne, son of the man slain twenty years ago by KC-Bar men sent by her father to run him off the range he had claimed for his Flying W brand. She had left no word at the ranch-house as to her destination. They would blame the storm for her absence. Her father would be frantic with fears for her safety . . . KC-Bar men would be searching the range for her lifeless body.

Lylah's eyes filled with tears. It was cruel of Jeff Wayne, detaining her in the circumstances. Almost was she tempted to give him the promise he demanded as the price of her liberty. But deep in her heart she knew the promise would not be kept. King Cole was a relentless inquisitor. . . . He would drag from her the full story of her adventures. It was not easy to deceive King Cole.

Reluctantly the girl put the thought away. She could not deal falsely with Jeff Wayne—not after what he had done that afternoon. Something had happened to her during those brief moments in his arms when her cheeks had pressed against that strong, steady heart. She wanted to hate Jeff Wayne with the relentless hatred that hardens the heart against the suffering of one's enemies. Instead she found herself passionately desiring to shield Jeff Wayne from the annihilating wrath of her father. What was this emotion that gripped her so profoundly?

Soberly she asked herself the question, her dreamy gaze on the lofty crags of the distant Sangre de Cristo Mountains. From somewhere in the old adobe house sounded the tread of booted feet. Lylah's heart began to beat wildly; she knew then the answer to her question. Her golden-brown eyes widened; she felt oddly breathless—and giddy; was conscious, too, of a strange fierce happiness that hurt.

Shaken by this self-revelation Lylah struggled to regain her composure. Jeff Wayne would never know her secret from anything she might say or do, she fiercely promised herself. She suddenly smiled. But if Jeff Wayne fell in love with her—ah!—that would be a different matter—and Jeff Wayne's wooing would be put to the test before he learned what she already knew. Another startling thought swept warmingly through her. Old King Cole would deny his daughter nothing—not even the love of Jeff Wayne. . . . It would mean peace—

not war—between the KC-Bar and the Flying W.

The radiance of her face quite startled Jeff. She saw the surprise in his eyes, and smiled demurely.

"You see, I can be fairly cheerful in spite of your cruelty in holding me a prisoner in your fortress," she greeted.

He looked at her searchingly, secretly perturbed, and wondering if she were hatching some plan of escape and was attempting to put him off guard with a show of amiability. She read his thoughts.

"So you doubt me?" she gibed. "Well, I haven't given you my parole not to escape if I can, have I? Or will you bind me in chains and lock me up in your dungeon unless I promise not to run away?"

"You'd not get very far," he warned sombrely. He hesitated. "Would you care to look round the place? Help pass the time."

"I was going to suggest it," Lylah declared. She jumped up from the bench. "We'll make believe that I'm an honoured guest." She laid her little hand in his hard brown palm. "At any rate, we can be friendly enemies for the time—"

Jeff chuckled. "You must see my Palominos," he told her. "You'll want to turn horse-thief when you lay eyes on them."

She looked with admiration at the two animals in the big loose-box especially built for them in the barn. Pale yellow coats shining like satin, and luxuriant tails and manes the colour of silver, they were as trim and graceful as blooded Arabians.

"Three and four years old," Jeff told Lylah, pleased at her enthusiasm. "A Mexican don down in Sonora thought I did him a favour once, and gave them to me. The mare was a yearling—the horse just turned two."

Jeff was soon to learn that Señor Ricardo Gonzales was still mindful of that favour, and that its memory was to have a singular bearing on his twenty-year feud with Lylah's implacable old father.

"They're both beauties!" exclaimed the girl.

"Gentle as kittens—both of them," he assured her. "No bronco-buster has handled them. . . . Trained them myself, and a child can ride either of 'em."

"I suppose you wouldn't sell the mare," she observed longingly.

Jeff shook his head. "She was a gift to me," he said, "but if you will be a good neighbour and drop in now and then I'll let you ride her," he promised.

"Not much chance of that," retorted Lylah, assuming a hauteur she was far from feeling. "I am afraid you will never see me here again, Mister Jeff Wayne."

She was secretly delighted at the sudden gloom on his face, and could not refrain from twisting the knife. "You mustn't take too much for granted merely because I am trying to make the best of an unpleasant situation," she went on cruelly. "In your relentless determination to get the best of my father you have not stopped to think what it means for a girl to find herself forced to spend the night in a strange place, with only strange men for company. My father and brother will hunt you down like a dog—"

The blood rushed to Jeff's face; he stared at her with horrified eyes. And Lylah saw with amazement and relief that this aspect of the affair had not until this moment entered Jeff's mind. His own innate decency and cleanness had been the cause of his seeming callous indifference to the chance he was taking with her reputation.

"I'll never tell them," she added, in a softened voice. "You saved my life this afternoon—"

"It's not that . . . I'm not scared of your men," he said, in a low voice. "Just afraid I'm an awful dumb animal—" He strode to his saddle on its peg behind a stall in which stood the big roan horse.

"Why—what are you going to do?" she asked, in a startled voice.

"Get you back home if we have to swim every creek between here and the KC-Bar," he said gruffly.

"Listen!" exclaimed the girl. "Somebody coming—riding fast—"

Jeff's hand left the saddle. The sound was unmistakable; the dull thud of furiously galloping hoofs. He leaped from the stable door, hand reaching down to six-shooter. Lylah followed

49

close on his heels, in time to see Brazos make a flying leap from his saddle and dash into the ranch-house. His excited voice came to them:

"Jeff! Jeff!"

He reappeared—saw Jeff and the girl running across the yard. "Jeff!" bellowed the old cowboy, "hell's done broke loose in the valley! . . . Ol' King Cole an' his bunch of gun-fighters has nabbed our boys at West Pass. . . . Saw them pull the play through the glasses. . . . They're ridin' this way hell-bent to git us—"

Lylah's heart shrivelled; she began to tremble, her frightened white face turned to the owner of the Flying W.

"He must not see me here!" Jeff and Brazos were looking at her. In the kitchen doorway appeared the rotund Barbecue. "He—he will kill you—if he finds me here. . . . Oh, I just know he will!"

She fled into the old ranch-house, saw the fat cook take down a huge Sharps buffalo-gun from the wall, and turn to one of the loopholes that pierced the thick adobe walls on either side of the main door. The sight of this businesslike preparation brought her to a pause, shuddering. Barbecue threw her a cheerful grin.

"Yuh'd best keep clear o' the door, ma'am," he warned. "No tellin' when plenty hot lead'll be flyin'."

She stood irresolute. Brazos hurried in, slammed the heavy door shut, and crouched at the other loophole, leathery face grim, hairy hands caressing a Winchester. Lylah's heart stood still. . . . Jeff Wayne was remaining outside—would face single-handed those rapidly approaching KC-Bar riders led by turbulent old King Cole. Alas for her beautiful plans to bring about a lasting peace between these warring clans of the range!

CHAPTER V
AFTER TWENTY YEARS

ONE sensed sinister intent on the part of the score or so of horsemen bearing down on the young owner of the Flying W. They came on confidently, obviously contemptuous of any resistance that could be opposed to their numbers. Routing out "nesters" and kindred unwelcome invaders of the range was just another job to the efficient riders of the KC-Bar. Perhaps the presence of the "Big Boss" was an added fillip to self-assurance. As with Napoleon and his Guards, so it was with King Cole and his hard-riding warriors. KC-Bar men never doubted the issue when the "Big Boss" rode in the battlefront.

Jeff's narrowed gaze shrewdly appraised the weazened little man who was the formidable King Cole—and the father of Lylah. The seventy odd years that had grizzled his hair and long, drooping moustaches had not despoiled the slight, bony frame; time had merely toughened and seasoned him, as it toughens and seasons good, honest hickory or oak. He rode easily, in perfect accord with the movement of the great black stallion under him, his gaze boring down on the young man coolly waiting in front of the ranch-house door. A beetling nose gave him a bold, predatory look. Unlike the others, he wore neither guns nor chaps, and the boots encasing black trousers were guiltless of spurs.

Closely following the old cattle baron rode two men whom Jeff surmised were Lylah's step-brother, Steve, and Bart Sladen, the KC-Bar foreman. Both men were in the late thirties, and both aroused in Jeff a quick and abiding dislike. There was nothing of the eagle-eyed Cole in Steve. He looked mean and vicious. Jeff was to learn that he was both.

The giant foreman was a more formidable person. There was bull-strength in those mighty shoulders and ruthlessness in the small, intelligent black eyes. A capable, but dangerous, man, Jeff sensed.

Fifteen yards now separated him from those approaching sinister visitors. Oddly enough his thoughts went to the girl hiding behind the adobe walls of the ranch-house. She was young to be the child of this old man riding towards him on the big black stallion. Vaguely he recalled that King Cole had married a second time, in his early fifties—a señorita of Old Mexico—which accounted for Lylah's blue-black hair and dark eyes. Hers was the flawless beauty so often the fruit of these mixed unions.

The trampling of hoofs on soggy ground hushed, and the jingle of spurs, the squeak of damp saddle leathers.

"So—Jefferson Wayne's son has come back—"

There was an odd note of satisfaction in the old man's dry, rasping voice, a sardonic gleam in his cold blue eyes.

"I promised I would come back—some day," the young man reminded him quietly.

King Cole leaned forward, his hands resting on the high pommel of his saddle, sardonic amusement in his searching gaze. "I've been waiting for you, boy." He smiled. "Twenty years is a long time, but I knew you'd be back some day—and I've been waiting." The old cowman chuckled. "Got your message once a year . . . got all twenty of 'em saved up—telling me you'd be back. . . . Yes, I've been waiting—and ready for you—"

"Meaning just what?" queried Jeff, taken aback by this gentle irony. His watchful gaze went to the clustering riders, saw with some astonishment that they shared his own perplexity at King Cole's inexplicable mood. Surprise was plain on their hard faces, and there was an exchange of uneasy glances between Sladen and the sullen-faced younger Cole.

53

"Are you a fool? Do you think for a moment that I haven't known what has been going on here in Crater Basin these last months?" The old cattleman's voice was suddenly harsh. Implacable hostility glared from those fierce blue eyes.

The impact of that menacing look shook Jeff, sent a sickening wave of doubt through him. This old man was more than formidable—he was irresistible. Lylah had warned him aright. As immovable as the mountains, she had said. Yes, that was King Cole of the KC-Bar.

The momentary panic left Jeff. "So you've known all along, huh?" His smile was derisive. "Mighty nice of you to drop in, mister." Jeff's glance flickered over the tensely listening cowboys. "But why the army? You must be a heap worried of meeting trouble in this valley . . . ghosts, maybe—"

Stifled gasps from the cowboys and the darkening scowl on the old cattleman's face told Jeff that his reference to the sinister affair of twenty years earlier was plain to all. His tone hardened.

"Also, Mr Cole, I'm asking you about three of my men you must have run into back at West Pass. Be just too bad if anything has happened to them."

"What we foolin' for?" grumbled a voice. "Let's finish this job pronto—"

King Cole glared round at the speaker. "Shut up, Steve!" he rasped angrily. His fierce, warning scowl swept the KC-Bar contingent. "Back! . . . All of you. I'm talking to this young man alone."

Bewilderment on their faces, the men swung their horses to a position midway between ranch-house and corrals, Steve Cole and Sladen reluctantly following at a fierce gesture from their glowering chief. A stealthy movement from the adobe wall caught Jeff's alert ears. Barbecue's big Sharps rifle had shifted to cover the distant group of riders. He glanced slyly at the other loophole; the muzzle of Brazos' Winchester likewise peeped inconspicuously at the visitors. Unless King Cole wore a concealed shoulder-gun there was nothing to fear from him, and Jeff Wayne had not yet met the man who could beat him to the draw.

If King Cole was aware of those rifles menacing his men he made no sign. Jeff was confident he had not observed them. The loopholes were cunningly contrived; only searching scrutiny would betray their presence.

"So—you are Jefferson Wayne's boy," mused the old cattleman, in a softened voice.

Jeff shrugged his shoulders, eyed him impatiently.

"He was a good man," said King Cole surprisingly. "You're the image of him, boy—"

"He lies less than two hundred yards from here—in the grave I dug after you murdered him!" blazed Jeff.

"I had no hand in it," interrupted the owner of the KC-Bar.

"I was only nine," went on Jeff relentlessly. "I saw my father and his men slain, his Flying W cattle driven away. I was too young then to fight, but I swore that some day I would be back, and that Flying W cows would again cover Flying W range. I sent you that message every year for twenty years, and now I'm back—to stay."

"I got your messages," said King Cole. "Was hoping you'd keep the promise. And listen to me, Jeff Wayne. . . . I had no hand in the death of your dad. We weren't friends . . . we didn't see eye to eye 'bout range rights; but he was a good man 'cording to his lights, and I never have shot down his sort on his own doorstep or anywhere else—"

"I was there," broke in Jeff. "I saw the men, Mr Cole . . . the horses they rode wore your KC-Bar iron. Don't tell me you had no hand in my father's killing! You didn't do the job in person, but your hired gun-fighters did it for you under your orders."

"Not under my orders," denied the cattleman. "I'd warned your dad there would be trouble if he didn't keep his cows off KC-Bar range . . . told him there would be no trouble so long as he kept to the valley here. Plenty grass here in the valley for all the cows wearing the Flying W iron."

The young Flying W man's smile was mirthless. "Generous, weren't you?" he retorted scornfully.

"There's all of a hundred thousand acres lying between these hills," asserted King Cole. "He could have run two or three thousand head the year round and kept them fat."

"He was aimin' to spread out some," Jeff told him mildly. "Maybe his mind worked in a big way, Mr Cole . . . same as yours does—and the way my mind works. I'm aimin' to spread out some myself, now I'm back."

King Cole's smile was bleak. "I come here to talk peace, and you go makin' war talk," he complained.

"I don't want peace on your terms," declared Jeff. He looked significantly at the waiting KC-Bar riders. "Sure looks peaceful that outfit of yours, armed to the teeth." His face hardened. "I was asking you about those three boys of mine back at West Pass. . . . You ain't answered—"

"Needn't worry none about those *hombres*," chuckled the old man. "You'll find 'em a bit peevish, maybe, on account of us having to hog-tie 'em so they wouldn't get hurt." His tone changed. "Now, you listen to me, young feller. . . . There is one thing you've got to take my word for. I had no hand in the killing of your dad. Some of the boys riding for me did the killing, sure enough, and the man that put 'em up to it was an *hombre* name of Sam Staver—"

"He was your foreman," charged Jeff.

"Not after what he did," growled King Cole. "Seems that Sam Staver was runnin' with the wild bunch—turned rustler. Your dad caught him red-handed, and was aimin' to tell me what was goin' on under my nose. So Sam Staver tells the boys I said go and fill Jefferson Wayne full of hot lead." He shook his head sadly. "Everybody knew I'd warned Jefferson Wayne to keep off KC-Bar range, and they just naturally reckoned I'd taken the easiest way to keep him off."

The old cattleman's earnestness impressed Jeff. The story rang true—was true; and for some unexplainable reason he was suddenly glad to know it was true.

"This Sam Staver—" he began.

"I always hang a rustler," King Cole told him bluntly. "Sam tried it once too often, and I nabbed him. When the rope was round his neck he came clean with the truth about the killing of your father."

Jeff nodded. There was a dazed look in his eyes. For twenty years he had regarded this man as the murderer of his father, and now—

"I'm sorry to have misjudged you, sir," he said simply.

"You believe me, then, Jeff Wayne?" Vast relief was in the old man's voice.

"Yes, sir, I believe you."

King Cole leaned down from his saddle. "We'll shake on it," he said huskily.

CHAPTER VI
A STETSON HAT

THEY clasped hands, to the amazement of the watching cowboys, and to the relief of Brazos and Barbecue, straining eyes and ears at the loopholes. The former grinned round at the tensely listening girl.

"They've shook hands," he whispered.

Lylah gave him a smile. Her straining ears too had caught the gist of the conversation between her father and Wayne. She could have hugged the grizzled old puncher.

"Now listen to me some more," went on King Cole's voice. "From the day I learned the truth, after I got your first message telling me you aimed to be back some day, I've held Crater Basin sacred to the time of your return . . . closed West Pass and the Gap against my own cows. 'It belongs to Jefferson Wayne's boy,' I told myself, 'and until he comes back to it no man shall enter.'"

Jeff stared at him, too astonished to speak, but understanding now, as Lylah too was understanding, why no KC-Bar cattle were to be found grazing the wild grasslands of Crater Basin.

King Cole's eyes twinkled. "Knew when you came last year to look things over." He chuckled. "Knew when your outfit rode in last June and set to work fixing the place up. Not a day has gone by without a report of your doings, Jeff Wayne."

"Never spotted anybody watching us," marvelled the young man.

"No one ever sees Chaco when he aims not to be seen," stated Lylah's father. "Chaco's a Yaqui Indian. He can't be beat for trailin'. Knows things about these parts that none of us ever will know."

Jeff grinned. "Reckon this Chaco *hombre* told you I've got a trail herd heading this way . . . coming up from the Pecos."

"Reckon Chaco did," admitted the old KC-Bar man. "All right with me, so long as you keep 'em in the valley."

"The valley's a good place for 'em—after the long drive up from the Pecos," agreed Jeff. His steady gaze met the old cattleman's frown squarely. "Soon as they get back some of the fat they'll have lost I aim to push 'em through West Pass back into the Don Carlos Hills country, and south down to Honda Creek."

"You're as mulish as your dad," growled King Cole. "Listen to me, young feller. . . . You won't find many of your cows come next round-up."

"Makin' war talk, sir?"

"Not war talk," rasped the KC-Bar owner. "Just giving you some facts. Far as I'm concerned you can run your cows anywhere you please. . . . I'll make concessions to Jefferson Wayne's son that I wouldn't make to any other man I know. I'm warning you for another reason. You don't know this country—and I do. I've been fighting here for nigh on forty years, and King Cole's brand is safe where another man's ain't safe. You've heard plenty hard tales about me, I reckon, but you'll find the folks that tell those tales are the thieves and rustlers and killers that come out of No Man's Land looking for plunder. They've got reason to hate me." He gestured towards the east. "You're less than fifteen miles from Cottonwood Wells, lying just across the border, and you'll find more bad *hombres* in that onery rustlers' town than fleas on a mangy coyote. There is no law in No Man's Land, 'cept the law of Judge Colt, and won't be until Congress includes the Public Lands Strip in the Oklahoma Panhandle as a *bona-fide* part of Oklahoma Territory. Right now she's nothin' but No Man's Land."

"Don't aim to run my cows east of the Line," Jeff declared. "Plenty range here on the New Mexico side of the border." He shrugged wide shoulders. "Can't scare me out, Mr Cole."

"You're a young fool!" snorted the old man. "They don't bother me much, 'cause I've put the fear of King Cole into their black hearts. . . . But they will be down on you like a pack of wolves on a yearling maverick . . . rustle you to the bone." He indicated the length and breadth of the valley with a sweeping gesture. "No chance losing cows to rustlers here in the Basin. No way to get in or get out 'cept through West Pass or the Gap."

"You say these rustlers don't bother you *much*," Jeff drawled. "Mean to tell me that you're losin' cows to 'em?"

King Cole scowled. "Losing more than seems reasonable," he admitted. "Last two round-ups seem to indicate that KC-Bar cows have quit having calves, or else some thieving outfit is slappin' a brand that ain't mine on the hides of the said calves. And that ain't the worst of it. . . . Last round-up tally-sheets show me short more'n six hundred prime three-year-old steers."

"Any idea who's raidin' your range?" queried Jeff, vastly intrigued. It was news indeed to learn that not even the mighty King Cole was immune from the depredations of cattle rustlers.

"Got my suspicions," growled the old man, "and said suspicions point to a mysterious *hombre* they call El Toro Grande. Trouble is nobody seems to have laid eyes on him. Reckon there's plenty in Cottonwood Wells that could call him by his real name if they'd a mind to."

"El Toro Grande—the Big Bull, huh," mused Jeff. He shrugged his shoulders, eyed King Cole narrowly. "Well, mister, thanks for all the kind advice, but the same don't change my plans none. I've got other plans for the Basin. . . . Aim to save the grass for fattening beef shipments. Also old man Perry of the Frying-pan is sending me five thousand stock cows to handle on shares. Be here in a couple of months. The Flying W is due to be a real outfit, Mr Cole." Jeff's voice lost its soft drawl, was suddenly hard. "As for this El Toro Grande, or any other border ruffian rustling me to the bone—well, they won't be the first rustlers I've run up against. Was foreman of the Frying-pan for five years, and rustling wasn't so popular down in the Pecos country when I left to come up here. And every man of my outfit is sure poison for the sort of scum you say hangs out across the border. They eat rustlers for breakfast, and yell for more." Jeff smiled grimly. "The Flying W is just that kind of salty outfit."

"Don't say that I didn't warn you," grumbled the old KC-Bar man, secretly delighted by this he-man talk. Anything less would have hardened his heart against Jeff Wayne, resolved him to close the range against the Flying W as he had closed it to other would-be neighbours. King Cole would not tolerate a weakling for a neighbour. A weakling might be tempted to steal his neighbour's calves. The KC-Bar domain covered enough territory to swallow comfortably one of the smaller New England states. The vast, lonely ranges offered plenty of opportunity for a brand-blotting neighbour to increase his herds. And times were changing. Lylah's wise old father knew that he could not much longer maintain his title as sole lord of the princely territory he claimed for the KC-Bar. Land-hungry settlers were yearly more troublesome, an ever-growing problem to the old-time cattle kings. Desperadoes of the worst type were daily growing more numerous in the Oklahoma Panhandle, better known as No Man's Land—safe haven from the long arm of the law. Cattle-stealing was on the increase, his own vast herds were no longer immune from organized rustling. King Cole knew men, and saw in Jeff Wayne the resolute courage and sterling honesty he demanded in the man who was to share his range and have voice in the never-ending conflict with the cattlemen's common foes —rustlers and "nesters."

"Don't say I didn't warn you," he repeated gruffly. The old man was determined not to show his hand at this early stage of the game. Not for one moment must young Jeff Wayne think he could count on support from the powerful KC-Bar. "And don't come runnin' to me for help. I've got enough troubles, without wastin' time on a young buck that won't take advice any way."

"The Flying W can make the grade without calling on you, mister," drawled the young cattleman. He smiled cheerfully at the gnarled, weather-bitten face glowering down at him. "The boys will be plenty disappointed when I tell 'em the KC-Bar has handed us the warm hand of friendship. They kind of figgered on a real excitin' range war, and now the only excitement looming on the horizon is the prospect of hanging a few rustlers."

Jeff's casual acceptance of the KC-Bar's friendship in no way deceived or displeased the grim old range lord. Loud protestations would have irked him. King Cole knew that the young cattleman was both pleased and relieved. He would have been staggered could he have guessed the full measure of Jeff's relief.

He nodded brusquely, wheeled the black stallion, and signalled with uplifted hand to his waiting men.

"Boys," rasped the owner of the KC-Bar as the riders spurred up and drew rein, "listen close. . . . The Flying W and the KC-Bar outfits are friends and neighbours from now on. Flying W cows will range west to the Don Carlos Hills and south of Carrampao Creek clear to the Honda." He glared round at the encircling impassive faces. "Those orders stand—until I say different," he added significantly.

The news was received in silence, most of the men apparently indifferent. Some of them grinned, threw Jeff friendly nods. Two among them evidenced displeasure—the younger Cole and the giant Sladen. Sullen anger was in the look the former bent upon his stepfather, a fleeting dismay in Sladen's restless, piercing black eyes. Only for a moment did the latter's broad, swarthy face betray undue emotion. Jeff shrewdly sensed

65

in the KC-Bar foreman a craftiness and cunning that would make him a far more dangerous foe than the merely vicious Steve Cole. The latter spoke in a sulky tone:

"We've got a lot of stuff down in the Honda bottoms, two-year-olds. Take a lot of work gettin' them out, and combin' the canyons over Don Carlos way. Or are you aimin' to let things ride till the fall round-up?"

"Up to Jeff," decided King Cole curtly. He looked at Sladen. "Bart, you and Mr Wayne get together in a day or two and figger things out to suit yourselves—"

"Suits me to let things ride till fall round-up," broke in Jeff. "We can throw our outfits together then and comb out all your KC-Bar cows without going to a lot of extra work."

The big KC-Bar foreman nodded assent to this plan. "Your say-so goes with me, Mr Wayne," he said, pleasantly enough. His smiling gaze went to Steve Cole, who was staring with curious intentness at the house door. "What's eatin' yuh, Steve? Seein' ghosts—or somethin'?"

"That hat!" shouted young Cole. He flung a furious look at Jeff. "How come that hat lying there on your bench, Wayne?"

Chill foreboding prickled down Jeff's spine. Slowly he turned and stared at Lylah's white Stetson, lying on the bench where she had placed it to dry out in the sun. He glanced quickly at the girl's father. Incredulity, growing rage, had replaced the old man's former friendliness.

"That's my daughter's Stetson," he said, in a harsh voice. "What is my girl's hat doing here, Wayne?"

"Your girl's hat?" Jeff forced an unconcerned grin, uncomfortably aware that the clustered horsemen were regarding him with hostile attentiveness. "Well, now," he parried, "sure is queer about that Stetson." He shrugged his shoulders. "What makes you claim it is your daughter's, sir?"

For answer King Cole motioned to his stepson, who spurred quickly up to the bench, his hand reaching down for the hat. Unconsciously all eyes followed the movement, and none noticed Jeff's hands slide down to his holstered guns.

"It's Lylah's! Got the KC-Bar marked on the inside band!" triumphantly cried Steve. He flung Jeff a malevolent look. "Talk up, Wayne!"

"Let's take a look." Jeff moved towards him, and stared swiftly at the hat-band. "Right you are, mister—that's the KC-Bar brand, large as life." He swung round, the carefully planned movement placing him with his back to the ranch-house door, hands close to gun-butts, grey eyes raking the circle of suspicious, scowling faces.

"Told you it was queer about that Stetson," he said, smiling thinly at Steve. "Run into it down in Carrampao Creek, and seeing it was a mighty nice Stetson, and seeing that man-sized cloudburst heading down, I just brought said Stetson hat home with me, instead of leaving it to head for No Man's Land on top of a fifty-foot flood of storm-water."

There was a silence, broken by a startled oath from Bart Sladen. "She was down there in the creek!" he cried.

The old cattle king's seamed face was a grey mask of anguish. Jeff silently cursed the sharp eyes that had betrayed the presence of the unfortunate Stetson, and forced him to arouse such dreadful fears in a father's heart. He had told as much of the truth as he dared. To have said more would have betrayed the girl's presence in the Flying W ranch-house. She had chosen to conceal the fact of her presence. He could not do less than respect her wish. There was nothing he could do to reassure her stricken father.

The men were restless, shaken by the thought of the idolized daughter of the KC-Bar having perished in the flood-waters of the Rio Carrampao. Impatiently they reined their restive horses, anxious eyes watching their old chief, sitting with bowed head on the tall black stallion.

"Let's get goin', boss," urged Sladen. "No sense wastin' time here. If she's safe at home we sure want to know it—"

Slowly the grizzled head lifted, the old man's gaze travelling across the trampled wet ground. Suddenly the cattleman's lean body stiffened, and for a brief moment King Cole's eyes held the absorbed look of one who has uncovered a startling truth. The next instant his gaze was boring full on Jeff.

As the latter met that penetrating, searching stare he saw with surprise that suspicion and black rage no longer distorted the old cattleman's features. There was sternness, and a curious, unfathomable expression that had Jeff wildly wondering.

Steve Cole's voice cut the silence. "Your story don't make the grade, Wayne," he sneered. "Get away from that door. I'm takin' a look inside your shack."

"You're talking out of turn, Steve!" rasped King Cole. "When did you get to be boss of the KC-Bar?" His fierce glance swept the others. "All right, boys. Let's get goin'."

He swung the black stallion away, and with a quick trampling of hoofs the KC-Bar riders followed. All but Steve. The latter snarled an oath and flung from his saddle.

"We ain't ridin' from here till I've looked inside that house!" he shouted. His hand darted down to his holstered gun.

CHAPTER VII
THE WISDOM OF KING COLE

CHUCK WALLIS morosely watched the big vulture soaring effortlessly against the patch of bright blue sky that roofed the great chasm in the west wall of Crater Basin. Chuck's prone position was ideal for sky-gazing. The view called for no exertion, no neck-twistings. Nothing to do but open his eyes, and there was that bit of vaulted blue, the ceaselessly circling vulture. An artist might have found a certain charm in the picture. Not so Chuck Wallis. He was heartily weary of sky and bird. The patiently watching vulture depressed him. Vultures fed on dead things . . . dead men . . . picked out their eyes first. He knew. Once he had driven one of the carrion birds from the body of a desert prospector, had seen the ghastly eyeless sockets in the thirst-tortured face. The sight had bred in him a deep and abiding hatred for buzzards.

"You son-of-a-gun," he muttered, "waitin' up there . . . waitin' up there—"

"I can think up worse names than that," growled the long, lanky cowboy stretched out by Chuck's side. His voice droned on.

"Feller, you sure can swear when yuh is real peeved," admired the stocky, black-haired puncher lying on Chuck's other side. "Never knowed yuh could use such burnin' words, Tom Collins."

"Shouldn't be usin' such langwidge," dolorously observed a sad-faced individual sitting on a near-by boulder. He cocked a gloomy eye up at the soaring vulture. "Them buzzards is wise . . . awful wise. Can smell corpses a long ways off." He shook his head. "You fellers ought to be sayin' your prayers, 'stead of cussin'."

The three bound Flying W men cast venomous glances upon the speaker. The latter grinned, patting the rifle across his knee. "Never seed such bad-tempered *hombres,*" he lamented. "Sure gives me the creeps—the way you fellers look at me." The KC-Bar man simulated a shudder, patting the rifle again. "Sure would be right skeered settin' here if it weren't for this bee-utiful weepon."

Chuck Wallis longingly eyed the "bee-utiful weepon," which happened to be his own prized Winchester.

"You'll be lookin' into the wrong end of that gun some day, mister," he promised, in a choking voice. "An' yuh won't have time for no prayer talk."

"Plumb out of his haid," mourned the guard. "An' him so young an' han'some. I sure could weep . . . I sure could weep." He sighed gustily, and grinned at his glowering charges.

Chuck's gaze returned to the ominous black spectre floating in the blue void above. A thoughtful expression crept into his eyes.

"She's a good gun, that Winchester," he soliloquized, as though unconsciously voicing bitter thoughts. "Too good for that slab-jawed coyote that calls himself a cowboy."

"Sure she's a good gun," complacently agreed the guard, unruffled by the insult. "That's why I'm keepin' the purty darlin'."

"A good rifle means nothing to you," derided Chuck. "Might as well be an Injun trade musket for all thc shootin' you can do."

The KC-Bar man snorted, visibly annoyed by the gibe. "Yuh'd be plumb surprised how straight I can shoot," he averred boastfully.

Chuck sneered. "Got a twenty-dollar gold piece in my jeans that says you can't wing that ol' buzzard," he challenged.

Ace Peters and Long Tom Collins were suddenly tense. They knew the cunning of Chuck Wallis. Never was he more dangerous than when he spoke in that lazy drawl.

"Yuh say yuh've got a twenty-dollar gold piece?" The guard's voice was thoughtful.

"I got another twenty that says the same," suddenly spoke up Ace Peters, resolved to back Chuck's play. It would not be the first time that good old Chuck had bluffed a pat hand.

"Me too!" echoed Long Tom Collins. "Sixty

dollars against the ol' buzzard, yuh dang horse-thief!"

The three bold gamblers slyly eyed the baited KC-Bar man, saw with joy the avaricious glitter in the sunken, smoky eyes. Chuck flashed a warning look at his friends. Unspoken words flowed between them.

"An' to think I never thought of lookin' yuh over," the guard was bitterly reproaching himself. He rose from his boulder, carefully leaned the Winchester against the face of the cliff. "Fellers," he chided, "I don't hold none with gamblin'. Gamblin' is a sin, so I ain't makin' no bets with yuh." His grin was sly. "It's plain duty starin' me in the face . . . duty that says I must take them big shinin' pieces of gold so yuh won't be tempted in your evil ways."

He shambled towards them confidently, long six-guns slapping against gaunt thighs. He had no reason to expect violence from his securely trussed prisoners. Grinning, he stooped over Ace Peters, stretched full length on Chuck's right. Instantly, as the lanky guard's head bent low, Chuck spun on his back; his legs, bound at the ankles, opened wide between the knees, forming a noose of muscle and bone which clamped in a lightning movement over the KC-Bar man's head.

With a startled, choking cry the surprised cowboy attempted to regain an upright position, and went sprawling on his back as Ace Peters

73

hurled his one hundred and sixty pounds against his legs. Ace promptly lay across the thrashing legs, while Chuck, dragged by the fall, now sat fairly on the guard's chest, knees firmly clamped around his neck.

"Lemme up!" he howled. "Yore spurs is rippin' me!"

He attempted to pull his gun-hand from under Chuck's muscular thigh; the latter bore down heavily, pressing the other's back against the upturned rowelling spurs.

"Yuh've got me!" choked the KC-Bar man. He groaned out an oath; his body went limp, unable to bear the torture of those spurs grinding into his back.

"Now, Tom—" gasped Chuck.

The long Flying W cowboy made a double roll that brought him alongside the captive. In a moment the fingers of his bound hands were working at the knots of the lariat wound round Ace Peters' arms and body.

"Sure are clumsy with your fingers," complained Ace.

"Shut your mouth," grunted the long cowboy. "You couldn't untie these dang knots with *both* your hands loose."

"Hurry up, feller," begged the suffering guard. "These dang spurs is drawin' blood—"

"Reckon that bronc yuh ride would sure laugh to see yuh now," chuckled Long Tom. He addressed

74

the stubborn knot luridly; fingers twisted and pulled. "There she comes!" he grunted.

Ace sighed with relief as he felt the binding rope go slack. In another moment one hand was free and reaching for the big clasp-knife in his pocket. He opened the blade and slashed Long Tom's bonds; the latter got to his feet, rubbed chafed wrists, and waved his arms to restore circulation.

"Get his guns," directed Chuck.

Armed with the two guns, the long cowboy speedily liberated his friends. Grunting dismally, their captive got to his feet, his lugubrious face a picture of woe.

"Keep your paws elevated," warned Long Tom. He glared fiercely at the man. "What's your name?"

"Smith." The prisoner threw Chuck Wallis a sly grin. "Some calls me Sinful Smith." He shook his head sadly. "Could have used that sixty dollars . . . was aimin' to high-tail it over to Cottonwood Wells to-night. Can always get a good game at the Longhorn." Sinful Smith sighed. "You gents is sure actin' onery."

"What'll we do with the ol' horse-thief?" demanded Long Tom of his friends.

Chuck looked up thoughtfully at the vulture. "Seems like we owe that dang buzzard a good supper," he mused.

"Sure do," agreed Ace Peters gravely.

Chuck nodded, walked over to the cliff, and

retrieved his Winchester. Sinful Smith's gaze followed him nervously.

"Get your broncs, Ace," called Chuck. "No time to lose. Got to be high-tailin' it pronto."

The black-haired cowboy hurried towards the group of horses tethered to the bushes.

"Drop your cartridge-belt, Sinful," rasped Chuck.

The KC-Bar man unbuckled his belt and let it slide to the ground. A startled, incredulous expression was in his eyes.

"Now, listen, fellers," he said earnestly, "I was only jokin'. Yuh never was in no danger. Yuh heard what the Boss said . . . just to keep yuh here till they come back—"

"Get movin', Sinful," ordered Chuck, in a relentless voice. "I'm givin' yuh a hundred yards start through the Pass, then I'm pumpin' hot lead. On your way, feller!"

With a frightened oath the gangling KC-Bar man started through the Pass; Chuck called off the approximate yards as he fled.

"Ninety-eight, ninety-nine!" he yelled. "Run— yuh ol' jack-rabbit!" He lifted rifle to shoulder, and as the rocky walls of West Pass echoed the crashing reports of the .44 Sinful Smith went leaping and bounding like a startled buck, dodging and weaving to escape the hail of lead he fancied was spurting after him. If he had taken time to look up at the blue arch of sky he would have seen the buzzard cease its soarings and plunge earthward.

"Reckon he won't stop running till he's clean through the Pass," observed Long Tom. He grabbed up Sinful's cartridge-belt and ran towards Ace and the horses. Chuck raced after him. He saw with relief that their guns and holsters were hanging on the saddle-horns. The raiders had not despoiled them. Even the other two rifles were in their scabbards.

"Jeff said I was to head over to Ute Canyon an' head Buck off from the Gap," Ace reminded the others as they swung into their saddles.

"Jeff's needin' us at the ranch-house," said Chuck curtly. "On our way, boys. Got to stop at Lone Butte and signal Curly and Slim at the Gap . . . like Jeff said to do if trouble come a-runnin'."

They tore out of the wide mouth of the Pass and across the rolling valley-land, true-blue warriors of the wild grasslands, riding to the aid of their boss and making naught of the odds against them.

Five miles found them at Lone Butte, the tough little cow-ponies blown and trembling from the terrific pace. Before hoofs slid to a halt the Flying W men were out of their saddles and racing up to the flat top of the pinnacle.

In a few moments a small fire was going, skilfully fed with damp grass to make plenty of black smoke. Chuck seized the long brass telescope from its niche in the rocks.

"Now, fellers," he told the others, "get busy."

Using a blanket, they made the desired puffs of smoke. Chuck anxiously watched the Gap through the telescope. Suddenly he exclaimed contentedly, "Good ol' Curly, right on the job! Now, the signal . . . trouble at ranch-house . . . come a-runnin'. . . . They got it! All right."

Boots stamped out the little fire and went clattering and sliding down to the floor of the valley. Freshened by the few minutes' rest, the horses carried them swiftly towards the ranch-house hidden behind the trees.

"Curly an' Slim have 'bout the same distance to go as we have," observed Chuck as they raced neck and neck. "We'll run into 'em back of the house. That KC-Bar won't be lookin' for trouble in that direction."

"How long do you figger we was tied up?" asked Ace.

"Not more than twenty minutes after they left us," estimated Chuck. "We're ridin' a lot faster than they would. Reckon we won't be more'n fifteen minutes behind 'em." He smiled grimly. "Sure will give that ol' range robber a pain in the neck when he finds himself looking down the muzzles of our guns."

Silence fell upon them, each man intent on his own thoughts. The wind flattened back the broad brims of their hats. Young reckless faces set in hard lines, they swept along to the rhythmic beat of drumming hoofs.

Angling in from the north-east flashed two riders. With one accord Chuck and his comrades veered to meet them.

"There's hell to pay!" Chuck yelled as the five horsemen met and swung abreast. In terse sentences he passed on the news of the raid to Curly and Slim. Their eyes narrowed—the resolute look of fighting men.

"Twenty of 'em, huh?" grunted the hard-visaged Curly. He slapped his low-hanging gun. "Fellers, I'm takin' six of their scalps."

"Long Tom," Chuck snorted. "There's five of us—an' five don't go into twenty more'n four times."

"Not to say nothin' of Jeff an' ol' Brazos," chimed in the wiry Slim Dally.

"An' ol' Barbecue's buffalo-gun," added Ace Peters.

Blithely, confidently, but none the less warily alert, the five Flying W men entered the thick grove of trees behind the ranch-house. Chuck's lifted hand signalled for a halt.

"Best tie our broncs," he advised. "Don't want 'em headin' in for the corral and giving us away."

Quietly they made their preparations for the surprise attack, loosening their six-guns and examining Winchesters. Curly refused to take his rifle. He preferred the short gun—one in each hand.

"Ready, fellers? Lct's go."

Silent as Indians, they wormed through the undergrowth. Chuck and Curly crawled round the right side of the house; the other three took care of the opposite end. Chuck suddenly halted, and pressed close to the adobe wall.

"They're riding off," he whispered.

The two cowboys stared at each other in wide-eyed surprise. An angry voice lifted above the sound of trampling hoofs.

"We ain't ridin' from here till I've looked inside that house!"

Even as Chuck and Curly leaped round the corner another voice rose above the din. "Steve's right. We're taking a look inside the house!"

The big KC-Bar foreman wheeled his horse. "Come on, fellers!"

"Stay where yuh are," warned the high-pitched voice of Barbecue behind his loophole. "I've got yuh covered, mister!"

"Yuh bet we've got yuh covered, the hull caboodle of yuh!" roared old Brazos. His rifle menaced them from the other loophole.

From both sides of the house sounded the shrill war-cry of the Flying W riders; then the lazy drawl of Chuck Wallis.

"Reckon that's right good advice, gents."

The confounded KC-Bar men goggled at the

menacing guns. Hands went up. There was grim determination in those hard eyes—those bristling guns.

Chuck glanced curiously at Steve Cole, crouched in front of Jeff Wayne, hand clutching half-drawn six-shooter, fear-filled eyes staring at the two Colts in the young cattleman's hands.

"Take his gun, Chuck," rasped Jeff. "The fool tried to pull a fast one on me."

His face a sickly green, Steve dropped the gun and lifted his hands. Chuck reached for the weapon and backed away.

"Get on your bronc," ordered Jeff.

Steve climbed into his saddle. Jeff's gaze raked the KC-Bar riders clustered behind Sladen. A little beyond them old King Cole watched in grim silence.

"Brazos! Barbecue!" called Jeff. "Keep 'em covered. First man that lowers his hands—fill him with lead. All right, fellers, two of you get their guns."

"Leave their guns alone, Wayne," said King Cole, in a crackling voice. "I'll answer for my men—"

"Think I'm a fool!" retorted Jeff angrily. He motioned to Curly and Ace. They moved grimly to the task.

"Stop!" rasped the old cattle baron. He lifted his hand imperiously, and rode past his men towards the young owner of the Flying W. Curly and Ace halted uncertainly.

"Shall I let him have it, Jeff?" Barbecue's big buffalo-gun swung to cover the black stallion's rider.

"Keep your Sharps aimed where I told you," muttered Jeff. "Cole ain't wearing a gun."

Barbecue's rifle swung back to cover the prisoners. Lylah's father drew rein close to Jeff.

"Wayne," he warned, in a low voice, "taking their guns from 'em will breed bad blood. Don't do it. A word from me, and they will ride away in peace."

"How do I know they will ride away in peace?" demanded Jeff bitterly. "You told 'em to get going a few moments ago, and what happened? Your fool stepson went for his gun—would have killed me if I hadn't beat him to the draw. At that there would have been killing done if my own men hadn't come in time to take a hand. Looks to me as if your rannihans don't listen close when you give orders, Mr Cole."

"I'll answer for my men," repeated the old man. "There'll be no more gunplay, Jeff." He smiled down into the other's furious eyes. "You see, they think a heap of my little girl. Steve kind of caught them off balance when he lost his head."

Jeff hesitated. There was truth in King Cole's words. It was not unreasonable in these men to wish to convince themselves that their little princess was not being held a prisoner. In fact, King Cole's willingness to accept his story about the Stetson hat and ride away without demanding further proof had astonished him.

His decision came swiftly. His gaze went to the waiting Ace and Curly. "You heard, boys. Seems there's been a mistake." His smile swept the KC-Bar men. "All right, fellers. No need to reach for the sky. The war's over."

Grinning sheepishly, King Cole's riders lowered their hands. They entertained no hard feelings. Jeff sensed from their big foreman's sulky expression that he was displeased at the result of the encounter. The Flying W had drawn first blood; the prestige of the KC-Bar was left somewhat tarnished.

Relief was in King Cole's eyes. "Looks like you kind of out-smarted old Sinful Smith," he chuckled to Wallis. "Didn't do no harm to the old reprobate making your getaway, did you, young feller?"

Chuck grinned. "Mister, that long-legged cowboy is the champeen runner 'tween here an' the Pecos. Never did see a *hombre* cover ground so fast."

The old cattleman nodded. The unbelievable escape of Chuck and his fellow-prisoners, their cool counterattack, proved the mettle of the Flying W outfit. Dangerous enemies these soft-spoken young Texans—or invaluable allies. His glance signalled Bart Sladen. The foreman nodded sullenly, and with a word to his men rode away, the outfit clattering at his heels.

"Chuck," said Jeff, "you can hand that gun back

to the man you took it from." He eyed Steve Cole unsmilingly as the latter sullenly holstered the returned six-shooter. "Won't be handing it back to you a second time," he warned.

"Another time you won't be taking it," sneered Steve.

His horse rearing under the cruel jab of his spurs, he dashed away.

"Your stepson ain't caring none for my looks," dryly observed Jeff.

"Steve's a fool," grunted Cole. "Never had no judgment." He swung his horse, reined round, his eyes beckoning Jeff. The latter went to him; the cattleman leaned down mysteriously.

"Should have wiped out those bootprints," he whispered. "Lucky the boys ain't as sharp-eyed as the old man, eh?"

Long grizzled moustaches twitching with silent laughter, he rode away.

CHAPTER VIII

A NEW FRIEND

THERE was a startled expression in the young cattleman's eyes as he turned back to the house. The door flew open, and Brazos and Barbecue clattered out, shouting loud greetings to their comrades. Jeff waved them away. He wanted to think.

Bootprints!

They were unmistakable! Clearly stamped in the wet soil in front of the door. No man's boots could have left those dainty marks. The keen eyes of Lylah's father had observed them. The wise old man had surmised the entire truth. Jeff understood now the meaning of the curious look in King Cole's eyes, his willingness to ride away with his men. He knew and trusted his daughter, guessed that Jeff had sheltered her from the storm, and had sympathized with her reluctance to be discovered in the company of a man she believed was her father's enemy.

Blessing the sagacity and wisdom that had prevented the humiliating disclosure of the girl's presence at the ranch, Jeff called softly through the open door.

She came out timidly.

"I've been terrified," she told him simply.

"Wish you could get back home ahead of your dad's outfit," he worried. "No chance of making it down Lobo Canyon, yet—"

"I think," she said, "that you are wonderful, Jeff Wayne."

The tone of her voice, the lingering softness in the warm brown eyes, oddly stirred him.

"Might have been worse," he rejoined, assuming a gruffness he was far from feeling. "That brother of yours came close to making a mess of things."

"Steve's queer," she admitted. "Father is worried

about him lately. He—is only a stepbrother," she added. "Father's first wife was a widow, and Steve is her son. He is not a Cole really."

All of which informed Jeff that Lylah was not fond or proud of her stepbrother. He nodded absently. Night was coming on them. It was imperative he devise some means of getting this girl back to her home before the KC-Bar men discovered her absence.

"We'll give them a chance to get through West Pass, then head for the KC-Bar the same way," he told her.

Lylah looked dubious. "It's awfully far that way—"

"Only thing we can do. You can't stay here all night."

She laughed.

"It's no laughing matter," Jeff said crossly. "Your dad knows you are here."

She looked at him, speechless.

"He trusts me to get you home."

"Dad—knew—"

"I figure he thought you'd be some upset to have the boys know you were in my house."

Lylah suddenly smiled. The knowledge that her fiery old father had willingly left her in the care of this young man was proof that Jeff Wayne had indeed won his powerful friendship. The thought fluttered her heart.

"You know," she said softly, "I overheard some

of the talk. I—I was so surprised—and pleased—"

"It's been one surprising day," agreed Jeff. He returned to the problem of getting her home. "I'll have the boys throw saddles on the Palominos. Sure would like to get you to the ranch ahead of that stepbrother of yours." He hurried away to the bunkhouse, to which place the Flying W men had tactfully withdrawn.

Warm sunshine bathed the bench by the door. Lylah sat down and examined the unfortunate Stetson hat, which Jeff had retrieved and returned to the bench. Her carelessness in leaving it for all the world to see had nearly caused the spilling of blood. She clenched a little fist and gave the damp crown an angry punch. She felt that she hated that Stetson for the trouble it had brought to Jeff Wayne. And she could not wear it home—not after what had happened. Steve and the others would ask how she had regained it so quickly, would guess the truth. A faint smile curved her lips. Blessed old hat. It would bring Jeff Wayne to her soon. He would be obliged to return it to her at the KC-Bar. And if he dared to send it by one of his riders—she would never speak to him again.

The girl's slim body suddenly stiffened. The sound was unmistakable—a faint scuffle of stealthy feet.

Lylah sprang from the bench, tense gaze fastened on the corner of the house, hand clasped over the ivory butt of her little six-shooter.

The stealthy movement had ceased; no sound reached her straining ears. Only the soft twitterings of birds and the murmur of voices from the corral where Jeff and the boys were saddling the horses. She was imagining things, Lylah told herself. The past unbelievable hours had left her a bundle of nerves. The explanation did not satisfy her. Lylah knew that she was not a bundle of nerves, that she was not imagining things. She knew positively that she had heard the sly approach of stalking feet.

She stood irresolute, screwing up courage to go and look round the corner of the house.

"*Señorita!*" came a cautious whisper. "*Señorita!*"

Lylah's dark eyes widened; stifling a startled cry, she ran quickly to the corner.

"Chaco!" she exclaimed, in a glad, incredulous voice.

"Speak softly," cautioned the old Indian in Spanish, the mother tongue of the little dark-eyed *señorita* wooed and won long years ago by Lylah's father.

The faithful Yaqui had accompanied his beloved mistress from the ancient Alvarez *hacienda* in Old Mexico to the new home of the great *gringo* chief in New Mexico. Lylah's coming within the year had claimed the life of the beautiful Carmela, to the lasting grief of the devoted Yaqui. All the more reason for Chaco's fierce devotion to the motherless daughter of King Cole. His love had guarded her through the years that brought the baby girl to young womanhood. In the old Yaqui's eyes his little *señorita* lived again in the daughter.

"I must not be seen," he warned her. "Quick, *señorita*, come with me—before it is too late."

Amazement still held the girl. She stared at him, saw that his breath was laboured, as though he had run a great distance. The dark, coppery skin of his heaving, massive chest gleamed with perspiration. Chaco's dress was simple, a pair of beaded moccasins and soft doeskin trousers buckled round his lean waist. Despite his great age there was still strength and endurance in that magnificent, tawny-skinned body.

"Come, my *señorita*," he repeated. "Chaco will take you where the *gringo* men cannot follow—"

"What brings you here?" she demanded, addressing him in the tongue of her mother. "There is no danger," she assured him. "The *gringo* men are my friends, Chaco."

"Friends?" His voice was disbelieving. "For months I have watched these *gringos* from the hilltops. Their comings and goings I have seen and nightly reported to the Señor Cole, as he demanded. Surely these *gringos* are enemies?"

"They are friends, Chaco," the girl reassured him, "but I am glad that you came."

She told him briefly of the pact of friendship between the two outfits. The Yaqui seemed relieved and pleased. He gestured to the north.

"Chaco saw the big *gringo* bearing you across the valley on his horse. Fear filled the heart of Chaco when he saw the little *señorita* in the hands of her father's enemy. Chaco swore to have the *gringo*'s life if harm came to her—" He touched the wicked-looking *machete* thrust inside his belt.

"You have come all the way from Sentinel Peak on foot?"

Lylah knew it was all of ten miles to Sentinel Peak, and realized that the devoted Yaqui must have run the entire distance to have arrived so soon.

"It is nothing," he said simply. "Chaco's heart is glad that all is well with the *señorita*."

"How did you get into the Basin?" she questioned him. "There is no way to enter, except through the Gap or West Pass."

"There is one other way—known only to Chaco," he answered.

A thought came to her. "Chaco," she asked excitedly, "this way—known only to you—is it a short cut to the KC-Bar ranch-house?"

The Yaqui answered that the secret trail known only to him would cut off many miles to the KC-Bar, but was not a safe one until the high mesa, where he had left his horse, was reached.

She explained the urgent need of arriving home before the return of the KC-Bar outfit. Chaco's smoky eyes narrowed when she told of Steve Cole's attempt to shame her in the eyes of the men. The Yaqui had little liking for Lylah's stepbrother.

"The big *gringo* will give us horses," he said. "We will ride quickly to the Place of the Winding Stair."

"They are bringing horses now!" she exclaimed. She clasped the Indian's brown hand and led him round to the front of the house. Jeff was coming up from the corral, followed by Chuck and Curly, leading the Palominos. The Flying W men threw astonished glances at the big Yaqui.

"He's Chaco," the girl explained. "Chaco has been my friend and guardian angel ever since I was born."

"Chaco, huh!" Jeff smiled. So this was the man who had kept watch over the doings of the Flying W in Crater Basin. Chaco, the secret eyes of old King Cole.

The Yaqui eyed him keenly. What he saw evidently satisfied him. He returned Jeff's smile.

"The Señor Wayne has been good to the *señorita*," he said gravely, in Spanish. "Whom the little *señorita* loves Chaco loves, and is their friend and servant."

"He says he is your friend," translated Lylah, the colour waving into her cheeks. She wondered if Jeff understood Spanish. The twinkle in the grey eyes told her that Jeff did.

"Chaco knows a short cut to the KC-Bar," she hurried on. "He says that over there"—she pointed

91

towards the northern rampart—"is a place he calls the Winding Stair, which leads to the high mesa on the other side of the Rio Lobo. He has a horse there. You see," she added triumphantly, "I can take Chaco's horse and be home before they arrive—"

"Ain't possible!" snorted Curly, who believed nothing his eyes had not seen. "The Injun's crazy. No way in or out of this valley 'cept through West Pass or the Gap."

"You don't know everything about this valley, Curly," reproved Jeff. He was thinking fast. If Chaco's story were true Lylah could easily reach the ranch before the arrival of the KC-Bar outfit; her presence there would put an end to the suspicions aroused by the Stetson hat.

"Curly," he rasped, "climb out of your saddle. Chaco is needing a bronc, and you're loaning him yours."

Purple shadows were creeping down the western rim as they set their horses for Sentinel Peak, rising like a cathedral spire in the north. Led by the old Yaqui on Curly's fast buckskin, the Palominos flew across the wild grasslands.

Jeff's pulse quickened as he glanced at the lovely flushed face under the wind-blown, dark curls. And suddenly, as they rode swiftly towards the shadowy hills, he became aware of a great reluctance to part with this girl who had so dramatically entered his life.

CHAPTER IX
THE WINDING STAIR

THE Indian's story of the Winding Stair interested Jeff. His own careful explorations of the mountain-walled valley had failed to disclose a break in the towering cliffs that rimmed the some two hundred square miles of wild grasslands he had wrested from old King Cole. West Pass and the narrower Lobo Gap in the north-east rim actually afforded the only means of entering or leaving Crater Basin.

There was no doubt in Jeff's mind that Crater Basin had once cradled the waters of a great lake, fed by numerous springs and streams flowing from the hills lying to the south and west. Some violent disturbance of the earth's crust had released the impounded waters in a cataclysmic deluge that had torn out the great gash now known as West Pass Canyon. Possibly the same gigantic upheaval explained the origin of the funnel-like Lobo Gap, and had formed the many underground channels through which the springs and creeks emptied into the Rio Lobo.

The character of the country changed as they neared the frowning northern battlements under the three-thousand-foot spire of Sentinel Peak. The rolling grasslands gave way to brown, sun-parched flats, across which sprawled a vast network of bony ridges studded with eroded sandstone. Here and there a stunted scrub-oak rose above a sparse undergrowth of mesquite and juniper. For the most part the ridges were low and narrow, reaching like grasping fingers down to the floor of the valley. Others rose with gorge-like aspect, their steep slopes gashed with slides of eroding sandstone. Coveys of quail rose in short, bullet-like flights at their approach; a coyote slunk away, to top one of the smaller ridges and to pause for an inspection of the intruders before melting into the undergrowth. Long-eared jack-rabbits popped up, darting this way and that.

Turning sharply to the left to avoid the numerous gorges pushing down to the valley floor, the Yaqui led his companions westerly towards an elbow of mountain. The broken surface of the ground made haste an impossibility; numerous potholes, tumbled boulders, and the occasional patches of thorny brush forced them to allow their horses to pick their own way.

A low, grumbling roar came to them as they neared the shouldering mountain. Lylah's eyes questioned Jeff.

"Waterfall," he told her. "Drops all of a thousand feet."

"And to think I've lived all my life less than ten miles away and not known there was such a place as Crater Basin!" she marvelled.

"You've never been in the Basin before," he pointed out. "You heard what your dad said . . . that he had held the Basin sacred against the day I came back to it . . . closed West Pass and the Gap to cows and humans—"

"I can't help feeling a bit shivery," Lylah confessed. "There is always something so appalling about the tremendous symphony of a big waterfall. I'm simply overwhelmed, an insignificant atom in the presence of a Titan. This one sounds like the thunderous moaning of some great wounded god of the mountains. It's really frightening," she declared.

The barrier of ridges was suddenly a vast swamp running along the shouldering mountain ridge, and reaching for several miles towards the western wall. Lush grass grew in the bottoms, but for the most part the terrain was desolate marsh-land overgrown with tules.

The Yaqui reined in the buckskin. "Plenty bad," he warned them, in his broken English. He gestured at the vista of swamp. "Plenty queeksan' . . . catchum horse . . . no good. Follow Chaco close . . . queeksan' no catchum horse."

They rode on through the giant tules. Evening shadows crept up the western wall—deep blue pools at the base, delicate pink and lavender at the peaks. The sullen face of the swamp took on a glittering, jewelled splendour; flashing bursts of amethyst and ruby lights twinkled at them through the breaks in the tule; the titanic salvo of the falls beat with deafening impact upon their ears.

The wonder of the falls brought a little cry from the girl. She reined in the Palomino mare, and gazed up with mingled awe and delight at the thousand-foot plume of avalanching waters. The Yaqui glanced back, lips moving, his words lost in that stupendous symphony of sound. He pointed towards the setting sun, and gestured up the towering mass of Sentinel Peak, rising more than three thousand feet above them. Lylah understood; they must hurry before the light failed.

They rode past the foot of the falls, where the turbulent waters of the giant whirlpool roared down a deep, narrow chasm that thrust south and became a broad, swift stream. Following its winding course, marked by cottonwoods, Lylah saw that the creek described a gradual arc back to the northern wall, where some vast underground channel bore its flood under the mountain ridge, to flow into the Rio Lobo.

Suddenly they found themselves on a shelf-like ledge directly behind the silvery curtain of the falls, veiled from the outside world by clouds of pearly, smoke-like mist. In front of them yawned the black mouth of a cave into which the Yaqui spurred his snorting horse. His voice came to them from the darkness.

"Wait!"

A match flamed in his fingers, and in another moment the flare of a torch lighted the scene.

"We leave the horses here," Chaco told them in Spanish. "We have reached the Winding Stair."

Jeff saw with relief that the great cavern would shelter the horses from the drenching mist. He swung from his saddle and turned to help the girl. She slid down lightly.

"Of all the spooky places," she laughed. "I can't imagine what will happen next!"

"No wonder I never spotted this place," Jeff rejoined. "Who would think of looking behind the falls!" He glanced at the Yaqui, stolidly waiting by the buckskin, the flaring torch clenched in a brown fist. "How long will it take us to get up this Winding Stair?"

"Maybe half-hour," answered Chaco.

"Must tie the horses," Jeff said. He took down his lariat and looked round for means of securing the animals. The dripping sides of the cave were worn smooth by the action of some long-ago subterranean stream. "Nothing to tie to," he muttered.

"Horses no run away," Chaco told him. He gestured at the dark curtain of descending water. "Horses afraid." He eyed the coiled lariat in Jeff's hand. "Winding Stair heap bad climb . . . we must take rope for the little *señorita*."

Lighted by the Indian's flaring torch, they scrambled up a short, steep incline to a narrow, high-walled passage that pitched sharply up into the bowels of the mountain.

In some long-gone era—perhaps when Crater Basin was still a vast lake—the passage had been a subterranean channel feeding the lake with the waters now cascading down the face of the mountain. The torrent's furious descent had shaped a series of stair-like ledges that corkscrewed up not unlike the winding stairs of a tower. Ascent would have been impossible but for those stair-like ledges.

Step by step they crawled up between the dripping walls of the ancient water-channel. The Yaqui proceeded cautiously, lighting each turn with his torch, his fierce eyes anxiously watching the girl as she laboured up, hands clinging to the lariat Jeff had made fast to her waist. Without its help the girl could never have worked her way up the climb.

The passage widened, became less steep, and seemed to run in a fairly straight line. Chaco grinned over his shoulder at them.

"Soon be at top," he promised.

The girl's cold fingers tightened over Jeff's hand. "Is it my imagination, or do I really feel the ground trembling under me?"

Jeff had already divined the truth. The Winding Stair had led them some twelve or fifteen hundred feet above the floor of the valley, and probably two thousand feet north of their starting-point.

The almost perpendicular climb had brought them considerably above the crest of the falls, and the gentle northerly ascent of the prehistoric bore was now traversing a great natural bridge high above the rushing waters of the Rio Lobo, hundreds of feet below. He questioned the Yaqui.

"*Si, señor.* Soon we come to Burro Mesa, other side of river."

They pushed on rapidly; yellow sunlight filtered through a tangle of underbrush barricading the mouth of the ancient watercourse. Chaco discarded the torch, and hacked the bristling growth with his *machete*, enlarging an opening through which the girl and Jeff wriggled. The Indian followed.

Directly above them towered the rugged crags of Sentinel Peak, from which point Chaco had kept his watch over the valley. The great pinnacle marked the southern line of the rolling uplands of Burro Mesa, reaching north to the Burro Mountains, some ten miles distant. Lylah must ride north-east, the Indian told her, and head for the low twin peaks that marked Beaver Pass, where she would strike Beaver Creek Canyon. The rest of the way would be familiar ground. Beaver Creek flowed within a few hundred yards of the KC-Bar ranch-house.

Lylah was in no hurry to be on her way, she said. Her father and his riders had three times the distance to cover, and she could easily make the ranch before their arrival. She had never been in the vicinity of Sentinel Park. The place thrilled her, she declared. Giants had once sported here, or perhaps had engaged in furious conflict, tearing down mountain peaks to hurl at each other. She was sure she had never seen such utter chaos. Sentinel Peak alone survived the fury of the gods, a majestic monument to its fallen fellow-peaks.

"You needn't contradict me," she warned Jeff. "I know you are dying to tell me that Crater Basin was once a volcano that toppled over a few mountains when it blew its head off; but I like my story better." She gestured at the majestic panorama. "Behold the Garden of the Gods!"

They gazed in silence at the awe-inspiring scene. The sound of rushing waters was in their ears.

"That's where our waterfall takes the big jump," surmised Jeff.

They left old Chaco and scrambled over big boulders to the brink of a deep, narrow gorge, where the swift waters gathered momentum for the spectacular thousand-foot plunge down the face of the cliff. Once this same furious torrent had boiled down the subterranean channel now known as the Winding Stair.

Fascinated, they followed the course of the gorge, and soon were standing on a wide ledge overlooking Crater Basin. Far below they could hear the deep boom of the unseen falls. Jeff felt the girl's slight form lean against him, bracing to withstand the force of the wind. Quite naturally his arm went round her slim waist. She seemed not to notice, and, wordless, they stood there, looking across the vast panorama of Crater Basin.

Suddenly she was looking up into his face. "It's yours," she said softly, "all yours, Jeff Wayne!"

"I'm really seeing it for the first time," he answered in a hushed voice. "Seeing it—with you—standing by my side." He met her look with a grave, wondering smile. "You were asking what would happen next. I am asking the same question—wondering what will happen next—"

His steady grey eyes held her warm brown ones in a long, lingering look.

"I think," she said, a little unsteadily, "I think quite enough has happened—for one brief day—and I really must go now."

They returned to Chaco, who had been making a hasty readjustment of the stirrups. Lylah climbed into the saddle.

"*Adios*, Señor Wayne!"

She was gone, with a gay little wave of her hand, a warm, flashing smile. The old Yaqui watched her for a moment.

"Be dark before she makes the ranch," worried Jeff. The Indian looked at him.

"Chaco be close to little *señorita*," he said simply. "Chaco go now."

He was off at a dog-trot that Jeff knew would make naught of the miles.

Reassured, the young owner of the Flying W made ready for his descent of the Winding Stair by fashioning and lighting a torch similar to the one carried by Chaco. Now that King Cole's daughter was being safely escorted homeward there were other matters to trouble Jeff. The trail herd, for instance. He was worried about the trail herd. Buck Saunders had not been warned of the conditions at Lobo Canyon. Plenty of trouble in store for Buck unless they got word to him. And this rustler—El Toro Grande. According to King Cole the man's daring was notorious. Anything might happen to Buck and the trail herd with a rustler like El Toro on the prowl.

By the time he reached the ranch-house Jeff had come to a decision. The ride in from the Winding Stair had taken him a good hour; night rushed at his heels, trailing jewelled banners across the darkening sky. He found Chuck Wallis and Curly Stivens at their suppers. The other men had already left for night-shift duty at the Gap and West Pass, Chuck informed him.

Barbecue appeared from the kitchen with a fresh pot of coffee and a plate of hot venison stew. Jeff suddenly realized that he was ravenous. He had not tasted food since early morning.

"We're taking a ride," he told the two cowboys. "Get your broncs saddled, and tell Brazos to throw my saddle on the roan."

"What yuh mean—takin' a ride?" grumbled Curly.

They listened with grim attentiveness while Jeff told them what he had learned about the elusive rustler masquerading under the *nom de guerre* of El Toro Grande. Curly was sceptical.

"King Cole was pullin' yore laig," he scoffed. "The ol' range-grabber aims to skeer yuh plumb off his territory." Curly chuckled. "His friendly greetin' of the Flying W don't fit in with all the talk I've been hearin' 'bout King Cole."

Jeff shook his head to this. Lylah's father was not deceiving him. The old cattle king had pledged his friendship. He spoke curtly.

"Get your horses ready. We're riding now."

Curly pretended dismay. "An' me all set for a long night's snooze in me downy bed," he groaned.

"Poor li'l mommer's angel child," gibed the fat cook. "Sure is a cryin' shame 'bout yuh, Curly."

The blond cowboy grinned. "If yuh wasn't so fat an' useless, Barbecue, we'd sure invite yuh to come on the party."

Barbecue glared after him indignantly. "Fat an' useless, huh?" he snorted. "Yuh'll be regrettin' them words come next meal-time, me young rannihan!" He looked at Jeff. "Man—what a day! Cloudbursts an' gunplay an' rustlers an'—" The fat cook gave his young boss a sly grin.

"And what else, Barbecue?" For all his careless tone Jeff's tanned face was suddenly red.

"An' the purtiest gal I ever laid two good eyes

103

on," declared Barbecue solemnly. "The sweetest li'l prize heifer of 'em all—an' she sure took a shine to ol' Barbecue!" He nodded mysteriously. "I got me a keepsake . . . somethin' she left behind." Barbecue vanished into his kitchen.

He was back in a moment, triumphantly bearing Lylah Cole's white Stetson hat.

"Sort of figger that some day I'll be over to the KC-Bar an' hand it back to her," chuckled the cook. "She'll sure be tickled to get her Stetson back . . . mos' likely will kiss me. Must have cost all of fifty good dollars of her pa's money." Barbecue grinned maliciously at the glowering boss of the Flying W.

"You've got it figgered out all wrong, Barbecue," said the young man coldly. He pushed back his chair and got to his feet. "Just to save your poor old brains from working too much overtime I'll take charge of that Stetson, feller."

"Meanin' you figger to collect that kiss yore own self," jeered the cook.

"I'll kiss you with the toe of my boot!" roared Jeff. He snatched the Stetson and stalked to his bedroom.

Barbecue winked solemnly, heaved an exaggerated sigh, and proceeded noisily to gather up tin plates and cups from the table.

"Back for breakfast, boss?" he queried when Jeff reappeared.

"No tellin'. Brazos will run things till I get back."

"Sure hope yuh're all wrong 'bout them rustlers bein' on the prod to-night." Barbecue looked reflectively at his big buffalo-gun. "Would like to be ridin' with yuh," he added wistfully.

Jeff's pretence at sternness vanished; he threw the Flying W's fighting cook an affectionate smile. "Got to leave some good men to hold things down at the ranch, you old fire-eater," he called over his shoulder.

And presently drumming hoofs told the listening Barbecue that his three friends were riding towards Crater Basin's western gateway.

CHAPTER X

THE MAN WITH THE BLACK BEARD

IN the picturesque parlance of the cowboy Honda Creek was "on the prod." Ordinarily a somewhat ineffectual trickle, the Honda was now running bank full, a swirling, turbid flood.

Buck Saunders, canny veteran of the long trail, had too often seen the costliness of impatience; one look at the turbulent stream told him that now was one of those times to refrain from just such impatience. Until the storm-waters subsided there would be no crossing of the Honda.

Unaware of Jeff's changed plans to swing the herd up Ute Canyon and enter Crater Basin by way of West Pass, the lanky cattle boss accepted the delay with his usual philosophic calm. These things were all in the day's work. He could not know that circumstances had prevented Ace Peters from bringing instructions that would have kept the big herd moving up Ute Canyon. Knowing nothing of the altered conditions, Buck saw no reason to abandon the agreed plan to push up Lobo Canyon, the shortest route—and the safest from discovery by KC-Bar riders.

"Won't hold us up more'n a day or two at the most," he prophesied to Tex Malley, his close friend and lieutenant. Like himself, the red-headed Tex had left the Frying-pan outfit to share the fortunes, good or ill, of the Flying W.

"Sure thought we was due for a stampede when that thunder and lightning hit us," Tex chuckled. "Them dogies was just too plumb tired to do anything but hump theirselves and drift some."

"Seen worse drives than this one," the lanky foreman observed. "No rustlers, no thieving Injuns cuttin' out beef on us. We ain't lost more'n a dozen head all told." He stared reflectively at the great herd slowly spreading out across the rolling uplands. "Tex, I'm leaving you in charge of things. Johnny is sure going to die if we don't get him to a doc. Don't like the way his leg has swelled up."

"Blood-poisonin' works awful fast," agreed Tex.

He scowled. "Sure would like to meet up with the gent that put that slug in Johnny's leg."

"Leave it to the kid to run foul of trouble," growled the Flying W foreman. "My fault at that. . . . Ought to have known better than let the young fool go hellin' round in Hidalgo without you or me along. Serve him right if he cashes in."

Tex grinned, entirely undeceived by Buck's roar. It was well known that the lanky, blunt-spoken foreman had a deep affection for the irresponsible young Johnny Wales, whom he regarded as a son. Johnny's latest escapade in attempting conclusions with a quick-shooting gambler had resulted unfortunately for Johnny. Despite Buck's skilful first-aid treatment the bullet wound had developed a dangerous infection.

"Where do you aim to locate a doc?" queried Tex as they turned their horses and rode towards the chuck-wagon.

"Cottonwood Wells." Buck gestured to the north-east. "Figure it ain't more than fifteen miles. Can make it come sundown. If I don't get back time the creek is down enough to swim the cows across you can push on. I'll overtake you. Aim to stay in Cottonwood Wells till I know Johnny ain't losing a leg—or worse. I'll find him a room in some hotel where he can be took care of good."

Tantalizing smells of frying steaks and hot coffee pleasantly assailed them as they rode into camp. Buck turned his animal over to the horse-wrangler, instructing the latter to catch up three fresh mounts from the remuda.

"Throw Johnny's saddle on one of 'em," he directed. "Johnny and me is riding over to Cottonwood Wells soon as I get a cup of coffee." He lowered his voice. "Cut out that old Baldy horse for Johnny. . . . Baldy'll ride him in easy."

Johnny's indignant glare as Buck joined the group lounging round the camp-fire told the foreman that he had been overheard.

"Might think I was a stove-up ol' cripple the way you talk," fumed the youth.

"You'll sure be a one-legged cripple if you don't mind me," reproved Buck. He speared a piece of steak on to a tin plate and glared fiercely at the rebellious Johnny. "You're riding ol' Baldy if I have to rope you to the saddle. How does she feel, son?" he asked, in a softened voice. "Hurting bad?"

"Don't feel so good," admitted the wounded cowboy. "Feels like I got toothache in my leg—"

"The doc will fix you up," the foreman reassured him. He drained a second cup of coffee, and got to his feet. "Slinger—you're riding with us to Cottonwood Wells; and while I'm gone the rest of you boys are taking orders from Tex."

"Slinger," a dark-browed, wiry little man, hurried off to help the wrangler saddle the fresh horses. The two heavy guns swinging low against his thighs indicated that his nickname was not without significance. Perhaps the thought was in Buck's mind when he made the selection. Cottonwood Wells lay across the border, in No Man's Land—and anything could happen in No Man's Land. Buck was secretly perturbed at the thought of visiting the notorious rustlers' rendezvous, but it was Cottonwood Wells—or the life of Johnny Wales.

Followed by the affectionate gibes of Johnny's secretly worried friends, the three rode away. Two men lying on their stomachs behind a boulder on the slope west of the camp watched the departure with much interest.

"That's Buck Saunders," muttered one of the watchers. "I'd know him a mile away. Ain't forgot the time he plugged me." The speaker swore fervently. "Next time it'll be him—and not his gun arm, either." He looked at his smaller companion. "I'm goin' down there and kind of get the lay of things. You stay here, Pascoe. . . . One of them *hombres* might know you for an ol' Frying-pan hand." He crawled stealthily away, and disappeared into the thick bushes.

The expression in Tex Malley's blue eyes was none too pleasant as he watched the approach of the burly, black-bearded rider. The latter drew rein and bestowed the customary greeting of the country.

"Howdy?"

Tex grunted a surly acknowledgment of the salutation. The stranger grinned affably.

"Flood held yuh up, huh?" His gaze strayed to the herd grazing under the watchful eyes of four Flying W riders. "Right smart bunch of beef yuh've got there, mister. . . . Goin' north to Abilene with 'em?"

"Maybe yes—and maybe no," Tex told him gruffly.

The stranger shrugged, and glanced carelessly at the half-dozen men sprawled round the camp-fire. "Not meaning to pry into your business none," he laughed. "Was hoping maybe yuh could use 'nother hand."

"No chance."

"Well, no harm asking," grinned the man. He sniffed hungrily. "That coffee sure smells good—"

"Help yourself, mister," invited Tex, more civilly.

"Don't need to hear them words twice," chuckled the visitor. He slid easily from his saddle and swaggered to the big coffee-pot, ignoring the unfriendly scrutiny of the Flying W men. Strangers were apt to be regarded with suspicion by riders of the long trail. And in this case the Flying W outfit was not to be blamed for their hostility. Every salty man of them was aware of Jeff Wayne's intended invasion of King Cole's range. For all they knew this apparently jobless cowboy was a KC-Bar man—and therefore a potential enemy.

"Heading for Cottonwood Wells?" queried Tex carelessly.

"Not me," grunted the black-bearded stranger. "Too many of El Toro's killers in that town to suit me." He grinned at his watchful listeners. "Me, now—I'm plumb peaceful."

Tex pricked up his ears. "What about this jasper yuh just named—this El Toro?" he wanted to know.

"He's one tough *hombre*," proclaimed the man. "I've been hearin' tales that King Cole would give a thousand dollars to lay his hands on him."

"Never heard of him," Tex declared.

The black-bearded man's gaze went to the grazing herd. "Maybe yuh'll hear of him plenty before yuh cross the Honda." He wagged his head. "I'm tellin' yuh . . . keep a look-out on the border to-night, mister. Never can tell when El Toro Grande and his gang'll come swooping out of No Man's Land."

"Ain't worrying none about El Toro," Tex rejoined coldly. "We carry plenty rope for rustlers."

"El Toro is no common rustler," boasted the black-bearded man. "Don't seem like the rope is made that'll fit his neck."

"Who is this bad *hombre* you call El Toro Grande?" demanded Tex.

"No man knows," said the stranger solemnly. "No man has seen the face of El Toro."

"Where does he hang out?"

"Only El Toro himself could tell you. . . . They say that those who do his bidding are to be seen any day or night at Cottonwood Wells. El Toro makes the law for Cottonwood Wells."

Doubts assailed Tex as he realized the significance of this morsel of border gossip. Cottonwood Wells was likely to prove a death-trap for the unsuspecting Buck Saunders and his two companions. Tex was too good a poker-player to betray his thoughts; no hint of his mental turmoil leaked through the impassive mask of his face.

"Sounds like a big toad in a dirty puddle, this El Toro," he sneered.

The black-bearded man shrugged his shoulders. "Don't say you wasn't warned, mister," he said indifferently. He swaggered to his horse and swung up to his saddle.

"So long, gents."

With a careless nod he rode away, and was lost in the depths of a gorge.

"What yuh make of the jasper, Tex?" The cook spoke in an injured tone. "Did yuh see what he done? Empties three cups of my coffee down his big gullet an' high-tails it away without so much as a thank yuh kindly for the same. If that black-whiskered jasper is a gent, then I'm a ring-tailed chimpanzee."

"Chimpanzees don't wear tails," drawled a tall cowboy.

"Chimpanzees is monkeys, ain't they?" challenged the cook haughtily. "An' did yuh ever see a monkey that wasn't wearin' a long tail?"

"Chimpanzees ain't monkeys," maintained the cowboy. "Chimpanzees is apes, like your ancestors was."

The cook glared angrily. "Dang yuh hide! Aimin' to make a monkey out of me, young feller?"

"Meaning you claim to be a chimpanzee?" queried his tormentor, in a gentle voice.

"I'll chimpanzee yuh!" bellowed the enraged cook. He snatched up a meat cleaver.

"Quit the monkey business!" rasped the worried Tex. He frowned at the grinning cowboys. "No sense plaguing a top-hand cook like Hank." Tex paused, and rolled a cigarette thoughtfully. "Any of you boys notice the iron that black-whiskered gent's bronc was wearing?"

"Looked like a Box-RG," promptly spoke up the tall cowboy. A chorus of voices confirmed his statement.

Tex shook his head. "Never heard of any outfit using a Box-RG iron," he declared. "What you boys make of that *hombre*?"

"A low-down killin' coyote," pronounced the same tall cowboy. "The nice kind of gent that plugs yuh in the back when yuh ain't looking."

"Wonder what his game is," muttered Tex. He

shook his head. "If that bronc was wearing the KC-Bar iron I'd say he come down here to look us over."

"Maybe he's this here El Toro he was yippin' about," opined a bow-legged rider.

"One thing about him is that he don't mean any good to this outfit," decided Tex. He fixed his gaze on the bow-legged cowboy. "Bandy, you fork a bronc and high-tail it after Buck. Tell him what that black-whiskered gent was saying about El Toro being the big boss of Cottonwood Wells. No figgering what will happen if Buck and the boys get into the hands of that gang of killers running things in Cottonwood Wells."

The bow-legged puncher started at an awkward run for his horse. Tex hurried after him. "Bandy— if Buck figgers he's got to get Johnny to Cottonwood Wells in spite of hell or El Toro you trail along with 'em."

Bandy nodded. "I get yuh, Tex," he said grimly. He patted his two low-hanging guns. "Leave it to Slinger an' me to tame them wolves." He spurred away.

Tex slowly turned, and stared moodily at the remaining members of the outfit. Three of them were saddling fresh horses, making ready to relieve the four men riding herd. Counting himself and the cook, there were ten men left to guard Jeff's big trail herd, every rider of them a veteran in rustler warfare. It seemed absurd to worry, but the black-bearded man's visit had profoundly disturbed Tex, aroused gloomy forebodings.

Behind the brush-concealed boulders on the slope overlooking the Flying W camp the burly, black-bearded man was holding earnest conversation with the weasel-eyed Pascoe. The two were watching the small moving dot that was Bandy Higgins riding furiously to overtake Buck Saunders. They had quickly surmised the reason for the Flying W man's hurried departure.

"We gotta stop," growled the black-bearded man. "Won't help our play to have Buck Saunders heading back to the camp. Sure fits in with our plans to have him off in Cottonwood Wells to-night."

"That was Slinger ridin' with him," muttered the ex-Frying-pan man. "We sure don't want Slinger back here to-night, nuther. . . . Me—I don't aim to be round where that shootin' fool is."

"Only one thing to do," decided the big man. "You sneak back to your bronc, Pascoe, and make for the upper bend of the creek, where you'll be out of sight. The creek is wide there, and you can swim your bronc across easy. There's a deep barranca that will take you through them low hills . . . cuts off a good five miles from here to Cottonwood Wells, if Buck Saunders had known it. This jasper that's riding to warn Saunders will have to go clean to Buffalo Crossing before he can ford. You'll be waiting for him up there in the rimrock."

The little killer's weasel eyes glowed with a reddish light; and with the stealth of a weasel he slithered into the bushes. His companion's hoarse whisper followed him:

"And, Pascoe—mind yuh keep your rifle dry. . . . You'll be using that rifle—"

A low malevolent chuckle oozed from the black beard; and presently the burly plotter moved cautiously towards his concealed horse.

CHAPTER XI

THE TALKING SMOKES

THE sand-bar known as Buffalo Crossing proved passable; from this point Buck and his companions rode north-east from Honda Creek, following an ancient trail cut deep by the sharp hoofs of countless buffalo. Many an Indian war-party had passed along that primitive wilderness highway; later had come the adventurous fur brigaders, with their long rifles, vanguard of the paleface horde that was to claim the West for the white man. Buck knew that somewhere beyond the high ridge in front of them lay the town of Cottonwood Wells.

Innumerable deep ravines gashed the steep, boulder-strewn slope. The dark-browed Slinger voiced the thought that was in Buck's mind.

"Good country to get buckwashed in," he observed. "If there was some jasper didn't like our looks he could easy sneak up on us from one of these gulches."

"Reg'lar ol' woman," derided Johnny, "that's you, Slinger. Always imagining things!"

"Some day maybe yuh'll grow up and get some sense," retorted the little gunman coldly. "I repeat—if I did my killin' that way I'd sure choose me one of these nice little gulches and wait for my man to mosey along the trail; and by the same line of reasoning I'm moving up ahead of this party a couple o' hundred yards." Catching Buck's nod approving the precautionary measure, Slinger put spurs to his horse.

"Might think there was Indians huntin' our scalps," jeered the irrepressible Johnny.

"We're in No Man's Land, feller," Buck reminded him. "Slinger is right. . . . No sense taking chances."

A few minutes' stiff climb brought them to the crest of the ridge, where they found Slinger perched on a big boulder smoking a cigarette.

"Some view," he observed laconically.

Below them stretched a vast desert-like country, seamed by arroyos—a bleak expanse of mesquite and cactus. Looking back, they could see the silvery line of the Honda twisting through the flats to the darkening blue shadow that was the mouth of the Honda Canyon. Somewhere in those gathering pools of blue was the Flying W camp—the trail herd. Sunlight still touched the towering pinnacles of the Sangre de Cristo and the rugged crags of Saw Tooth, far to the west. The sun would be dipping behind those peaks within the hour; already the soft shadows were creeping up their eastern slopes.

Slinger's keen eyes fastened on a fly-like object moving across the flats lying between them and Honda Creek.

"Some one riding this way," he said.

"Looks like he'll cut the trail just where she starts to climb," commented Buck. His gaze went to the vast wastelands reaching towards the eastern horizon. On the northern rim of the desert—perhaps some five miles distant—was a huddle of buildings, the town of Cottonwood Wells, nestled at the foot of a low range of bleak hills. Buck was conscious of a huge relief as he stared down at that smudge of green and grey. . . . Another hour would see a doctor fishing for that troublesome bullet in Johnny's leg.

Slinger spoke softly. "What yuh make of that smoke yonder, Buck?"

The foreman stared with narrowed eyes at the thin column of smoke rising from the crest of a high ridge overlooking Honda Canyon, and about six miles from the sheltered valley at the canyon's mouth, where the trail herd would be bedded down that night.

"There's another of 'em," Johnny said.

The second spiral of smoke rose from a more distant peak lying to the south, and was barely visible. It faded for a moment, then again it hung against the horizon. Instinctively the three Flying W men looked at the nearer ridge; the column of smoke wavered, and spurted up blackly in a series of short and long puffs.

"Injun smoke talk!" exclaimed Johnny.

Buck's gaze went quickly to the low bleak hills lying to the north of Cottonwood Wells. A third column of smoke was curling up from one of the bare ridges back of the town.

"What yuh make of 'em, Buck?" There was an uneasy note in Slinger's voice as he repeated his question.

"Don't like the looks of 'em," muttered the foreman. "Shouldn't be surprised but what them smokes is talking about us?" He looked at Johnny. "How's the leg feeling, feller?"

"Don't feel so good," admitted the young cowboy reluctantly. "What yuh mean them smokes is talkin' about us, Buck?"

"Not about us personal," explained the older man; "more likely it's the cows somebody is interested in."

"Rustlers!" Johnny scowled. "We're heading back to camp pronto!" he declared. "To hell with my leg!"

Buck shook his head. "You'd only be in the way,

Johnny," he pointed out gently. "A one-legged cowboy is plumb useless round a cow-camp when there's rustlers on the prod."

"Don't see that feller that was down on the flats," called Slinger, in his curiously soft voice. "Saw him a minute ago—and now he's gone—"

"Spotted us up here on the ridge," surmised Buck. "He's laying low in one of them brush-draws till he's got us figgered out." The foreman's gaze swept the horizon. "The talking smokes have done talking," he added. "All right, Slinger . . . fork your bronc and high-tail it back to camp. Johnny and me don't need you riding herd on us in Cottonwood Wells."

The Flying W's premier gunman demurred. "We can be in Cottonwood Wells inside of forty minutes," he pointed out. "Won't take the doc more'n half an hour to fix Johnny up, then me and you can hit the trail back to camp. Won't need to worry about Johnny getting into trouble while he's laid up in a hotel bedroom. You can fix it with the doc to keep an eye on him."

Buck hesitated. He keenly felt the responsibility for the safety of Jeff Wayne's big trail herd. Also he realized that the life of young Johnny Wales depended on the prompt removal of the poison-breeding bullet. The wounded cowboy's own suggestion that he proceed to Cottonwood Wells without the aid of his friends was not to be considered. Iron fortitude had brought Johnny thus far on the journey. He had made light of his sufferings, but Buck knew, and the cold-eyed Slinger knew, that the youth was enduring intolerable agony. There was no telling when sheer weakness would bring about a collapse. Another thought was turning over in the foreman's mind. If rustlers had designs on the herd, as he suspected, the smoke signal behind the town indicated that the plot had its source in Cottonwood Wells. Slinger and he might pick up information that would effectively aid in forestalling an impending raid.

Slinger, cannily sensing what was in Buck's mind, pressed his argument. Slinger had his own reasons for desiring to accompany the others to Cottonwood Wells. He was highly dubious regarding the welcome in store for them in the town. The place was nothing better than a hang-out for border ruffians and rustlers; if it were true that the trail herd had been spotted and marked down for a raid there was good reason to believe that the arrival of strangers in their midst would greatly interest certain persons in Cottonwood Wells.

Slinger sensed sinister possibilities in the situation, wherefore it was his firm belief that his own pair of six-guns would considerably increase Buck Saunders' chances against suddenly joining the silent colony resident in Boothill Cemetery.

"Won't hurt none to learn what's going on in

that town," he urged craftily. "If there's a wild bunch figgerin' to rustle us we sure want to know it. No chance of 'em pulling off a raid before we get back to camp. I can do a heap of scoutin' while yuh're getting Johnny fixed up."

"Maybe yuh're talking good sense, Slinger," agreed the foreman reluctantly. "All right, let's ride."

Buck was to regret his decision. A tragedy might have been averted had he stuck to his first resolve to send Slinger back to the camp. Scarcely had the three men dropped below the brow of the hill when Bandy Higgins splashed across the sand-bar of Buffalo Crossing and turned his tired horse into the long hill trail. Had the others delayed their departure another minute, or had Bandy made Buffalo Crossing a minute sooner—but so closely is woven the pattern of Life with the pattern of Death.

Bandy's horse was too weary to take the long, steep ascent at anything faster than a walk. The cowboy relaxed to an easy slouch, and proceeded to roll a cigarette. Shadowy blue pools lay in gully and crevice. Overhead a buzzard winged lazily against deep blue sky; from somewhere in the distance a coyote sent up its wild, yipping cry.

"Move yore laigs, feller," Bandy admonished his weary horse. "I got me a message to get to ol' Buck."

He licked the cigarette and struck a match. From behind a boulder down in one of the shadowy gullies curled thin blue smoke. The match suddenly fell from Bandy's fingers, and, like a limp bag of meal, he tumbled from the saddle. Startled by the sharp crash of the rifle, the horse whirled round and tore down the trail.

Minutes passed; the thud of frantic hoofs died away in the distance; the hush of twilight deepened; and presently a wide-brimmed hat lifted above the boulder, and a pair of weasel eyes peered intently at the huddled heap lying across the trail. A grin distorted the killer's face. Rifle in hand, he moved warily towards his victim. Pascoe did not believe in overlooking a possible gold piece. The limp heap in the trail stirred, and as the gun in Bandy's hand roared Pascoe pitched forward, a look of silly surprise on his vicious face.

The Flying W man lifted his head with an effort, and peered closely at the limp, sprawled body of the killer. What he saw apparently satisfied him, and with a contented grin his own head sank lower and lower—lay very still against the damp, hoof-torn trail.

The reverberating report of the murderer's rifle faintly touched the ears of the three men descending the opposite slope of the ridge. Buck reined his horse.

"Somebody shootin'," he said uneasily.

"That feller we saw down on the flats," surmised Slinger. "Taking a shot at the coyote we heard yippin' a while back."

It was the second shot—the shot Bandy's friends did not hear—that killed a "coyote."

They pressed on towards the squalid huddle of adobe buildings that was the border town of Cottonwood Wells.

CHAPTER XII

GUNFIRE

THREE men rode down a moonlit canyon trail that followed the easterly descent of the Honda. Saddle-leathers squeaked, spurs jingled softly against the ceaseless roar of the storm-stressed stream.

Alertness marked the horsemen; they sat tensely erect in their saddles, eyes wary, searching out the dark pools of hollow and crevice, suspiciously scrutinizing each moon-silvered bush and boulder. One of the riders threw an appraising glance at the roiled waters of the creek.

"Honda is sure on the prod to-night," he declared. "Jeff, I'm bettin' yuh a fifty-dollar Stetson that Buck ain't got them cows across. We'll find 'em camped out on the wrong side of this hell-roarin' creek."

"My bet lays the same way, Curly," Jeff told

him. "You won't get you a new hat out of me on that gamble."

Chuck, riding on Jeff's right, suddenly reined his horse. "Listen!" he exclaimed softly.

They eyed him apprehensively. Chuck Wallis was noted for a pair of uncannily keen ears.

"Guns a-poppin'," muttered the cowboy.

Faintly the sound reached their straining ears—the unmistakable crackle of six-guns. They looked at each other with shocked eyes. Curly Stivens swore softly.

"El Toro!" he grunted.

Jeff's horse was already leaping into full stride; and, reckless now of ambush or treacherous footing, the Flying W men went drumming down the winding canyon trail.

CHAPTER XIII

TRICKERY

TRAGEDY stalked the moon-bathed mesa below Honda's frowning cliffs. Tex Malley lay prone behind his dead horse, a bullet in his left shoulder, the thunder of a trail herd's stampede shocking his ears. The pangs of his hurts were as nothing compared to the pangs of shame that gnawed the red-headed cowboy. Wounds of the flesh would heal—never this appalling blow to his pride. He had failed Buck Saunders.

Some twenty yards away the fair moonlight vaguely outlined a shapeless, dark mass that might have been a boulder or bush, but which Tex knew was another dead horse. Behind that inert carcass crouched the man who had shot Tex down, and the Flying W puncher was resolved to get that man if it were the last thing he did. Six-shooter gripped in his good right hand, he grimly waited for the rash movement that would deliver his enemy unto him. From afar, fading in the distance, came the last rumbling thunders of the stampede—an occasional crack of a six-gun. Off to the right a red glare below the bluffs told Tex that the chuck-wagon was in flames.

Red fire streaked through the moonlight; and as the rustler's gun roared Tex heard the thud of lead sinking into the inanimate flesh of his barricade. His own weapon spurted answering flame. The exchange tightened his caution; that one careless lift of his head when he glanced at the burning chuck-wagon might have cost him his life. The desperado across the way was on the alert, was lightning-fast with his gun. Tex settled down for another period of watchful waiting.

The last reverberating echo of the thundering hoofs faded into the distance; and suddenly another note beat softly across the hushed mesa. Wild hope surged through Tex. That faint, rhythmic beat was the drumming of horses' shod feet.

A doleful voice hailed him. "Let's call it a day, cowboy. You go yore way an' I'll go mine. No sense us layin' hyar."

Tex grinned, shrewdly surmising the reason for the speaker's sudden anxiety to be on his way. The sound of those drumming hoofs was not to the rustler's liking. The thought cheered Tex. Something whispered loudly in his ear that those approaching riders were Flying W men. The dolorous voice hailed him again.

"Talk up, cowboy. . . . Plumb foolish—us layin' out hyar when thar's good likker to be had over at Cottonwood Wells. No hard feelin's on my part for this night's work."

The sound of the drumming hoofs faded. Tex guessed the riders had halted to view the burning chuck-wagon. They may, or may not, have heard the recent exchange of shots; the chance was small that his plight would be discovered unless their attention was gained. It was difficult to distinguish a dead horse from bush or boulder in the deceptive moonlight. It was desperately vital to secure that attention. Tex tilted his gun, counted to three between each shot, and pulled the trigger three times. An answering flash winked through the darkness, and again the cowboy's .45 spat red flame skyward. This time three answering flashes winked back, telling Tex that the distant riders had correctly interpreted his signal and located his position. He listened tensely; drumming hoofs

127

again beat faintly at his straining ears. He counted off ten seconds, and fired another shot into the air. A single flash winked in return. Tex dropped the emptied gun and snatched up his second Colt. For the third time his hidden enemy addressed him, this time plaintively.

"Them yore friends, cowboy?"

"Figger it out for your own self, mister," Tex called cheerfully.

The dull thud of galloping hoofs drew towards them; vague shapes topped a distant rise and floated down the long slope. Tex sent a shot crashing into the night; the bark of a .45 came on the heels of the answering flash. The riders were coming fast and furious now, and hard on the roar of the six-guns came the rustler's dejected voice.

"Yuh've got me, cowboy. . . . I'm a-comin' out."

A shadowy form lifted from behind the speaker's dead horse.

Tex smiled grimly. No fool—that rustler. As Tex's prisoner he could hope for a chance—a slim chance—to keep on living; otherwise his doom was sealed. It was immediate surrender, or those horsemen would come with guns smoking.

"Keep your paws elevated," Tex warned the approaching rustler. "No tricks, mister." He moved warily round the carcass of his own horse.

"Yuh got me all wrong, cowboy," mourned the prisoner. "Me—I'm plumb peaceful—ridin' all happy an' care-free to Cottonwood Wells—just a honest cow-prodder with a month's pay burnin' holes in my pants pocket—an' danged if I don't ramble spang into this hyar rustler's shindig an' git my bronc shot from under me. I ain't no rustler, mister. . . . Me—I'm just a inner-cent bystander."

"Yeah?" Tex was frankly sceptical.

The prisoner glanced nervously at the rapidly approaching riders. He was a tall, stoop-shouldered, middle-aged man, and the pale moonlight revealed that his long, lugubrious face wore an expression of injured innocence. "I'm talkin' solemn truth," he groaned. "Stick up for me, young feller. . . . Don't let 'em make me dance on air when I ain't done nothin' but perteck myself. Was hightailin' for cover when yuh come smokin' yore guns at me. Ain't your fault I ain't lyin' there stark an' cold 'longside my poor bronc."

There was just enough truth in the man's story to raise a doubt in the cowboy's mind. While it was unlikely, it was not impossible that he was the victim of evil circumstance.

"Yuh won't dance on air none if yuh can prove your alibi," he gruffly assured his sad-faced prisoner. He stared doubtfully at the oncoming riders. He was not positive of their identity. Were they friends or foes? If the latter—well, there were four bullets left in his gun. Tex Malley's lean fighting jaw set in grim lines.

The three horsemen spread out as they came within gunshot; a voice hailed the two men standing between the dead horses.

There was no mistaking Jeff Wayne's voice; all doubt fled from Tex. Joyfully he sent out an answering shout.

"It's Tex!" yelled the voice of Curly Stivens; and in a moment the newcomers were spurring up through the moonlight. The lanky prisoner turned a ghastly face to his captor. "Stick up for me, feller," he implored. "I'll be dancin' on air if yuh don't—"

"What yuh got there, Tex? A rustler?"

Jeff swung from his saddle, his scowling gaze on the prisoner.

"Claims he ain't," stated Tex honestly. "Claims he was headin' for Cottonwood Wells when the rustlers stampeded us. I spotted him, and we shot it out. He got my bronc and I got his."

"Sure is the truth," affirmed the prisoner, in his mournful voice. "An' if yuh ain't objectin' none I sure crave to lower my hands. Gits kinda tirin' reachin' for the sky."

An astonished grunt from Chuck Wallis drew their eyes. The cowboy was peering intently at the captive.

"Know the jasper, Chuck?" rasped Jeff.

"Huh! Sure do!" The cowboy's voice was ominous. "Sure have heard your sad voice before, feller, and I've sure seen that long horse-face."

130

Chuck slapped his thigh. "Sinful Smith!" he announced triumphantly.

The KC-Bar man grinned. "That's me," he admitted. "Right glad to meet yuh again, mister. Yuh kin vouch for me to these other gents."

Jeff and Curly Stivens pricked up their ears. They had heard the story of the encounter with Sinful Smith at West Pass. Hot anger blazed in Curly's eyes.

"What d'I tell yuh, Jeff?" he cried. "Didn't I tell yuh King Cole was framin' yuh—him an' his hand of friendship!"

"Tie the man up," ordered Jeff briefly. There was a dazed, unbelieving look in his eyes. Was Curly right? Was the old lord of the KC-Bar playing cat and mouse with him?

"Where's Buck Saunders?" he asked Tex.

He listened patiently to the cowboy's story of the foreman's decision to rush the suffering Johnny Wales to Cottonwood Wells for medical treatment, the visit of the mysterious black-bearded stranger, the latter's warning to watch for raiders from No Man's Land, and his own fears for Buck's safety in Cottonwood Wells, where the notorious El Toro Grande was said to hold sway.

"Didn't seem right for Buck to go ridin' into that rustlers' nest and not know what he was up against," concluded Tex. "Sent Bandy Higgins chasin' after him. . . . Told Bandy to go along with Buck. Bandy's awful fast with a gun—most as good as Slinger."

Not a word of reproach from Jeff. He knew Buck Saunders, and he knew Tex Malley. What had happened was beyond their powers to foretell. He could have done no better than they. The raid had been cunningly planned—and executed. The fact that the one man taken was a KC-Bar rider was damning proof of old King Cole's duplicity. Jeff reluctantly found himself accepting Curly's theory. The story of El Toro Grande was a fable contrived to hoodwink him and keep clean the skirts of the KC-Bar.

"Wasn't expectin' no trouble from the west," Tex told him gloomily. "Had all but a couple of the boys posted between the herd and the border. First thing we knew a bunch of riders come hightailin' out of the Honda, smokin' their guns as they tore into the herd."

Jeff nodded. He could visualize what had happened: the sudden roar as that great herd rose to its feet, the clicking of horn on horn, the thunderous rumble of stampeding hoofs.

"They got old Windy Bill," he informed the downcast Tex. "Saw him lying there across his Winchester by the burning chuck-wagon."

"Windy was always sayin' he'd die with his boots on," muttered Chuck Wallis. "One he-man cook was old Windy." Chuck glared at Sinful Smith, whose bony wrists Curly was none too gently binding with a buckskin thong. "No sense wastin' time with this jasper," he said darkly. "Not when there's trees handy." Chuck gestured significantly at a gaunt-limbed cottonwood.

Jeff shook his head. It was in his mind to confront King Cole with his captured minion. "When Sinful dances on air he'll have plenty company," he promised Chuck.

"Mister—yuh're doin' King Cole wrong, an' yuh're doin' me wrong," insisted the captured KC-Bar rider earnestly. "It's like I said—I was ridin' plumb peaceful to Cottonwood Wells when I runs into this shindig." Sinful appealed to Chuck. "Wasn't I tellin' yuh I aimed to set in a card game to-night over at the Longhorn?"

"Yuh said somethin' of the sort," admitted the cowboy, recalling the incident of the twenty-dollar gold pieces.

"I'm awful truthful," declared Sinful solemnly. "Yuh kin ask ol' King Cole. He thinks a heap of Sinful Smith's word."

"We aim to ask him," Jeff assured him dryly. His voice sharpened. "You didn't tell us you stopped a bullet, Tex!"

"Nothin' much . . . no bone busted," scoffed the cowboy.

Jeff made a hasty examination of the wound, and with Chuck's expert aid contrived a temporary bandage. "How many you figger was in that gang?" he asked as he deftly fashioned a sling for the injured arm.

"Was too far away to see much," Tex told him.

"Judgin' from the gun-flashes, I'd say all of twenty or more. Pat Hogan and three of the boys was ridin' the border about a mile south of here. Don't know what happened to 'em. I'll bet they're hangin' right on them rustlers' tails— unless they caught some of that hot lead. Looks like the rest of our outfit is wiped out," he added, in a low voice.

Jeff nodded gloomily. Not until the bright light of day could he be sure of the fate that had overtaken his outfit. The cook, he knew, lay dead by the smouldering embers of his chuck-wagon; others had doubtless shared the cook's fate, or had been captured by the outlaws. The calamity that had overtaken his venture was a blow too stunning to be immediately comprehended in all its hideous completeness; and woven through the turmoil of rage and despair that beset him was the thought of the girl who was the daughter of the dastard who had struck this ruthless and foul blow.

Tex was staring disconsolately across the moonlit landscape. "Done run off the cavvy along with the cows," he mourned. "Sure made a clean sweep of the Flying W outfit!"

"How many horses did you bring along?" questioned Jeff, who had left the matter of the horse herd to the experienced Buck Saunders.

"Buck figgered on a string of eight broncs to a man," Tex told him. "I'd say there was about a hundred head in the cavvy, not counting Windy's two broncs and the chuck-wagon mule hitch." Tex swore softly. "And here I am set afoot in the middle of nowhere!"

The loss of the horse herd was a serious blow. Jeff knew that Chuck and Curly were chafing to pick up the trail of the outlaws. Every moment's delay in taking up the pursuit lessened hope of eventual recovery. Unless the chase was hard-pressed the stolen cattle would soon be safely hidden in some unknown canyon, where brands would be altered and the cattle either scattered over the almost trackless range or else pushed south-west, across the Mexican border.

Another thought greatly perturbed the young owner of the Flying W. Buck Saunders was in Cottonwood Wells, which, according to all reports, was a dangerous place for an honest cowman. The fact that Bandy Higgins and the cold-eyed Slinger, two of the outfit's fastest gunmen, were with Buck failed to allay Jeff's fears. It was imperative that he know the situation in Cottonwood Wells, and the only way to gather information was for himself to proceed to that reputed rustlers' roost.

"Curly," he told the blond cowboy, "you're riding with me to Cottonwood Wells, and Sinful Smith shares your bronc. Tex'll ride double with me, and, Chuck, you pick up that trail and follow it till you locate our cows. And mind what I say— don't pull off any play on your own account. All I

135

want to know is where those cows are holed up. When you locate them high-tail it back to the Honda. If we ain't here you hit the trail for Cottonwood Wells."

"Yuh're all mixed up, Jeff," protested Curly. "What yuh mean is for Chuck to ride to Cottonwood Wells with yuh an' for me to hunt them rustlers down. Chuck—he's that careless he'll ride plumb into a hunk o' hot lead, an' then where'll our cows be?" He grinned maliciously at the slim, cool-eyed Chuck.

"We're riding like I say," rasped Jeff. His voice softened. He knew the blond Curly's love of battle. "Maybe you'll be throwin' plenty hot lead yourself before we get out of Cottonwood Wells," he comforted the fire-eating puncher. "From what Tex says old Buck and the boys are sure needin' friends in that town. All right, let's ride."

"Listen!" hissed the lynx-eared Chuck. "Somebody shootin'!" He stared tensely into the south. "Sure is guns poppin'," he muttered.

Their eyes swept across the misty landscape. A flash winked through the darkness, and a second later came the faint bark of a gun. Curly's own six-shooter leaped into his hand, sent flame rocketing skyward. Three more shots flared from the south, and from a position slightly to the right winked a brighter flash, followed by the heavier crash of a rifle.

"Pat Hogan!" exclaimed Tex, in a jubilant voice.

"I'd know the yelp of that old Sharps of his anywhere."

Jeff and the others were already leaping into their saddles, and, guns winking their beacon flares, they dashed away.

Tex watched them enviously. An unhorsed cowboy was a pitiful thing, especially at such moments, when a man craved action. Muttering maledictions, the Flying W man flung a dark look at the cause of his horseless condition.

"If you swing—I'm pulling on that rope," he promised.

Sinful Smith gave him an uneasy grin. This talk of ropes and hangings was wearing on the nerves. Sinful knew the hair-trigger temper of the cowboy. He was of the breed himself. No knowing what might happen. The KC-Bar man stared gloomily at the gaunt cottonwood-tree.

"Yuh got me figgered all wrong, mister," he complained bitterly. "Wait till yuh kin ask folks in Cottonwood Wells about me. There's plenty folks in that town that kin tell yuh I ain't no friend to outlaws an' cow-thieves. That's all I ask . . . just wait till yuh kin larn about my honest, peaceable nature—" Sinful Smith broke off, cocked a listening ear. "Sounds like yore cavvy," he added, grinning round at Tex.

That low thunder rolling across the mesa could mean nothing else. Tex listened tensely, heard the faint yip of the distant riders. The horse herd, or a goodly part of it, had been salvaged from the stampede. Tex loosed an exultant yip of his own, and began hastily to strip off saddle and bridle from his dead horse.

The cavvy took form in the moonlight, came drumming up, and was skilfully manoeuvred into a narrow coulee, where two of the riders held the band of horses secure.

Swiftly the Flying W men roped fresh mounts, changed saddle gear, and rejoined Jeff and Tex. Curly was leading a big buckskin.

"Got yuh a real hawse," he told Tex, with a grin. "Lucky yuh've got one good arm, cowboy. Yuh'll need all yuh've got if this bronc gets notions."

"Don't yuh lose strength worryin' about me," retorted the wounded puncher cheerfully. "One arm is plenty unless an *hombre* aims to pull leather like yuh most always does."

He swung into the saddle, grinning at his indignant friend.

"All set, boys?" Jeff eyed his crew. "Chuck, Pat rides with you. Pat says the last he saw of the herd it was heading due south-west up the arroyo below Rocky Point. Keno"—Jeff's gaze went to one of the newcomers—"you stay with the cavvy . . . hold 'em where the camp was. The rest of you fellers and Sinful Smith ride with me to Cottonwood Wells."

Disappointment sat heavily on Tex. He stared glumly after the departing Chuck and Pat. "Seems like I ought to be ridin' south with Chuck," he demurred. "Ain't carin' much to face Buck—after me lettin' those cows get away," he added, in an undertone for Jeff's ear.

The latter shook his head. "You're going to that doctor in Cottonwood Wells," he declared firmly. He spurred away. With a clatter of hoofs the others fell in line; and soon only the recovered cavvy and the lone guard marked the scene of Chuck's encounter with Sinful Smith.

CHAPTER XIV

TWO DEAD MEN

THE elongated KC-Bar man's knowledge of the trails was an unlooked-for boon. Sinful yearned to be in Cottonwood Wells, had urgent reasons of his own for haste. If Jeff could have glimpsed the workings of the cunning mind masked behind Sinful's lugubrious countenance he would unhesitatingly have left King Cole's scheming henchman swinging under the nearest convenient tree. Jeff was yet to learn that Sinful Smith was a dangerous combination of sly fox and vicious wolf. The KC-Bar man's earnest protestations of innocence, coupled with a clinging shred of belief that King Cole was not the instigator of the night's ruthless affair, perhaps influenced the young owner of the Flying W. He wanted Sinful

Smith to prove his innocence, for that proof would also clear the owner of the KC-Bar. If his prisoner could produce reputable friends in Cottonwood Wells who would vouch for him, so much the better for Jeff's own peace of mind.

The grey dawn found them in the rimrock north of Buffalo Crossing. They rode steadily up the bleak slope, the same winding trail traversed the previous evening by Buck and his two friends. The sky lightened, pale gold flushed the eastern mountain rim, and suddenly the sun came up in a hot, angry glare. Curly, riding in advance of the others, reined in his horse and turned a startled face to his companions.

"Bandy!" he exclaimed. "It's Bandy Higgins—layin' here dead in the trail!"

They crowded up, staring silently at the lifeless form sprawled across the trail.

"Died throwin' hot lead at the skunk as dry-gulched him," muttered Tex, noting the gun in the dead puncher's clenched hand.

The four Flying W men dismounted and gathered sorrowfully round the earthly remains of their late comrade. Sinful Smith watched them uneasily, fear in his pale, bulging eyes. He sensed peril in the situation.

Jeff gently pried the gun from the stiffened fingers. "Fired one shot before he passed out," he told the others after a brief examination.

"Bandy wasn't one to waste lead when he pulled

a trigger," Tex said grimly. "Reckon we'll find that killer layin' somewheres below the trail."

"An' there he lays!" exclaimed Curly. He went clattering down the side of the gully. The others watched, heard his surprised oath. "Boss—it's that Pascoe *hombre* as was wrangler for the Frying-pan until yuh kicked him off the ranch."

"Pascoe, huh!" Jeff's face hardened; he turned and eyed Sinful Smith. "You know this jasper, fellow? Was he riding for the KC-Bar?"

"Never heerd tell of him afore," declared the lanky KC-Bar man stoutly.

"Lucky for you," muttered Jeff. He followed Tex down to the killer's body, his glance directing the remaining Flying W cowboy to keep guard on the prisoner.

"Bandy's bullet got him between the eyes," announced Curly, straightening up. "Reckon he dropped Bandy first with his rifle, and was comin' over to make sure he was dead when Bandy pulled the trigger. See—there's Pascoe's tracks, leading from that boulder."

"Funny thing—him laying behind that boulder— waitin' to get poor old Bandy," murmured Tex. "Sure don't figger it out how he knew Bandy was heading this way after Buck."

"Your black-bearded friend," said Jeff. "There's your answer, Tex. He saw you send Bandy high-tailing after Buck, and sent this rat to dry-gulch him. Didn't want Buck to get your message."

Curly swore softly. The mystery was getting too deep for him.

"I'm bettin' yuh've guessed it right, Jeff," muttered the unhappy Tex. "If I'd only figgered what he was up to things might have worked out different."

"Nobody's blaming you, Tex," Jeff told him curtly. "None of us can know everything."

"Should have used my gun on him," mourned Tex. "Would have been no cow-stealin' if I'd used my gun on him." His gaze flicked back at the watching Sinful Smith. "Reckon Pascoe'd have a horse cached somewheres near here." The cowboy's eyes glittered. "If that bronc wears the KC-Bar iron I'm voting for a hangin'-party right here and now." His glance again flickered significantly at Sinful Smith. The latter licked suddenly dry lips.

"My vote goes the same way," growled Curly. He vanished into a thick growth of juniper. "Here's Pascoe's bronc!" came his voice. The saddle under their prisoner squeaked as he stirred uneasily. Curly spoke again. "Don't wear the KC-Bar iron, though." Disappointment was in Curly's voice. He reappeared, leading a dejected, gaunt-flanked sorrel. Relief looked out of Sinful Smith's pale eyes.

"Strip the gear off and turn him loose," directed Jeff. "Sure would have starved to death if we hadn't run across him."

They had another task to perform, and when they rode on their way a pile of stones marked the spot that was Bandy Higgins' last earthly resting-place.

The killing of the messenger sent to warn Buck added fuel to Jeff's fears. Gloomy forebodings weighed heavily on him. The fact that the killer was a former Frying-pan man told a disquieting story—a story that explained much concerning the previous night's raid. Pascoe knew of the proposed trail-drive, and had carried the information to King Cole. Jeff could think of no other explanation. Lylah's ruthless old father was behind the whole affair. He had been a fool, a simpleton, to believe for a moment that King Cole would surrender a princely domain without a fight. With one hand he had offered friendship, and with the other had knifed Jeff in the back.

Jeff winced; for behind his bitter thoughts was the memory of a slim, dark-eyed girl, whom he knew now was all the world to him, and whom he knew, with a desolating certainty, must be banished for ever from his mind and heart. He could not hope to win the daughter of the man upon whom he must make relentless war.

They topped the ridge, from which point Buck and his companions had viewed the mysterious smoke signals the previous evening. Below them, on the desert's rim, sprawled the grey adobe walls of Cottonwood Wells.

CHAPTER XV
COTTONWOOD WELLS

S UNLIGHT streamed through the bars of the small window set about the height of a tall man's head in the adobe wall. Buck Saunders was a tall man, and by clinging to the bars with both hands and rising on his toes he was able to obtain an unobstructed view up the wide, dusty street that was the main thoroughfare of Cottonwood Wells.

The buildings sprawled along the street, which at this early-morning hour showed no signs of life, were mostly squalid adobe hovels, with here and there the gaunt, false-fronted frame structure common to the border West. None of these last had known paint, although some of the more pretentious places of business and pleasure showed signs of whitewash, long since weather-stained and scarred by blistering sun and fierce desert wind.

Stretched across the end of the street, which was several short blocks in length, rose a decrepit two-storey frame building, identified by a large sign swung from the balcony as the Great Western Hotel, and of course was for the comfort of paying guests. It had been Buck's plan to enjoy briefly the luxuries of the Great Western Hotel as advertised by the swinging sign. He was not at all pleased with the private room he now occupied. The adobe building that blocked the lower end of the street directly opposite the hotel was also a hostelry of sorts, but, unlike the Great Western, no charge was made for board and room. Here one could enjoy, or otherwise, the hospitality of Cottonwood Wells without the expenditure of a penny. In fact, Buck's temporary place of residence was Cottonwood Wells' municipal bastille—otherwise the gaol.

Dejection sat heavily on the tall foreman's face as he stared gloomily up the squalid street. Apart from the fact that he had never before occupied a gaol-cell, he was frantic with apprehension about the trail herd. He should have heeded the warning of the "talking smokes" and avoided Cottonwood Wells as one avoids the plague.

He could see his mistakes with horrifying clarity now that it was too late. He should have used stealth in getting Johnny Wales into the town—in fact, Slinger and he should not have entered its confines in the circumstances. Johnny could have made the last half-mile without their help. Johnny's condition would have precluded any attempt at violence upon his person. He was a sick man, and as such entitled to the consideration of even the ruffian citizenry of Cottonwood Wells. Johnny was due for a hard time of it, the doctor had said. It was a toss-up whether Johnny would pull through. . . .

Buck's eyes filled with pain at the thought of Johnny dying; a lump rose in his throat, and his fingers, clenched round the iron bars of the narrow window, tightened in a fierce grip that brought white blotches to his knuckles. Buck loved harum-scarum Johnny Wales.

A mongrel dog crawled from under the planks of the pavement, and after blinking inquiringly up and down the street sat down and leisurely scratched first one ear and then the other. Three dejected cow-ponies stood at the hitch-rail in front of one of the more gaudy saloons, evidently forgotten by their drunken owners. A blanketed Indian stalked from a sort of alley between two adobe buildings. A squaw followed him, and after a brief word with her lord shuffled through the dust towards the ramshackle hotel at the end of the street.

The buck sat down on the edge of the pavement, evidently of a mind to bask in the warming sun while waiting for his spouse to forage food from the hotel kitchen. Noises began to emanate from other buildings—voices, and the clatter of booted feet, the banging of doors. Cottonwood Wells was awakening—that portion of it not sleeping off the debauches of the long night.

Buck withdrew his gaze from the dreary scene, and eyed the slumbering Slinger Downs, sprawled on a pile of dirty straw. There was a smear of dried blood on the dark-browed puncher's face, and after a moment's scrutiny Buck stooped and ran his fingers through the thick thatch of black hair. Light as was the touch, the cowboy stirred, and sat up with a jerk.

"Feller, you sure got a lump where that jasper's gun hit yuh," Buck told him. "If yuh ain't got a headache I'm a sheepherder."

The little gunman scowled, and felt the bump gingerly. "Some *hombre*'s goin' to get worse than a headache when we get out of this lousy hole." Slinger fumbled in a waistcoat-pocket, and gave a dismayed look. "Took my smokes off of me—the thievin' coyotes!" he complained disconsolately. He got to his feet. "Take your baccy too, Buck?"

"They wasn't taking chances on us settin' fire to the straw," Buck told him. "Wouldn't want us burnin' down their nice *cuartel*."

"Huh!" Slinger shrugged his shoulders. "Fire won't burn these 'dobe walls. At that all a fire could do would be to suffocate us good. No, suh, they done took our baccy just to be low-down mean an' onery."

He went to the window, and drew himself up to the bars for a glimpse of the street. The loss of his cigarette tobacco was the least of Slinger's woes at this moment. He knew without a word from Buck that the latter was suffering torments over the outcome of this visit to Cottonwood Wells.

Despite the uneasiness caused by the mysterious smoke signals, their arrival had apparently attracted no undue attention. Buck's first concern was to get Johnny into a comfortable bed. Ignoring the patient's earnestly expressed desire to tarry at one of the drink palaces, the foreman had hustled Johnny into the hotel, and Slinger had gone in quest of a doctor.

"You'll mos' likely find the doc over at the Longhorn Bar," was the information gleaned from the hotel proprietor. "Doc Mosby mos allus settin' in at a poker game when he ain't probin' for bullets. He sure acts peevish if yuh make him lay down a good hand, so don't rile him if yuh can help it. Let him play his cards out if he's a mind to."

The Longhorn Bar proved to be Cottonwood Wells' most ornate pleasure establishment. Always cautious, Slinger, without appearing to do so, made an inspection of the exterior. Information regarding doors and windows and where they led to was a first principle rarely neglected by the salty little gunman.

A casual stroll round the long frame building told him all he wanted to know. After a sharp glance up and down the street to note if curious eyes were unduly interested in his movements, he pushed through the swing-doors.

For so early in the evening the Longhorn was well patronized. Slinger paused for an instant just inside the door, alert eyes making a quick survey of the place. Some half-score of men were lined up at the bar, which ran the full length of the left wall, and was presided over by a beefy individual with a red, perspiring face. Apart from a furtive glance he showed no interest in the newcomer. Slinger's gaze travelled down to the far end of the long room, and fastened on a group seated at a card-table. There was no need to have Doc Mosby pointed out to him. The short, pudgy man wearing a white goatee, rumpled linen suit, and wide-brimmed straw hat could be none other than the poker-loving doctor. One would have guessed correctly that Doc Mosby had originated somewhere below the Mason-and-Dixon line.

Satisfied that he had found his man, Slinger went swiftly towards the poker-players and bent over the object of his search.

"Doc Mosby, suh?"

The doctor looked up with sleepy-lidded eyes, remarkably blue and clear, under white-thatched brows.

"Got a sick man over at the hotel, suh," whispered the Flying W man. "Blood poisoning." Slinger grinned apologetically. "Right sorry to bother yuh—but yuh're the only doc in this man's town."

The doctor snorted. "Bother me! Who you're bothering me, young man?" He tossed his cards on the table, and broke into a good-natured chuckle. "My friend, you save my life. These gentlemen are taking me to the cleaners." Smiling genially, the doctor pushed back his chair and reached for a worn black bag. "What's your outfit, suh?"

"He's a young feller as got shot up a while back," evaded Slinger, conscious of listening ears.

The doctor nodded, and trotted briskly towards the street door. Slinger followed, secretly mystified at the singular lack of interest exhibited by the patrons of the Longhorn in his hurrying the doctor away from his card game. The remarkable absence of curiosity vaguely troubled the gunman. This indifference to a stranger among them, and to the errand that demanded a doctor's immediate attendance, impressed Slinger as unnatural. Something told him that his presence was no cause for surprise to these men; their avoidance of his eyes was too studied to be real.

As the swing-doors closed behind Slinger and the doctor one of the men rose from the card-table and sauntered across to the bar, where he spoke briefly to a swarthy half-breed. The latter nodded, and hurried into the street. After a brief whispered conference with the red-faced barman the man rejoined his companions at the poker-table. They gave him sly grins.

"Sent the marshal his orders?" The speaker chuckled.

The other man's smile was not pleasant to see. He was tall and thin, his bony, fleshless face covered with parchment-like brown skin. He was rather elegantly attired in a long, double-breasted black coat and dark trousers tucked into shiny black boots. His name was "Smoke" Hawker, and he was the proprietor of the prosperous Longhorn Bar—and Cottonwood's outstanding citizen.

"Yes," he said softly, "our town marshal has his orders." The saloon man deftly shuffled a fresh pack of cards, and continued to speak in a low voice. The others listened attentively, and presently two of them followed the half-breed into the street. Like most of the patrons, they wore the garb of the cowboy, and both carried two guns in their holsters.

Still puzzling over the reception accorded him, Slinger escorted the genial Doc Mosby to the hotel, where the doctor paused to speak to a pretty, fair-haired girl hurrying towards the dining-room door. Slinger judged she was the waitress.

"Hello, Nellie! May need you for some nursing to-night." The doctor chuckled. "Make a nurse out of you yet if one of these cowboys don't run off with you first."

The girl blushed prettily, a phenomenon Slinger observed with some surprise. Cow-town waitresses were not usually given to quick blushes. He eyed her curiously, realized that she was very young, and obviously new to the border West.

Chuckling at her confusion, the little doctor followed Slinger up to the first-floor room where Buck was firmly putting Johnny to bed.

"Reckon yuh'd better take our broncs over to the feed barn for a spell," the foreman whispered to Slinger as the doctor went to the bedside. "You and me is headin' back for the Honda as soon as the doc gets Johnny fixed up. Those broncs'll ride better with a feed in 'em."

Slinger nodded, and hurried from the room and down the rickety stairs to the street. It was quite dark now, and he had to inquire the way to the nearest livery barn from a half-breed lounging near the hitch-rail.

"Me show you," offered the man.

He led the way down the street, past the brightly lighted saloons, past a squat adobe building at the end of the street, where a burly man stood framed in the lighted doorway, above which was painted the words "OFFICE OF CITY MARSHAL." The man gave Slinger a sharp look, stepped quickly towards him.

"Hey, feller—"

The cowboy glanced back. The man hurried up, and Slinger saw that he wore a marshal's badge pinned to his black shirt.

"Yuh ain't wearin' them guns in this town, mister." The marshal's voice was decidedly hostile. "We got a new law agin strangers totin' guns."

"Try and take 'em from me," invited the little gunman softly.

Unfortunately for Slinger his back was turned to

his obliging half-breed guide; he failed to see the man's arm swing up. Something hard struck him with terrific force across the temple—he felt himself sinking into oblivion.

Infected bullet-wounds were an old story to Doc Mosby, and before Buck had cause to wonder at Slinger's non-return the troublesome piece of flattened lead had been skilfully removed from Johnny's leg.

The little doctor was not pleased with the outlook, it seemed. He beckoned Buck to follow him into the corridor.

"It's going to be a fight," he gravely informed the foreman. "As nasty a case of blood-poisoning I've seen in a blue moon. Another day—we couldn't have done a thing."

"Yuh mean Johnny's due to—to die, doc?" Buck's voice trembled.

"He has a chance—just a chance. Of course, we can amputate—"

The foreman gave him a horrified look. "Johnny'd rather hand in his checks," he muttered. His big hand clutched Doc Mosby's plump shoulder. "Don't yuh go cutting off his leg, doc! I got a little bunch of cows down on the Pecos. . . . Yuh can have 'em—have anything I got—if yuh get Johnny on his two feet again."

"He'll not die if I can help it," the doctor assured him. "I said the boy has a fighting chance . . . he's young and strong. Lucky you got him here before it was too late to do what little we can."

"Was aimin' to be on my way . . . got a big trail herd on my hands," Buck told him. "Sure hate to leave, with things looking so bad for Johnny."

"Not a thing you can do here," declared the doctor. "If he pulls through—and we'll make up our minds that he will—he won't be on his feet again inside of a week or ten days at the earliest. Might as well be attending to your business, and leave the boy in my hands, which is my business." Doc Mosby nodded vigorously. "You look after your cows, suh."

Buck knew the advice was sound. Waiting in Cottonwood Wells could avail Johnny nothing . . . and his duty to Jeff Wayne must not be slighted. Worry masked under a cheerful grin, he returned to the bedside.

"Be back in a day or two," he told the suffering cowboy. "Doc reckons you'll be right as rain in no time at all." The tall foreman chuckled. "The doc says he's fixin' up to have yuh a cute little nurse . . . don't want me round botherin' her."

"Don't need no nurse foolin' round me!" fumed Johnny. "On your way, feller. Jeff's cows is worth a sight more than a fool puncher like me. Go on—fork your broncs, you and Slinger. Something tells me there's rustlers ridin' the trail to-night."

Doc Mosby followed Buck to the door. "If you

154

see a girl with corn-coloured hair down in the office tell her to come up," he instructed. "She answers to the name of Nellie Blaine," he added. "If she's not around tell Hank Smithers at the desk."

The tall foreman clattered down the shaky stairs to the office, where he came upon the girl with the corn-coloured hair standing in the street entrance and gazing wistfully up at the star-jewelled sky. He addressed her bashfully.

"If yuh're Nellie Blaine, ma'am, Doc Mosby is wantin' yuh upstairs."

"Oh, yes, sir—I'm Nellie Blaine." She gave him a shy, confused look from eyes as blue as cornflowers. "I'll go right upstairs. . . . Sometimes I help Doctor Mosby."

Buck strode into the street, much pleased and relieved. He felt that he was leaving Johnny in safe hands. He liked Doc Mosby, and the thought of Johnny having the tender care of a good woman did much to lighten his heavy heart. He began to wonder why Slinger had not returned from stabling the horses. Perplexed, he stared up and down the street. From the hotel office came the tread of booted feet; Buck's gaze swung to the door. The three men emerging into the street were the same he had observed lounging at the desk. One of the trio, a burly, hard-faced individual, wore a marshal's star pinned to his black shirt. The latter muttered something to his companions, and all three moved towards the Flying W cattle boss.

"Howdy, stranger?"

Buck returned the greeting, suddenly sensing hostile intent on the part of these men. His gun hand slid down to holster; the marshal spoke in a snarling voice.

"Keep yore hands from yore gun, mister . . . up with 'em—an' keep 'em up."

His gun leaped into his hand—the guns of his two companions menaced the foreman.

"What's the idee?" Buck spoke coolly, halting the downward swoop of his hand.

"Yuh're under arrest," the marshal informed him gruffly. "Take his guns, fellers."

Something warned Buck that any attempt at an argument would only mean a speedy and unpleasant finish—for himself. Reluctantly he lifted his hands, allowed the confiscation of his guns. He had a pretty fair notion now of what had detained Slinger. "What's the charge?" he wanted to know.

"Yuh'll find out soon enough," growled the marshal. "There's plenty agin yuh, feller."

Buck fired a shot in the dark. "Maybe your two friends is from the KC-Bar," he said contemptuously.

The hard-faced trio exchanged sly glances; one of them snickered. The marshal swore, gestured with his gun. "Git movin'," he ordered curtly.

"It's the calaboose for you, mister." He gave his prisoner an evil grin. "Yuh'll find comp'ny waitin' for yuh. . . ."

One circumstance brightened the gloom that sat upon Buck Saunders and Slinger Downs—the fact that Johnny Wales had been placed in the competent hands of Doc Mosby before the sinister activities of the marshal of Cottonwood Wells robbed them of their liberty. The thought was in Slinger's mind as he looked round from the barred window.

"Might have been a sight worse," he reminded his companion philosophically. "S'posin' that onery marshal had grabbed us the moment we hit town—shoved poor Johnny into the calaboose 'long with us."

Buck nodded glumly. "Nothin's so bad but what it might be a heap worse," he agreed.

The little gunman's gaze went back to the street. "What yuh figger these coyotes aim to do with us?"

"Turn us loose when they've done what they've set out to do," replied the foreman, in a dejected voice.

Slinger glanced at him uneasily. "Meanin' when they've got Jeff's cows hid where we'll never find 'em, huh?"

"That's the way I figger their play." Buck shook his head. "We should have minded them talking smokes, feller."

The dark-browed Slinger scowled. "Somebody is goin' to pay good for this," he promised. "Do yuh figger it's the KC-Bar in this, Buck? Figger old King Cole's been laying in wait to grab Jeff's cows an 'bust him afore he gets the old Flying W on her legs?"

"Plumb sure of it," declared the Flying W cattle boss. "Jeff was taking a long chance bringing cows up here to KC-Bar territory. King Cole ain't letting no outfit horn in on his range. Look what he done to Jeff's dad when Jeff was a kid."

"Jeff won't take it layin' down," opined the salty Slinger. "Plenty gun-smoke due when old Jeff puts on war paint." Slinger's voice died away, and for a moment he stared in stunned silence up the dusty street.

"Buck!" The gunman's voice was exultant. "He's ridin' into the street now. . . . Jeff's ridin' into the street—an' Tex is with him, an' good ol' Curly, an' Andy Trigg—"

Others had observed the arrival of the Flying W men with their prisoner, Sinful Smith. Among the interested bystanders was the swarthy half-breed. The latter threw a startled glance of recognition at the dejected Sinful Smith, and hastily retreated through the swing-doors of the Longhorn Bar. Another barman had replaced the beefy drink-dispenser of the previous evening, an elderly, grizzled-moustached veteran, who was leisurely mopping the imitation mahogany bar with a soiled damp cloth. Save for two bemused cowmen snoring in chairs, with tousled heads bent over a card-table, the long room was empty of customers.

"What's on yore mind, Pedro?" The old barman eyed the half-breed attentively. Excitement was writ large on Pedro's broad, swart features.

"Gotta see the boss queek!" gasped the man.

"Smoke ain't up yet," the barman told him; his hand ceased its circular movement with the cloth. "Yuh knows the boss don't git outer bed afore ten o'clock—'less somethin' big's due to bust."

"Gotta see the boss queek," insisted the half-breed.

With a shrug indicating that the crime would be upon Pedro's head the barman dropped his wet rag, limped round the end of the bar, and knocked on the door of a room under the balcony that ran across the rear of the dance-hall. A voice answered, and after a brief moment the door opened an inch or two. The old barman backed away apprehensively.

"Pedro says he's gotta see yuh pronto," he informed the unseen occupant of the room. "Maybe thar's somethin' big due to bust loose."

The door opened wider, and the saloon man's death's-head face peered into the bar-room.

"What is it, Pedro?"

"*Señor!*" gasped the half-breed. "Beeg news I breeng you!"

Hawker's peculiar tawny eyes glittered, and at his gesture the half-breed glided up and vanished into the room. The barman returned to his leisurely mopping, his inquisitive gaze fastened on the closed door. It suddenly flew open; Pedro shot out, sped on cat-like feet to the swing-doors, and disappeared into the street. The barman eyed the vibrating doors thoughtfully for a moment, then took a gun-holster hanging on a nail, and buckled it round his waist. Limpy knew from long experience that events sometimes came fast and furious in Cottonwood Wells.

Unaware of the interest aroused by their arrival, Jeff and his friends continued down the street towards the marshal's office, pointed out to them by an obliging citizen. It was on Jeff's mind to turn his prisoner over to an officer of the law, if such an official was to be found in Cottonwood Wells. The arrangement was not entirely to his satisfaction. The law in Cottonwood Wells was apt to be a farce, and its enforcer a hireling of the desperadoes rumour said were in control of the town. Although it entailed the possible loss of his prisoner, Jeff considered the experiment worth trying. According to the measure of vigilance the marshal used in guarding Sinful Smith, so would Jeff measure the honesty of the marshal. Sinful Smith's escape from gaol would mean that the Flying W could not hope to find friends or obtain justice in Cottonwood Wells.

From the little barred window of their cell Buck and Slinger eagerly watched the approach of their friends, and speculated upon the identity of the prisoner. The fact that Tex Malley accompanied the owner of the Flying W struck the worried foreman as ominous. Tex, he saw, wore his arm in a sling. There could be only one answer to that . . . rustlers. Buck's heart sank into his boots.

The unexpected arrival of Jeff and Curly Stivens had the foreman guessing wildly. Buck had supposed they were miles away, guarding the secret of Crater Basin from KC-Bar eyes. Things had been happening since he left the trail herd to the care of Tex Malley. The foreman felt in his bones that what had happened had not been for the best. Slinger spoke softly in his ear.

"Yuh reckon Jeff's got wind of what that marshal's done to us fellers?"

"Search me," grunted the foreman. "One thing's sure—Jeff's going to know we're in here awful soon. Nothing to keep us from telling him our own selves. All we've got to do is talk up loud through these bars."

Alas for Buck's hopes! No sooner expressed than to be dashed to the ground. Unnoticed by the two engrossed at the window, the door behind quietly swung open; the marshal and the two men who had accosted Buck in front of the hotel stepped quickly through the entrance. Behind them scowled the face of the half-breed. The marshal spoke in a fierce whisper:

"Git back from that window, fellers— an' keep your traps shut—if you aim to live!"

The levelled guns in the hands of the speaker and his hard-eyed companions spoke louder than words. Glaring furiously at the marshal, but careful to refrain from speech, Buck and Slinger moved away from the window. The marshal addressed them again:

"Both of yuh lie down on that floor . . . flat on yore backs . . . an' mind yuh—not a whisper. One word outer yuh, an' we fill yuh with plenty hot lead pronto. I'm talkin' turkey to yuh."

The two Flying W men knew the marshal meant what he said; they could tell when a man was bluffing—and this cold-eyed representative of the law in Cottonwood Wells was assuredly not bluffing. Maintaining their sullen silence, they assumed the desired prone position on the straw-littered floor. The marshal motioned to his companions, who swiftly bound arms and legs with short pieces of rawhide brought for the purpose. Whereupon the half-breed deftly gagged them with pieces of dirty towelling.

The whole affair had taken less than three minutes. The marshal, with a muttered word to the half-breed, hastily withdrew, followed by his two friends. The door closed; the half-breed grinned at the two prisoners, and proceeded to roll a

162

cigarette, at which Slinger's eyes cursed him. The half-breed grinned again, and made himself comfortable by squatting on his haunches in front of the door. Through the barred window came the sound of trampling hoofs—the well-known voice of Jeff Wayne. . . .

"Howdy, marshal? . . . Got room in your calaboose for this jasper?"

There was no reason for Jeff Wayne to suspect that his trail boss lay bound and gagged within a few feet of him behind those thick adobe walls. The short ride down Cottonwood Wells' main and only street had discovered nothing to arouse suspicion. As yet the little border town was still somnolent, scarcely awakened to the activities of a new day.

The town marshal favoured him with an affable grin. "Sure—got plenty room, mister—but how come yuh're wishin' to stick ol' Sinful Smith behind the bars?"

"Got reason a-plenty," Jeff assured the marshal. He gave a brief account of the raid resulting in the loss of his trail herd, quite unaware that the story he told was adding to the distress of a much-troubled Buck Saunders. The marshal stared grimly at the sad-faced Sinful Smith; the latter's left eye drooped slyly.

"This right, Sinful?" barked the marshal. "Yuh was nabbed—after shootin' it out with this other jasper?" The marshal jerked his head at Tex.

"Ain't denyin' that part of it," answered the KC-Bar man, in his mournful voice. "Was like I said to Mr Wayne. . . . Was ridin' for town here an' got mistook for a rustler." Sinful Smith grinned sympathetically at Jeff. "Don't blame 'em none for suspicionin' me, an' maybe yuh'd best lock me up for a spell, marshal—'till I kin prove I'm an innercent man. Don't hanker none for these gents to git peevish an' of a mind to set me to dancin' on air." Again his left eye drooped a sly wink.

The marshal glared at him fiercely, and stepped from his office door into the street. "Maybe yore story's straight, Sinful—an' maybe yuh're a liar. Git down from yore bronc," he blustered. "Seems like there's nothin' else I kin do but lock yuh up. An' listen close, feller—if it's proved yuh turned to cow-stealin' in yore old age yuh'll sure decorate a tree awful soon. Fellers like yuh is givin' Cottonwood Wells a bad name."

He ushered the prisoner to the door, and turned him over to his deputies. "Watch him good," he warned. Unseen by the Flying W riders behind his back, the marshal gave Sinful Smith a sly wink of his own as the guards led him away.

"Seen anything of three fellers riding broncs wearing the Flying W iron?" queried Jeff when the marshal returned from handing over his prisoner. "One of 'em with a hurt leg and looking for a doc?"

The marshal considered for a moment. "Seems

like I did hear about 'em," he finally admitted. "Come to think of it, Hank Smithers over at the hotel was tellin' me Doc Mosby's tendin' a sick *hombre* a couple of fellers brought in last night. Reckon the other two pulled their freight . . . ain't seen nothin' of 'em myself." The marshal shrugged indifferently. "Maybe Hank can tell yuh about 'em."

Jeff eyed the marshal suspiciously. He was not impressed with the law officer; nor was he impressed with his story. "Know of a rustler they call El Toro?" he asked curtly. "Heard this town is El Toro's hang-out."

"Some *hombre*'s a liar," retorted the marshal angrily. "El Toro sure don't hang round in this town—not while I'm marshal."

"Then you know this El Toro, huh?" persisted Jeff.

"There's been some talk of him the last few months," admitted the marshal cautiously. "Some say there ain't no such animal. . . . Me—I ain't run into him myself."

"There's talk that he runs this town," broke in Tex softly.

"An' I'm talkin' loud that some *hombre* is a liar!" repeated the law officer. He threw Tex a sour look.

Curly Stivens spoke up: "Just the same, we lost a bunch of cows last night, mister marshal—"

"Meanin' what, feller?" blustered the officer.

"Meanin' there's rustlers in your territory," Curly sneered.

"I'm town marshal. What goes on outside of this town ain't my business," retorted the officer surlily. He swung on his heel, hesitated. "Say, yuh're Jeff Wayne!" He eyed the young cattleman with renewed interest. "Sinful Smith spoke yore name, but I didn't git yuh placed right off." The marshal grinned. "There's been talk of yuh, mister."

The four Flying W men eyed him intently, and Jeff said quietly: "What kind of talk, marshal?"

"That yuh was aimin' to horn in on the KC-Bar." The marshal wagged his head. "Maybe if yuh put two an' two together yuh kin figger out where yore cows has got to. King Cole ain't lettin' no outfit horn in on the KC-Bar." With this parting shot the marshal stamped into his office.

Curly Stivens looked at Jeff with blazing eyes. "That feller's talking turkey—which means it's a KC-Bar job!"

Andy Trigg of the saturnine countenance looked longingly at the gaol door. "Curly's right," he said judicially. "Yes, suh, Curly is sure callin' a spade a spade." Andy glanced at the gaol door. "I'm for yankin' that Sinful Smith *hombre* out of there an' hangin' him to a limb right now."

Jeff shook his head. He had his own good reasons for turning the KC-Bar man over to the marshal, and in any event the dour-faced Texan's plan could result only in complete disaster.

166

"No sense us committing suicide, Andy," he pointed out. "Come on, let's mosey over to that hotel and see Johnny. He'll tell us about Buck and Slinger. Sure want to get on the trail of those fellers."

They swung their horses about, and rode two abreast up the street, now showing an increased activity. Cowboys clattered noisily along the rough-planked pavements, some bound for hotel or restaurant, others vanishing behind the swing-doors of the several saloons. A buckboard whirled down the street, trailing a banner of dust, and halted in front of the big general store. Across the street was the gaudy front of the Longhorn Bar. As the quartette of Flying W men rode past Smoke Hawker emerged from the saloon, followed by an alert-eyed man wearing two guns. The two stared casually at the passing riders. The man with the guns looked inquiringly at his companion. Hawker nodded. The gunman gave a hitch to his holster, and sauntered slowly in the direction of the hotel.

Hawker's strange tawny eyes turned towards the gaol, from which the marshal was emerging. Apparently satisfied, the saloon man swung on his heel and vanished behind the swing-doors.

The marshal made his way up the street leisurely, nodding greetings to acquaintances, and pausing for a brief chat with the driver of the buckboard in front of the store. The marshal's eyes were busy as he talked, and presently, when Jeff and his friends had disappeared into the hotel, the officer hastened across the street and vanished behind the swing-doors of the Longhorn Bar.

CHAPTER XVI

WAR IN COTTONWOOD WELLS

JOHNNY was sure that he was dead—and in heaven. He was not surprised to find himself dead. Buck Saunders had often darkly prophesied his untimely demise; but to find himself in Paradise rather astonished him. Johnny had never been confident that when his time came the Pearly Gates would be opened to him. A border cowboy just didn't seem to belong in a place where there were angels—and yet here was an angel bending over him, an angel with beautiful golden hair and sweet blue eyes and tender smile. Johnny closed his eyes.

"Poor fellow," murmured the angel. "He's nothing but a boy, scarcely any older than me." Anxiety crept into the soft voice. "His fever's rising. . . . Oh, I do wish Doctor Mosby would come!"

Johnny's eyes opened. "Yuh was speaking, ma'am? Reckon yuh're one of them angels, ma'am, like my mother used to sing to me about when I was a kid. . . . She—come up here long time back. . . . Reckon I'll meet up with her round here somewheres. . . . She'll be right pleased to see her Johnny." The feverish voice was apologetic. "Awful sorry, ma'am—to come up here botherin' you angels—"

"Oh, please don't talk that way! I'm not an angel. . . . I'm just Nellie Blaine. Oh, why doesn't Doctor Mosby come!"

"Nellie . . . Nellie—" The delirious voice hushed, and presently the patient's regular breathing told the girl that he slept.

Relief sprang to her eyes; she looked down at the relaxed face, admired the healthy bronzed skin, the thick, wavy hair, the boyish yet singularly firm mouth, the powerful brown hand clasping her slender fingers. She feared to break that clasp; he was sleeping so peacefully now—for the first time—

The tread of booted feet echoed on the stairs. The girl frowned. Such a clatter. . . . Not Doctor Mosby. . . . Might be a regiment trooping up the rickety old stairs. . . . She'd give them a piece of her mind—only she couldn't—not while Johnny's big brown hand held her prisoner. She wouldn't risk waking him for anything less than a fire—

The tramping feet came on down the corridor, halted outside the door. And suddenly Nellie was frightened. Those men—what were they doing there at Johnny's door?

Three months in lawless No Man's Land had

considerably disillusioned her young girl's belief in the chivalry of men. She had seen dreadful things happen in Cottonwood Wells—seen the smoke of belching guns—seen dead and dying men in the street.

Nellie gazed at the door fearfully. Had these men come to take Johnny—come to kill him?

Low whispers reached her straining ears—a gentle knock. Nellie's terrified gaze came back to the peacefully sleeping cowboy. Slung over a chair at the head of the bed was his holster, with its two heavy guns. She reached quickly with her free hand and grasped one of the weapons.

Another and louder knock—a gruff voice. "Is Johnny here? We want to see Johnny."

The girl held her breath, and swung the gun to cover the door. The knob was turning.

"Ain't locked," muttered another voice. "Let's take a look, Jeff. Maybe the kid's lyin' in there dead."

The door opened, and disclosed four dusty, travel-worn cowboys crowding the entrance. Nellie spoke in a fierce whisper. "Don't you dare come in here. . . . I'll shoot—"

The four men gaped at her. She stared back, defiant, watchful, half crouched by the bed, one hand clasped in the sleeping cowboy's, her free hand menacing them with Johnny's heavy .45.

One of the men addressed her in a quiet voice. "We're Johnny's friends, ma'am. I'm his boss,

Jeff Wayne, of the Flying W ranch." The speaker smiled reassuringly. "No need to keep that gun on us, ma'am."

Another step sounded in the hall, unaccompanied by the jingle and rasp of dragging spurs and the swish of leather chaps. Doctor Mosby this time. The girl's tension relaxed.

"If you are his friends, please wait a moment. The doctor is coming. He may not want Johnny disturbed—now he is sleeping at last."

The gun continued to menace them. The blond Curly grinned at her admiringly.

"Ma'am," he said fervently, "I reckon we ain't had no call to be worryin' about Johnny—not with you looking out for him."

"Hello—hello!" Doc Mosby bustled in, astonishment on his jovial pink face. "Bless me, what's doing here!" His gaze went to the gun. "Put that cannon down, girl! Might go off and hurt somebody."

The six-shooter slipped from her limp hand. "I—I thought they'd come to—to kill him!" she gasped.

"We're Johnny's friends," explained Jeff as the doctor turned inquiring eyes on the intruders. "How is he making out, doc?"

Doc Mosby moved to the bedside and stared down intently at the patient. He gave the girl a surprised look.

"Bless my heart!" he muttered. "Sleeping like a

baby . . . and holding on to your hand like a drowning man to a rope—"

"I've been afraid to take my hand away from him," Nellie told him, in a low voice. "He was so restless . . . it seemed to quieten him." She flushed.

"Best thing you could have done," chuckled the wise little doctor. He beamed at the interested audience. "Thanks to this young lady your friend will be on his feet and well as ever inside of a few days—a very few days. Gentlemen, meet Miss Nellie Blaine. You can thank her for a miracle."

Wide-brimmed Stetsons were in their hands; and Jeff said earnestly, "We sure do thank you, ma'am. The Flying W won't forget all you've done for Johnny."

Nellie blushed. The frank admiration and gratitude of Johnny's friends left her rather breathless; she smiled faintly, downcast eyes on the sleeping cowboy. Jeff took pity upon her, and gestured to the others to retire outside. They tiptoed out, followed by Jeff and the doctor.

Jeff questioned the latter about Buck and Slinger. Doc Mosby seemed surprised.

"Understood they were leaving town soon as they could get away. . . . Said something about a trail herd," he informed the interested cowmen. "Queer you didn't meet 'em."

"The herd was rustled last night," Jeff told the

doctor. "Tex here will tell you that Buck and Slinger never got back to camp. . . . And where they are sure has us plenty puzzled."

"Looked in any of the feed barns?" queried the doctor. "The tall man, Buck, said something about getting a feed for their horses." He gave Tex a professional glance. "Come to my office before you leave, young man. . . . I'll dress that bullet-hole for you." Doc Mosby eyed the bedroom door worriedly. "That girl's been up all night . . . must send her off to bed."

With a genial smile of dismissal he bustled back into the sick-room.

"Something awful smelly in Denmark," muttered Tex as the four men went quietly down the rickety stairs. "We'd have met Buck and Slinger if they left this town last night. Sure don't like the signs."

"If Buck and Slinger were on the trail last night they'd have found Bandy," Jeff pointed out. "The fact that Bandy was still layin' there proves they never left town."

"Can't get round that argument," assented Tex.

"You boys go scout round the feed barns," Jeff told Curly and Andy Trigg. "If their broncs are in town we'll know for sure that Buck and Slinger have run into trouble."

"That marshal!" growled Curly. "Sure ain't carin' for his looks none. Got a hunch he was lyin' when he said he ain't seen Buck and Slinger." The blond cowboy swore. "Tex, yuh done said a mouthful . . . this business smells dirty."

Smells of food came to thcm as they descended to the office. Jeff eyed the dining-room door. "First thing we do is eat," he wisely decided; "then we'll go through this town and comb her out good."

"Always could fight best with a hunk of steak in me," grinned Curly, "an' something tells me that maybe guns will be smokin' before we see the last of this rustlers' roost."

They clattered into the long, narrow dining-room, and took possession of a table. The frightened-eyed man behind the desk slouched after them.

"Don't wait on table usual," he confided. "My niece is helping Doc Mosby nurse yore sick friend. Nellie is my dead wife's niece . . . a orphan. That's why she come from Kansas City to live with me. Ain't got no home of her own. Business sure has picked up since I put her to waitin' table. What's yore orders, gents?"

They ordered, and Jeff, realizing that this man must be Hank Smithers, questioned him about the missing foreman. The hotel man darted an uneasy glance at the door. Smoke Hawker's gunman was slouching in. With a nod that held a veiled warning the man took possession of an adjoining table. The hotel proprietor's leathery face went ashen.

"Ain't seen yore friends from the time they left my place," he declared loudly. "Must have been in a awful hurry . . . didn't stop to eat or nothin'." He slouched off to the kitchen. When he returned a piece of paper lay under the slice of bread on the plate he placed in front of Jeff. With nervous haste Hank Smithers backed away.

"What's yores?" he asked the man at the next table.

"Cup o' coffee, Hank. Already done et over at the Chinks. . . . His coffee is sure rotten." The man grinned across at the Flying W contingent. "You gents come to the right place if yuh craves good coffee."

"We'll be the judge and jury, mister," retorted Curly acidly, always quick in his likes and dislikes, and instantly conceiving a hearty dislike for this booster of Hank's coffee. He would have said more, but for Jeff's warning glance.

There was a curious expression on the latter's face as he stared down at the slip of paper on his plate. The message he read there was startling. "Maybe Smoke Hawker can tell you about your friends," ran the hasty pencil scrawl.

Jeff cautiously slid the piece of paper under his hand to Tex, who silently absorbed the message and passed it on to Curly and Andy. The latter, at a glance from Jeff, wadded the paper between thumb and forefinger and slipped it into his half-emptied coffee-cup. Curly pushed his chair back.

"Me—I'm full to the guards," he announced. "Only thing I craves right now is just one little snort of red likker, meanin' I hereby declares we drop in at the Longhorn for the same."

"Sometimes, Curly, yuh get right bright notions," approved Tex.

A four-horse stage was rocking down the dusty street as the four friends emerged from the Great Western Hotel. They watched it in silence for a moment, saw it swerve to the left, and whirl past the adobe gaol at the end of the street.

"Reckon she runs between here and Abilene," observed Tex. Not that he cared about the destination of the Cottonwood Wells' stage. The remark was for the benefit of the man who had followed them out from the dining-room. The Flying W men knew that their unwelcome companion was furtively watching them from the hotel door.

Curly yawned elaborately. "Well—thought we was goin' to sample red likker," he drawled.

"There's the doc!" exclaimed Jeff, glimpsing a rotund figure standing in the doorway of a low adobe building a short distance down the street. "Tex—you mosey over to his office now and get your arm fixed. The drinks can wait."

He gave the other two a significant look, and with answering flickers of their eyes Curly and Andy Trigg went clattering down the rough planks. They knew without a waste of words that their immediate job was to locate certain horses wearing the brand of the Flying W.

Tex glanced doubtfully at the doctor's office. He smelled danger, was uneasy at this splitting up of their forces. Jeff read his thoughts, and smiled grimly. "I'm waiting here in one of these chairs till you boys get back," he said loudly. "No use me getting all hot when there's nice shade here."

He lounged casually to one of the chairs lined against the wall. By which Tex knew that his young boss was taking up the duties of watch-dog. "This man is a spy," Jeff's eyes told him. With a brief nod the cowboy bent his steps towards the adobe office of Doc Mosby.

Jeff's lazy-eyed glance told him that the spy was uneasy. Apparently he was disconcerted by this split-up; and it was equally apparent that his chief concern was in the business that had taken Curly and Andy down the street, in which direction were to be found the town's two livery barns. It came to Jeff that somebody had blundered, had carelessly left certain Flying W horses where they should not be.

Unobtrusively Jeff's left hand loosened the gun on that side of his holster. The spy was on his right, between him and the hotel entrance. An attempt to follow Curly and Andy would bring him directly in front of Jeff.

The latter had not long to wait. The spy, after a sly glance at the sleepy-eyed man in the chair, lounged from the entrance, only to halt abruptly as a soft Texan voice addressed him.

"If yuh ain't in a rush, mister, maybe you can give me some information about things in this town—"

"Huh!" The spy glared suspiciously. "Ain't got time to chew the rag," he said ungraciously. He took another step, and halted again as Jeff's left-hand gun slid into view.

"Keep your paw away from that smoke-wagon, feller!" Jeff's voice had lost its soft drawl, was suddenly ominously chill.

The man's hand relaxed its clasp over the gun-butt. "What's the idee?" he growled sullenly. "Ain't carin' for your funny play, mister."

"Said I wanted to talk to you," returned Jeff quietly. "Fact is—maybe you'll tell me why you come spying on me and my friends."

"Anybody says I'm spyin' on yuh is a liar," declared the man defiantly.

"Maybe you take pay from El Toro—or is it King Cole you get your orders from?" sneered Jeff, watching him intently.

The man's eyes flickered uneasily. "Don't know either of them gents," he blustered. "I ride for the Circle Y, an' yuh'll swallow plenty hot lead when my outfit hears of this funny play."

"Smoke Hawker run the Circle Y?" Jeff's voice was ironic. "Just where does this Circle Y outfit run cows, cowboy?"

"Hawker don't run cattle . . . he runs the

Longhorn Bar. Hawker is a friend of mine, an' I'm tellin' yuh, mister, he won't like it none—you goin' on the prod with his friends."

The man's gaze went down the street, and the thick fingers curled convulsively.

"Keep your hands up," warned Jeff, not shifting his gaze to look down the street. The man's expression told him that Curly and Andy Trigg were returning—and not on foot. They were riding the horses that had brought the missing Buck and Slinger to Cottonwood Wells.

"Curly and Andy are awful peevish this mornin'," he drawled. "They don't like some things about this town—and you're one of 'em."

"Found 'em, Jeff!" Curly Stivens' voice was choking with anger. "Found the broncs over at the XL Feed Stables! I'm for takin' this town apart if they've done for old Buck an' Slinger."

"Tie the broncs with the others," Jeff ordered. He rose from his chair, careful to keep his attention on the spy. "Andy—you watch the horses. . . . Curly—you take this jasper's guns."

The blond cowboy swiftly removed the weapons, and at a gesture from his boss threw them under the flooring of the porch that fronted the hotel. Fortunately the location of the hotel at the end of the street effectively covered their actions. Chance observation from down the street would not arouse curiosity. They were just a group of cowmen in casual conversation. If

Hank Smithers was aware of any extraordinary proceedings taking place on his hotel porch he was careful to ignore the affair.

"Seems to me I noticed an old 'dobe shack off to the side of this hotel as we came up," drawled Jeff. "Kind of curious to take a squint inside that 'dobe shack . . . might be a real interestin' old ruin. What you say, Curly?"

"Got the same notion," grinned the cowboy, grasping what was in Jeff's mind. "Reckon I'll take a rope along. Always hanker to tote me a rope when I go explorin' old 'dobe ruins."

Jeff motioned to his thunderstruck prisoner to move on across the street.

"Maybe you'd like to take a look at the old shack yourself," he invited courteously.

They crossed the dusty street, the prisoner slouching between the two Flying W men. No chance observer would have guessed that one of the three cowboys strolling round the sun-blistered walls of the hotel was a prisoner.

As Jeff had surmised, the tumbledown adobe shack was tenantless.

"Nice place for tarantulas," Curly muttered as they ducked inside the gloomy interior. He gave the prisoner an ugly grin.

"No time to waste," Jeff said. "Get busy with that rope, Curly."

The blond cowboy worked swiftly with his lariat. "Gotta gag him," he grunted as he rose from the completed task. "Yell his head off if we don't close his trap."

"Maybe he'll do some talking first." Jeff leaned over the prostrate prisoner, and pushed a gun-barrel against the man's side. "Talk up, mister. Where's Buck Saunders—and Slinger Downs? You know who I mean?"

They read ghastly fear in the crafty eyes; the unshaven face was suddenly grey, beaded with sweat.

"El Toro'd kill me," muttered the man. "I ain't talkin'—"

The quick-tempered Curly was in a killing rage. He loved Buck Saunders—and Slinger Downs was as a brother to him. He bent threateningly over the bound man, the fingers of his hand curled round the worn butt of a six-shooter. "Who's this El Toro *hombre*? What's he done with Buck Saunders—an' Slinger?"

"Yuh ask Smoke Hawker," gasped the man, wilting under the impact of the cowboy's blazing eyes.

"Smoke Hawker seems to be the big wind in this town," Jeff said softly. "Is Smoke Hawker this here El Toro?"

"There's some talk he is," muttered the prisoner sullenly. "Yuh cain't prove it by me."

"All right! We'll ask Smoke Hawker that same question." Jeff smiled thinly. "We'll tell him you told us to ask him."

"Smoke'll kill me!" gasped the man. "Yuh cain't buck Smoke Hawker in his own town. He'll make cold meat outer yuh, an' me too, for givin' him away."

"Don't worry none about Hawker killin' yuh." Curly's grin was sinister, grim with dark promise. "I'm savin' that little job for myself, mister—if we don't find Buck an' Slinger enjoying their usual good health."

At a gesture from his boss he deftly gagged the prisoner with his own soiled bandana; and, leaving the weather-beaten, crumbling walls holding their secret, the two Flying W men drifted casually across the street to the hotel.

Tex had returned from Doc Mosby's office, his left arm neatly bandaged and supported by a sling in a manner that gave him the use of his bridle hand. He grinned cheerfully, waggling his fingers at them.

"Doc says no damage done, to speak of—"

Jeff grinned. "Looks like you'll be needin' that hand to help swing a few rustlers, Tex," he chuckled.

His gaze swept the street. Banners of dust beyond the gaol told him that horsemen were approaching from the west. The newcomers might be honest cowboys in for a Saturday night's fling, or they might be members of the rustler gang returning from their successful raid on the Flying W. The day was still young for the arrival of whooping, jubilant, pleasure-seeking riders from the more distant cattle outfits ranging the Cimarron country to the west and north, wherefore those lifting banners of dust impressed Jeff unfavourably. This affair of the missing Flying W foreman called for fast and furious action, while life still ran at low ebb in Cottonwood Wells. Another half an hour might see overwhelming reinforcements in the presence of those approaching riders. With a terse word to the others he swung up to his saddle.

Faces grim, cold eyes watchful, they rode down the street, Andy Trigg leading the two riderless horses. Swarthy faces peered furtively from the dark doorways of adobe hovels; two cowboys clattering along the planked pavement towards the general store stared curiously at the strangers. A tall, thin man wearing a wide-brimmed black hat and black frock-coat emerged suddenly from the swing-doors of the Longhorn Bar. At his back pressed the burly town marshal. The latter swaggered forward, raised his hand authoritatively.

"Hey! Whatcha aim to do with them two broncs?"

The marshal's hand slid down to his gun. "Them broncs ain't leavin' this town 'less yuh pay the feed bill on 'em."

Jeff, Curly, and Andy were swinging from their saddles as the officer spoke. Tex, handicapped by his wounded arm, remained in his saddle; his part would be to guard their horses. Jeff addressed the truculent marshal politely.

"You run the XL Stables?"

"Sure do! An' them broncs has a feed bill due—"

"That's funny." Jeff's voice was sarcastic. "Those broncs were ridden into this town by the two men you was telling me you hadn't seen hide nor hair of. How comes you ain't seen 'em—and their horses in your feed barn?"

With an oath the marshal reached for his gun, but changed his mind as three guns whipped up, covering him and his tall companion. From behind them Tex kept alert watch up and down the street. Faces stared curiously from doors and windows. If there were any spectators disposed to aid the marshal none apparently cared to challenge the menacing .45 in the good right hand of the vigilant-eyed Tex Malley.

"You're resistin' an officer of the law," blustered the marshal. "Could kill yuh legal for this—"

"Yeah!" jeered the irrepressible Curly. "You an' your tin badge! Where did yuh get that badge, feller? Ain't no law in this robber's roost."

The marshal threw an irresolute glance at his tall, frock-coated companion. The latter spoke softly, addressing the officer.

"Let me attend to this, Stiles. No sense starting gunplay over a feed bill." He smiled blandly at the glowering Flying W men. "Come in, gentlemen. Might as well talk things over in a friendly spirit. The drinks are on the house."

Jeff eyed the speaker intently. "You Smoke Hawker?" he asked curtly.

The tawny eyes flickered, perhaps not caring for the chill menace in the young cattleman's voice.

"That's my name, mister."

"Was told you can tell me what's become of two of my men. Found their broncs in the XL feed barn—but ain't finding Buck Saunders and Slinger Downs."

Smoke Hawker's gaze shifted for a brief moment in the direction of the lifting yellow haze nearing the outskirts of the town. Jeff's face darkened. The saloon man was expecting help from that quarter.

"Talk fast! I'm in one big hurry," he warned. "You know what's happened to my friends. That spy of yours spilled the beans, Hawker—or is it El Toro I'm talking to?"

The saloon man's death's-head face contorted malignantly, the strange tawny eyes glittered. With an effort he quickly recovered his urbane smile. "Just plain Hawker, young man—Smoke Hawker to my friends." The suave voice was suddenly a sneer. "As for your men—they're in gaol—charged with cattle-stealing."

"Yuh're a liar!" growled Tex from his horse.

Hawker's yellow eyes rested on him fleetingly,

185

as though marking the speaker. His voice rasped on:

"King Cole, of the KC-Bar, has been losing cattle to rustlers. He asked Marshal Stiles to be on the watch for suspicious characters. These three men, one of them wounded, answered the description, and the marshal nabbed two of 'em—"

Jeff's voice, cold with rage, interrupted the saloon man.

"Reach for the sky! The two of you! Curly, if that fake marshal makes a move—start your gun smoking. Andy, you take their guns."

Andy Trigg obeyed, removed a small but deadly Derringer from a shoulder-holster under Hawker's frock-coat.

"Now the gaol keys—"

"Got 'em," grunted the cowboy, withdrawing his hand from the marshal's pocket. He held up the keys triumphantly.

From somewhere above them sounded the roar of a six-gun. One of the led horses squealed, and went plunging away. Almost instantly Tex Malley's .45 belched smoke. A splintering crash followed the report of the heavy Colt; and those underneath the balcony, though they could not see, knew that a man's body was plunging through the gimcrack railing. The sickening thud in the street behind them announced that Tex Malley's bullet had found its man. The cowboy uttered an astonished exclamation.

"Jeff! That was Sinful Smith just tumbled off the balcony! Your marshal done turned him loose, like you figgered he would."

The street came to life. Men's excited voices, booted feet clattering on the board pavements. Shouts and oaths from the darkened interior of the Longhorn, a rush of heavy feet for the swing-doors. The three Flying W men under the balcony in front of the door closed round their prisoners. The swing-doors bulged, and suddenly swung back as Curly flung a shot through the panels. Jeff spoke grimly.

"Hawker, another shot from your crowd and you're a dead man—you and your hireling killer marshal! Tell 'em what I say—quick!"

There was a sudden silence in the street, which the cold-eyed Andy Trigg and Tex were menacing with their guns, a sudden silence inside the Longhorn Bar. The saloon man's thin, cold voice broke the silence. "No gunplay, friends. Stiles and I can attend to this matter. . . . Just a misunderstanding."

"Now, Hawker, you and the marshal walk in front of us to the gaol. I'll be right behind you. Curly, you and Andy look out for Tex and the broncs. All set, Tex? . . . Let's go!"

The strange procession moved down the street, the tall Hawker and the burly marshal side by side, Jeff with six-shooter at their backs. Tex followed, leading the horses under the ready guns of his watchful-eyed comrades.

The trailing dust-banner was nearer, lifting in quick spurts; sign that the gunshots had been heard by the approaching riders. Jeff's eyes spoke their message to Andy; the latter hurried to the oak door set in the thick adobe wall of the gaol. It was not locked.

Leaving Curly and Tex on guard outside, Jeff and Andy hustled the prisoners into the marshal's office. Flame streaked from the dark passage leading to the tier of cells. Echoing the thunderous clap of the half-breed's gun, followed the roar of Andy Trigg's .45. Gun-smoke filled the little office, bit at eyes and nostrils.

Smoking gun in hand, the Flying W puncher ran into the passage. Curly dashed in, saw that he was not needed, and returned to his post outside.

"Got the skunk plumb centre," came back Andy's satisfied voice. "All right, boss."

There was no need for the cell's key. The half-breed deputy had left the cell door open as he hurried into the passage to lie in wait for the men holding his chief a prisoner. The sight of his dead deputy did much to soften the marshal's truculence. His face bloodless, he meekly entered the cell, followed by the coldly contemptuous Smoke Hawker.

Andy was already busy freeing the two bound Flying W men. Buck got up stiffly, stretched aching muscles, and grinned at Jeff.

"How's Johnny making out?" were his first words.

Jeff assured him that Johnny was "on the mend." The tall cattle boss beamed, and eyed the sullen prisoners with lively curiosity.

"What you aimin' to do with these gents?" he next wanted to know.

"Serve 'em the way they served you and Slinger," Jeff informed him grimly.

"And I'm tyin' the knots on this onery marshal coyote," growled Slinger as he got to his feet. He glared at the self-styled marshal.

The cold menace in the eyes of these men told Smoke Hawker and his hired gunman that protests would be futile. Sullenly they lowered themselves to the hard earthen floor; and presently the four Flying W men were in the dark passage, the heavy door locked on their captives.

"You can throw the key away when we get outside," Jeff told Andy. "Throw it so far they'll never find it this side of Christmas."

They trooped into the office, ignoring the limp body of the slain half-breed deputy lying in the passage. The first thoughts of Buck and Slinger were for their confiscated guns and holsters. The sight of them adorning a nail on the office wall gladdened their hearts.

"And am I cravin' food!" mourned Slinger. "Me an' Buck ain't ate since yesterday noon. Gotta take my belt in a coupla notches."

They hurried out; Andy locked the gaol door, and for good measure hurled the keys into a distant patch of weeds. Curly came up, leading the horse stampeded by the bullet intended for Tex.

"Ain't hurt at all," grinned the cowboy. "That piece of lead just burned his hide some."

The sound of approaching hoof-beats came clear and loud. There was no chance now to get away unseen by the oncoming riders. Jeff's glance saw the open doors of the XL feed barn a little to the right of the gaol. With a gesture for the others to follow he leaped to his saddle and rode for the open doors. In a minute they were inside, putting to frantic flight a terrified Mexican, who went burrowing under a mound of straw.

"What are we running for?" Curly wanted to know, in an aggrieved voice. "There's six of us here now. Tex an' Andy each got 'em a man. I sure craves a couple of scalps my own self."

"Maybe this outfit that's riding in will give us plenty action before we say *adios* to this town," the foreman prophesied coldly. "Jeff don't do things without good reason, cowboy."

Jeff, who was watching through the partly closed door, looked round at them.

"One of you get Johnny's horse," he ordered. "Can't leave Johnny in this town after what's happened."

"I'm ropin' that doc and taking him along with us," murmured Buck Saunders. "Andy, you go get Johnny's bronc, and cinch that saddle good."

Drumming hoofs swept round the adobe gaol;

Jeff peered cautiously through the stable door. The men crowding at his back saw his long, lean body go suddenly rigid.

"Know 'em, Jeff?" The foreman spoke softly. Jeff looked round, and they saw that his face was troubled. There was a stunned expression in the young cattleman's eyes, and dawning anger.

"It's the KC-Bar outfit," he told them, in a strained voice. "Old King Cole himself." His gaze went back to the crack in the door.

It was not the sight of King Cole that had so shaken Jeff; nor the fact that with him rode Steve Cole and the giant Bart Sladen, with some half-score riders at their backs. It was the slim, boyish figure riding stirrup to stirrup with the grim old cattle baron—the unmistakable figure of Lylah Cole. The glimpse of her filled the young owner of the Flying W with heartsick longings, and at the same time tortured him. Bit by bit damning evidence had piled up against that little but formidable and ruthless old man on the big black stallion; evidence that in Jeff's eyes convicted King Cole of a cruel double-dealing and infamous conduct only to be avenged by the shedding of blood.

The haste shown by the self-styled marshal in turning loose the recently and suddenly deceased Sinful Smith positively linked the KC-Bar with El Toro's desperadoes. Jeff believed that the mysterious El Toro was Smoke Hawker—that

Hawker was in league with King Cole. The presence of KC-Bar men in town meant war. The temper of the Flying W outfit was strained to the breaking-point—his own heart was bitter against this lying old man.

His brain in a whirl, Jeff stared dumbly at the horsemen pressing up the street. Sladen and his punchers reined in their horses in front of the Longhorn Bar, but the foreman did not enter the saloon. Instead he crossed the street and joined King Cole, who had dismounted before a small building opposite the Longhorn. After a few moments' conversation the two men entered the building, which had a lawyer's sign above the door. Lylah and Steve continued up the street to the hotel.

Jeff decided swiftly. He must delay discovery of the fate dealt out to Smoke Hawker and the marshal, and he must have it out with King Cole—man to man—in private.

Grim, wordless, poker faces masking their thoughts, the Flying W men listened attentively to his brief instructions. Jeff pushed the wide doors open, and they rode out and up the street, compact, formidable, Jeff in the lead, the others riding two abreast, with Andy Trigg in the rear, leading Johnny's horse.

CHAPTER XVII
A SALTY OUTFIT

IT was Lylah Cole's first visit to Cottonwood Wells in six months. She detested the place, and would not have come to-day had not her presence been necessary to sign certain papers before a notary in the person of Lawyer Simmons, who held some sort of Federal position authorizing him to certify signatures. Lylah understood that the papers in question had to do with a deed of right-of-way to the railway of a certain strip in No Man's Land which King Cole planned to claim in her name when, and if ever, Congress included the Oklahoma Panhandle as an integral part of the new Oklahoma Territory. The land bounded the eastern line of the KC-Bar home ranch, and, as well as controlling valuable water-rights, lay directly across the path of the eagerly hoped-for railway, slowly reaching out from Kansas City. The coming of the railway would see the fulfilment of King Cole's dream to found a new town on the New Mexico side of the border, within five miles of the home ranch-house.

Lylah fervently hoped that day would soon arrive. Cottonwood Wells was the only town within a three-hour ride of the KC-Bar, and she loathed the dirty, sordid place, shrank from its leering, evil-eyed population.

Dusty and travel-worn, she lost no time in seeking the scant comforts of Hank Smithers' hotel. The thought of soaking in a tub of hot water quite cheered her as she followed the melancholy Hank up the rickety stairs to her room. It struck her that the sad-faced, bow-shouldered old hotel-keeper was more dreary than ever; Lylah was quite shocked at the haunting fear in his eyes, the look of sheer terror when he saw her stepbrother dismount in front of Juan Cordero's unspeakable *cantina* across the street from the hotel.

Lylah had no love for Steve, but she never feared him, except when he was drunk. She knew that Steve was partial to Juan Cordero's vile *mescal*, and would probably emerge the quarrelsome bully drink made of him. Even so, that was not sufficient reason for Hank's fright at the sight of Steve. There must be something else concerning Steve that worried the hotel man.

Suddenly depressed, the girl locked the door and flung herself on the bed to wait for the promised tub of hot water. If she could have guessed what was in her unlovely stepbrother's mind Lylah might have been saved much anguish. As it happened, she knew nothing of the presence of Hank Smithers' pretty orphan niece in the hotel. Nor did she know that Jeff Wayne was at that moment dismounting from his roan horse in front of Lawyer Simmons' office, a few doors down the street.

The young owner of the Flying W had been much in her thoughts; it had been a struggle to refrain from bringing up his name to her father.

King Cole had made no reference to what had transpired in Crater Basin. Not by word or look had he betrayed his knowledge of her presence in Jeff Wayne's ranch-house. His silence on the subject of Jeff Wayne, the amazing fact that there was to be a lasting peace between the Flying W and the KC-Bar, had considerably perplexed her.

Lylah thought it passing strange that King Cole chose to keep so important a piece of news from her. Even so, she was conscious of a warming happiness that filled her face with a new and radiant beauty whenever she thought of Jeff Wayne. Dismay would have utterly destroyed that happiness could she have witnessed the meeting between her father and Jeff Wayne in the office of Lawyer Simmons.

When the young cattleman swung down from his saddle in front of the lawyer's office Buck Saunders, followed by Slinger, Curly, and Tex, pushed through the swing-doors of the Longhorn Bar.

Perhaps some fifteen patrons were in the place, some drinking at the bar, others engrossed at the card-tables. Most of the convivial ones at the bar were the newly arrived KC-Bar punchers, who were keeping the grizzled Limpy doing a rush business for the moment. Limpy and his friends had taken Smoke Hawker at his word; apart from removing the body of the slain Sinful Smith from the street, Hawker's injunction to keep out of the affair was being rigidly obeyed by his satellites. They were to learn things about the formidable Flying W outfit.

The old barman, first to glimpse the newcomers, and sensing their sinister intent, promptly dropped the bottle in his hand and reached for the big .45 he had earlier that morning buckled round his waist. Buck's voice halted the downward swoop of the barman's hand.

"Reach for the sky—every man of yuh! Quick—stick 'em up!"

Slowly the barman's hands went up under the grim menace of those seven six-shooters in the hands of those four cold-eyed strangers—there would have been eight guns, but for Tex Malley's wounded arm—and, reading the threat of sudden death at their backs in Limpy's bulging eyes, the dusty KC-Bar riders were quick to follow his example.

Others, seated at card-tables, and apparently residents of the town, hastened to comply with Buck's second low-voiced demand. At a word from the foreman they left their chairs and bellied up to the bar. Buck's gun motioned to Limpy to line up with the others. Swearing under his breath, the indignant barman came out of his cubby-hole and took his place at the end of the line.

"All set, Curly. Get their guns." Buck's voice was businesslike. "Keep them paws high, fellers."

The blond cowboy slid down the line of dusty backs, deftly jerked guns from their holsters, and dropped them into a gunny-sack he had been holding in readiness under one arm.

"Feel like a ars'nal," he grunted as he dragged his load to the wall near the door.

"All right, boys. Each put your paws on the shoulder of the man in front of him, and you, tall feller, start the march round to the far wall."

They obeyed, moving off in a long line. Curly grinned.

"Look like a line of gaol-birds doin' the lock-step," he chuckled.

"Be doin' the lock-step your own self for this business," muttered one of the victims.

"No talk!" rasped Buck. "Belly up to that wall, and rest your hands up high. First man that moves or looks round dies where he stands. Not warning you a second time."

The foreman nodded to Curly, who now sped to the two rear doors and turned keys in locks. Tex and Slinger took positions on each side of the swing-doors. "No jasper goes out of here," Buck reminded them, "but any feller wants in gets in, only yuh takes his shootin' irons pronto, and lines him up 'longside the others."

The foreman backed to the door, and signalled Andy Trigg, waiting outside with the horses. The cowboy nodded, relayed the signal to Jeff, waiting across the street.

Andy's quickly raised clenched fist told Jeff that so far his plan was working smoothly, and that all was well in the Longhorn Bar. Guns loosed in holsters, he slipped quietly into Lawyer Simmons' office.

It was evident that the KC-Bar was due for a payday, for King Cole and his foreman were bent over a table counting gold coins from a canvas sack. The lawyer watched sleepily from his desk chair.

Jeff fell into a crouch, guns leaped to his hands. "Put 'em up!"

His voice was a rapier-thrust. The two men bending over the table looked up with shocked surprise, read relentless purpose in the cold grey eyes challenging them. King Cole's expression grew bleak.

"What's this, Wayne? A hold-up?" rasped the old man.

The young cattleman eyed him scornfully. "That's more in your line, Cole," he retorted. "Holdin' folks up goes right well with cattle-stealing."

The cattle king's seamed face darkened at the insult. "Gone plumb crazy, Wayne?" he barked. "What's the idea—walking in here and stickin' us up?"

"Before we do any talking, Cole, you unbuckle Sladen's holster. You and your lawyer friend ain't wearin' guns, I reckon."

The old cattleman obeyed with surprising meekness. Jeff sensed King Cole was not anxious to see Sladen attempt to start anything.

"I'm doing what this young fool says, Bart," Cole admonished the big foreman. "Keep your hands up and let me drop that gun-belt."

Guns and holster thudded to the floor.

"Now back up to the wall, and keep your hands high," Jeff ordered. "You too, mister." He threw a fierce glance at the lawyer, who hurriedly took his place in the line-up. Jeff reached for Sladen's holster with the toe of his boot and kicked it aside.

"Now we can talk," he said.

"We're listening." King Cole's voice was peevish. Talking with a gun covering him was something new to the cattleman. "Hurry and get done what's on your mind, young feller."

"My trail herd was rustled last night," Jeff said thinly. "Flying W men were shot—some of 'em killed." His eyes were bitter. "But maybe that's not news to you, Cole?"

"I'll say it's news!" barked Lylah's father. His eyes blazed. "What d'I tell you, Jeff? Didn't I warn you El Toro would be watching for you?"

"We nabbed one of the gang," continued Jeff, a bit wearily. "He was one of your own hands, Cole. . . . A KC-Bar man, name of Sinful Smith.

199

He shot one of my best men, killed Tex Malley's bronc, and mighty near killed Tex." Jeff's voice was scornful. "You still claim it's news to you, mister?"

The bewilderment on the old cattleman's face was so genuine that for a moment Jeff was assailed by disturbing doubts. King Cole spoke in a wondering voice:

"You meanin' to accuse me of stealing your cows, Wayne?"

Jeff shrugged his shoulders. "Sinful Smith is one of your men, ain't he?"

"You're sure of this, Wayne? You're sure this feller was old Sinful?"

"Chuck Wallis knew him minute he laid eyes on him. And Sinful Smith admitted his name and that he was a KC-Bar man."

Up to this moment Sladen's broad, swarthy face had presented an impenetrable mask. He suddenly smiled, shrugged amusedly.

"Reckon Sinful didn't tell you that I fired him last evenin', did he, Mr Wayne?" he asked courteously.

Jeff stared at him intently. "No, Sinful didn't tell me you'd fired him," he admitted.

The foreman nodded. "That sure explains a lot about this mix-up. Ol' Sinful went and joined up with the wild bunch—meanin' El Toro's gang."

"You've hit it plumb centre!" barked Lylah's father excitedly.

Jeff felt the ground falling from under his feet; he stared at the other men blankly. The explanation was not unreasonable. King Cole smiled sadly.

"So you was thinking I double-crossed you, huh?" He shook his head. "Can't say I blame you much. I'd sure like to lay my hands on that old scoundrel."

"You can put your hands down," Jeff said dully. He holstered his guns. "Seems like I'm barking up the wrong tree."

"Don't blame you," repeated King Cole, lowering his hands and rubbing them vigorously. "Where you got this Sinful Smith? Let me talk to the old scoundrel. We'll soon find out where they've got your cows."

"Sinful Smith won't talk no more," Jeff informed them. He briefly related the events leading to Sinful's sudden demise that morning.

"The ol' coot had it comin' to him," growled the KC-Bar foreman. There was a satisfied gleam in his smoky eyes. It struck Jeff that the man was both pleased and relieved to hear of Sinful Smith's passing. "Sure had it comin' to him," repeated the foreman. He looked at his chief. "That explains how we lost those steers last spring. Ol' Sinful was hand in glove with this El Toro *hombre*." Sladen swore. "One sly ol' fox, that Sinful Smith, drawin' KC-Bar pay an' helpin' El Toro rustle our cows."

"Huh!" King Cole gave his foreman a bristling look. "Figger there's any more of our riders pulling the same play, Sladen? Strikes me you getting plumb careless with your job—letting El Toro's rustlers get on the KC-Bar pay-roll."

The big foreman shook his head. "Reckon Sinful Smith was the only rustler slipped in on us, Mr Cole. If there's any more like him mixed up with the outfit we'll sure have a hangin'-party pronto."

"See that you do," fumed the old man. "And if Smoke Hawker's mixed up in this business I'll swing him too."

"Right now," chuckled Jeff, "you'll find friend Hawker and his marshal locked up in the calaboose." He continued his story of the Flying W outfit's activities in Cottonwood Wells. Admiration and something like awe gleamed in King Cole's eyes.

"You mean to say you've got my boys holed up in the Longhorn right this minute?" he marvelled. "By gosh, Jeff!"

The latter nodded gloomily. He was no nearer to solving the mystery of his lost herd than he had been hours earlier. Dismay dragged heavily at his heart.

Sladen's expression was thoughtful. "Smoke Hawkins and Stiles won't feel so good—you leavin' 'em hog-tied and locked up in gaol," he warned Jeff. "That Stiles feller is one fast man with a six-gun, mister. If I was you I'd high-tail it outer this town—you and your outfit. Stiles'll start his guns smokin' moment he lays eyes on yuh." The KC-Bar foreman nodded his massive head. "And I'd sure steer clear of Cottonwood Wells after this, Mr Wayne."

Mirth suddenly convulsed King Cole's leathery features. "Jeff," he cackled, "you and your outfit sure has guts, takin' the marshal's guns from him and lockin' him and Smoke Hawker inside their own gaol."

"Lucky we didn't do worse to 'em," muttered Jeff. "Gun-whipping Slinger Downs the way they did, and throwing him and Buck in gaol; and on top of that setting their spy on our trails. Near as I can figger it they was framing to clean up on us." The young cattleman looked at King Cole. "I got a hunch that this Smoke Hawker is behind this rustling job. How do we know he ain't El Toro himself?"

"That's purty wild guessing," responded the old man dubiously. "Never figgered Hawker that way. Always quiet and soft-spoken . . . makes good money out of his bar and dance-hall."

"Then how do you figger the play he and his marshal pulled on us?" puzzled Jeff.

Sladen spoke quietly: "Just mistaken judgment on Hawker's part," he said. "Hawker and Stiles knowed the KC-Bar has been losin' cows to rustlers. I'd told 'em myself to keep a look-out for

strangers in town. Your men come in last night—
one of 'em with a wounded leg. Hawker and the
marshal just natchcrly sized 'em up for rustlers
an' jumped 'em like they did. Then you and your
fellers come snoopin' round this mornin', and they
figgered you was more of the same gang. Yuh
can't blame Hawker and Stiles for actin' plumb
hostile, Mr Wayne."

Against his will Jeff realized the sound logic in
the KC-Bar foreman's deductions; the explanation
was identical with Smoke Hawker's own plausible
words. The deeper he pried into the mystery the
further he seemed to be from the truth. One stark
fact stared him in the face. He had lost a trail herd
of three thousand cattle and his riders had been
shot—some of them killed. Rustlers had raided
him—this mysterious, elusive El Toro was no
myth. If King Cole's skirts were clean, as he now
believed, then he must seek elsewhere for the
scheming brain masked behind the name of El
Toro. Jeff stared at the big KC-Bar foreman.

"What you think, Sladen? You figger it was El
Toro's gang that rustled me?"

"Looks that way," admitted the KC-Bar man
cautiously. "No tellin'. Might be some gang as
trailed yuh up from the south." Sladen's eyes
questioned his chief. "What's your notion,
boss?"

"El Toro," grunted King Cole.

"Any notion where this El Toro roosts?" Jeff

eyed Sladen closely. "Any idea what he looks like?"

Sladen shook his head. "If we knowed that we'd nab him awful quick," he said grimly. "El Toro is one sly fox. Nobody has ever seen his face."

"You said there were fellers in this town that could name him if they'd a mind to come clean," said Jeff, looking at King Cole. "That brings us back to Hawker—or that marshal of his."

"No evidence," grunted the grizzled cattleman. "Not that it ain't possible, but we need evidence before we can go charging Hawker with rustling cows." The ranchman frowned. "You're wasting time, Jeff. You should be down there on the Honda, readin' signs. You'll find these rustlers where your cows are hid."

Sladen nodded agreement. "Tell yuh what we'll do, Mr Wayne," he said, in his rumbling voice; "you an' your outfit get started . . . soon as we get back to the ranch I'll set the boys combin' those draws over Saw Tooth way. Now we're neighbours we gotta work together 'gainst these cow-thieves."

There was wisdom in the suggestion, and generosity in the KC-Bar foreman's offer, considering the high-handed treatment being accorded some half-score KC-Bar riders in the saloon across the street. Jeff gave the man a friendly smile.

"Reckon you're talking good sense, Sladen," he

agreed. "First thing you and me do is mosey over to the Longhorn and make peace talk with your boys. They'll be feeling awful peeved."

Sladen's answering grin was affable. "Leavin' town right off?" he wanted to know.

"Inside of fifteen minutes," Jeff told him, remembering Johnny Wales.

"We'll give yuh a half-hour's start before we turn the marshal and Smoke Hawker loose," chuckled the KC-Bar foreman. "They'll sure be on the prod when they come out of the calaboose."

"Ain't forgetting your guns?" reminded Jeff softly.

Sladen grinned and reached a long arm for the holster lying on the floor. He buckled it round his waist, eased the weapons in their sheaths, to make certain the misadventure had not left them resistant to the lightning pull that was apt to mean the difference between life or death.

"I'll walk across the street with you boys," wisely decided old King Cole. He glanced at the lawyer. "Be right back, Simmons. You can be fixing up them papers Lylah's got to sign." He picked up a couple of the gold pieces lying on the table and followed the two younger men into the street.

The Longhorn Bar's list of patrons had considerably increased by the time Jeff pushed his way through the swing-doors accompanied by the two chieftains of the KC-Bar.

"The show's over," Jeff said softly as Buck's cold gaze fastened on the armed Sladen. "We're on the wrong track. Seems like the KC-Bar ain't mixed up in this cow-stealing business."

Buck's gaze went to the twenty-five men pressing against the wall. "Looks like we got a bull by the tail," he muttered. "These *hombres* are goin' to act awful belligerent when we take our guns off 'em. That last bunch that come in just before you did are sure on the prod . . . belly-achin' to beat the band 'cause they ain't gettin' the drinks they come all the way in from the Cimarron to spend their pay on."

"Leave it to me," chuckled King Cole. "Boys," he called genially, "the war is over! . . . It's King Cole talking to yuh."

Twenty-five angry red faces turned and glared at the group by the door—twenty-five pairs of spurred boot-heels scraped the bar-room floor. King Cole's smile swept them amiably, and fastened on the veteran barman.

"Limpy, you come and tend to your bar. I'm standing the drinks for the crowd." The twenty-dollar gold pieces clinked on the bar. "Line up, boys . . . name your pizen!" The old man chuckled. "Been a mistake, and we aim to make things right with you."

The long line of cowboys and citizens stared resentfully at the men clustered near the door. Jeff suddenly smiled, and followed Cole to the bar.

"I'm Jeff Wayne, fellers. Been a fool mistake, like Mr Cole says." Jeff jingled two more twenties on the bar. "Line up, boys— I'm layin' my money 'longside his for the drinks."

An amused chuckle broke from the red-headed KC-Bar puncher, a loud roar of laughter as the long line disintegrated into groups; with a clatter of boot-heels and jingle and rasp of spurs the suddenly appeased cowboys surged towards the bar, led by the grizzled barman. Limpy's mollified grin bore witness to considerable satisfaction at the sight of the four gold pieces adorning his bar.

The big KC-Bar foreman edged close to the end of the bar, eyes furtively beckoning Limpy; the latter darted him an apprehensive look, and leaned towards the foreman, as though taking his order.

"What about Hawker and Stiles?"

The barman spoke in an undertone that only Sladen's ears caught in the uproar of voices and stamping feet. The foreman's swarthy, stolid face was a mask, but the gleam in the smoky eyes told Limp his question had been heard. Sladen flashed a cautious look at Jeff; and saw that he was in earnest talk with his own foreman. The barman made a pretence of sliding bottle and glass across the bar to the KC-Bar man's hand. The latter leaned closer.

"Hawker an' Stiles are down at the gaol. I'm goin' over to have a talk with 'em. An' Limpy— the play lays the way King Cole says. No more trouble to-night—" Sladen downed his drink, and with a brief nod shouldered towards the street, throwing Jeff an affable grin as he pushed through the door.

The young cattleman's narrowed gaze followed him doubtfully. Jeff had observed the little byplay between the barman and Sladen. He wondered what there was about the KC-Bar foreman that so persistently aroused his antagonism. The man was affable enough, always politely deferential—and King Cole seemed to trust him implicitly. With a shrug Jeff put the problem aside for the time. He had agreed to be out of Cottonwood Wells within fifteen minutes—the time was short.

Unobserved by the noisy celebrants, the Flying W men slipped into the street.

"I'm getting Johnny out of that hotel," Jeff told Buck Saunders. "It's fixed to hold Hawker and the marshal in gaol till we get out of town. Those two *hombres* are going to be on the prod. No telling what'd happen to Johnny if they caught him here alone." Jeff stared thoughtfully up the street. "Now, listen, Buck. You get the broncs in that yard back of the hotel, and wait there till I bring Johnny down. We'll come out by that door we saw in the dining-room . . . it opens into the back-yard. If the marshal and Hawker break loose from gaol too quick we don't want 'em to know we're still in town."

"I get yuh," nodded the foreman.

"And fetch my roan along. I've got to stop in the doc's office and fix things with him."

Jeff hurried up the street; the others turned to their horses.

"Sure will have a tough time breakin' loose outer that gaol," chuckled Curly as he swung into his saddle, "what with the keys lost and a three-inch oak door to bust in."

Jeff found that Doc Mosby was not in his little office. He strode on swiftly across the street, and into the hotel. The melancholy Hank Smithers was not in his customary place behind the desk. Jeff turned to the stairs, and halted abruptly.

Voices in the dining-room . . . a girl's frightened protests . . . a man's drunken laugh.

Jeff's face darkened. He knew that drunken voice—Steve Cole's. His heart suddenly constricted. Lylah was in the hotel . . . was being abused by her inebriated stepbrother! Instantly he knew he was wrong. He would recognize Lylah's voice among all the voices in the world.

Grey eyes blazing, Jeff headed for the dining-room. No matter who the girl might be, she was in trouble—

Recognition leaped into his eyes. The girl was Johnny's pretty blonde nurse—Nellie Blaine—struggling desperately to free herself from Steve Cole's embrace. Lying on the floor was the senseless form of Hank Smithers, blood oozing from a gash in his scalp.

Scarcely halting his stride Jeff flung himself at Steve; the latter heard the rush of feet, and lurched from the girl, his hand reaching for his gun. He might as well have reached for the moon. Smiling crookedly, Jeff's clenched fist lashed out; Steve's knees buckled, and down he sprawled. A glance assured Jeff that the man was senseless. He looked at Nellie. She tried to smile.

"He—he was terrible!" she gasped. "He—he hit poor Uncle with his gun!"

She ran to Hank Smithers, knelt by his side. The hotel man opened his eyes, tried to speak.

Trampling hoofs went past. Jeff knew that Buck and the boys had reached the seclusion of the rear yard, screened from the street by the hotel. The problem of what to do with Steve was solved. He bent down, picked the senseless man up bodily, and carried him out through the rear dining-room door.

"Hold the skunk here till we leave," he told his astonished riders curtly, "and take his guns off him." Jeff vanished into the dining-room.

Hank Smithers was on his feet, still dazed, but apparently unharmed.

"Ain't hurt at all," he was assuring his worried niece. "Just sorta stunned me some. Be all right in a minute." He grinned at Jeff. "Sure glad you happened in, mister. That drunk Cole feller's been pesterin' Nellie ever since she come to Cottonwood Wells."

"This town's no place for a decent girl," Jeff told him. "You get your niece away from here, Mr Smithers." He looked at the girl. "I got to take Johnny away with us . . . we're ridin' now. Johnny's life ain't safe in this town."

The girl gave a little gasp, and was suddenly very pale. "I'll—I'll go up to his room with you," she said quietly. "Doctor Mosby is there—"

She fled in front of him up the creaky stairs.

CHAPTER XVIII

WHAT LYLAH SAW

LYLAH wondered why Hank Smithers was so long about bringing the hot water he had promised. How was she to know the hotel man was having troubles of his own?

The sound of feet mounting the stairs sent her to the door. Hank was bringing the water at last! She edged the door open, peered through the crack. Her dark eyes widened.

A pretty girl with corn-coloured hair popped up the stairs, flew down the dingy corridor, and halted at one of the bedroom doors.

Lylah's face was suddenly ashen. The tall man following the girl was Jeff Wayne! She stifled a gasp; she wanted to cry out that it could not be Jeff Wayne . . . but it was Jeff Wayne. . . . He had paused by the side of the girl . . . the hussy was looking up at him, smiling in a sort of half-frightened manner, was speaking in a low, breathless voice—a guilty voice, Lylah told herself. Jeff was smiling down at her . . . he was opening the door . . . had gone into that bedroom—with that girl!

Lylah slowly closed her own door, stood there, pressing both hands on the knob, her eyes closed, as though she would banish that picture from her mind. She felt strangely dizzy—as though the floor was falling away from beneath her feet.

CHAPTER XIX
DESERT LOVE SONG

DOC MOSBY was dubious about Jeff's decision to remove Johnny Wales. He shook his grey mane, frowned, snorted, and wanted to know if Jeff had gone quite crazy.

"Johnny's tough as bull-hide," argued Jeff. "Seems like there's nothing else we can do but take him along with us. Maybe cost him his life if we leave him in town." He briefly related the circumstances regarding the ill-natured marshal of Cottonwood Wells. Doc Mosby scowled.

"That man Stiles has the instinct of a killer," he grumbled. "Something wrong about him. Landed in this cow-town six months ago, and inside of a week was strutting around with a marshal's badge pinned to his vest. My own opinion is that the man's nothing more than Smoke Hawker's hired gunman. Don't know what has got into Smoke Hawker of late. Wasn't half bad sort until this Stiles got chummy with him."

"Then you withdraw your objections?"

Doc Mosby said vigorously that he certainly did withdraw his objections. "Be insane for us to keep Johnny here with Stiles on the warpath," he declared. "If I know human nature, Stiles is a cold-blooded killer. The problem is, how is Johnny going to stand a long, hard ride in his present shape. He's had a close call. Only thing that saved him was his splendid physical condition." The little doctor glanced slyly at Nellie Blaine. "Not forgetting that maybe Johnny's nurse helped the miracle along."

The girl blushed in pretty confusion. "Johnny must get dressed—if he's really leaving now," she stammered. "I—I'll be waiting down in the office—to say good-bye." She gave Johnny a look, and turned to the door. Johnny sat up in bed, a curious, startled dismay in his eyes.

"I ain't going!" he exploded, his gaze clinging to the girl.

She stared back at him, wide-eyed. Jeff, conscious that time was flying, spoke curtly.

"The matter's settled. You're riding with us soon as you get into your pants and Stetson, mister."

Johnny glared at him. "Yuh ain't settled nothing," he declared vehemently. His gaze returned to the girl, clung with a curious, despairing intensity to her wide blue eyes.

The colour waved into her fresh young face, as suddenly receded; and as though drawn by an invisible cable she moved like one in a trance to the bedside. Johnny reached out a big brown hand that sought and clung to hers. It was plain that for that moment they had forgotten their speechless friends. They were alone—alone in a wonderful world of their own. Johnny spoke huskily:

"I'm not leavin'—without you—Nellie!"

She answered him in a breathless little voice, scarcely audible to the others:

"I'll—I'll go anywhere—with you—Johnny!"

Doc Mosby's chuckle broke the spell. "Bless my soul!" he marvelled. He gave the stupefied Jeff a twinkling look. "Seems to me Johnny has settled things to suit himself." The doctor wagged a forefinger at the beaming cowboy. "Scalawag! Just what are you going to do about this, and where are you going to take this young lady who says she will go to any place with you?"

Johnny's eyes clouded. "Why—huh—only one place we can go—" he stuttered. "Why—Nellie and me'll head right for the Flying W." Johnny looked hopefully at Jeff. The latter shook his head.

"Sorry, Johnny. You can't take Nellie to the ranch. You—you ain't married to her yet, Johnny, and there's no woman at the Flying W."

Doc Mosby frowned thoughtfully at the dejected

215

young faces, and suddenly snapped his fingers. "Nellie!" He beamed at the girl. "You run and pack what things you'll need. Johnny will be ready by the time you are packed."

"But we have no place to go," she interrupted, somewhat wildly. "Anyway, it's all too absurd! Johnny and I have no—no business being so foolish at such a time."

"Nonsense!" snorted the little doctor. "Best thing could happen for you to get away from this back door of hell. I know what you have put up with since you came to live with your uncle. If Johnny hadn't figured out something a lot better I'd have made Hank Smithers pack you away from this town in short order."

Doc Mosby beamed at his audience. "Now, listen, you two. We'll have a wedding!"

"A wedding!" Nellie's voice was startled. "How can we—have a wedding?" she faltered. "Why, Doctor Mosby, you know there is no minister in Cottonwood Wells!"

The doctor chuckled. "I haven't finished," he said. "Now listen some more. Back in the Sierra Madres Hills, just off the desert, is a little Indian *pueblo*—maybe twenty-five or thirty families, and a pretty decent lot. Have to be, with Padre Juan watching them like an old sheepdog. Padre Juan has lived with 'em for fifty years . . . an old saint if there ever was one; and those Indians kiss the ground he walks on."

216

Doc Mosby beamed round at his listeners. "That's where you'll go, my children, to this Indian *pueblo* . . . an easy ride for Johnny—less than ten miles—and won't do him any harm. The long ride over to Crater Basin would be too much for him . . . probably set him on his back for months. The doctor looked at Jeff. "Won't be much out of your way. Save time at that."

"You—you mean—" Nellie faltered, blushed.

Doc Mosby nodded. "Exactly. You and Johnny will be married by old Padre Juan. And you can stay at the *pueblo* until Johnny's leg is healed." The genial doctor's eyes twinkled.

Johnny grinned. "Where's my pants?" he demanded. "I crave to meet up with this Padre Juan!"

Nellie fled. "I—I'll be ready!" she called over her shoulder, in a breathless voice.

Doc Mosby picked up his shabby bag. "Be good to her, boy," he said solemnly. He drew a handkerchief from his alpaca coat and blew his nose vigorously. "You ain't good enough for her, Johnny. But, then, none of us is good enough for a good woman." The doctor looked at the young cowboy's still dazed employer. "We've just seen one of those miracles we read about in books," he said, "the blossoming of a beautiful flower—love at first sight."

"Johnny is mighty lucky," Jeff said, and, thinking of a certain great rock high above Crater Basin, where less than twenty-four hours earlier he had stood by the side of a dark-eyed girl and himself known the joy— and the pain—of that same miracle, he grinned with kindly fellow-feeling at the bridegroom-to-be. "They don't come better, or cleaner, than Johnny," he assured Doc Mosby.

"I believe you," chuckled the latter. He glanced back from the door. "I'll have my Indian boy saddle a horse for Nellie—and fix up a pack-burro to carry her things. José will go with you. He's one of Padre Juan's boys . . . you can trust José."

Johnny's eyes followed Doc Mosby reverently out of the door. "Jeff," he said softly, "that doc is one white man. Some day—I—I'll—" Johnny's voice choked; and he bent quickly to his boots, lying under the bed.

"Sure." Jeff grinned. "Some day we'll have a little Mosby Wales running round the place."

"I figger to get me a bunch of cows," declared Nellie's Johnny importantly. "You watch my smoke, Jeff. Little Mosby's dad is due to be a cattle king." Little Mosby's father-to-be let out a subdued jubilant yip, and reached for another high-heeled boot.

Nellie was waiting for them when they went down to the office. Accompanied by Doc Mosby and Hank Smithers, they hurried through the deserted dining-room to the Flying W outfit waiting in the rear yard.

José, a slim Indian youth, had Nellie's horse in

readiness and the pack-burro loaded with her few possessions. Sitting on the ground, leaning his back against the wall, was Steve Cole, nursing a bruised paw.

The parting was brief, wordless, in fact. Buck and his riders watched, poker-faced. Instinct warned them that now was not the time to betray astonishment, ask questions. The sullen-eyed Steve Cole alone gaped in blank amazement. His fuddled brain could reason out but one answer to the mystery. Hank's pretty blonde niece was going off with Jeff Wayne.

"Yuh'll find your gun layin' out in that bunch of weeds somewheres," Slinger Downs curtly told Steve as he spurred away to overtake the outfit. At a signal from Buck the little gunman had waited for the others to get a good start before turning Steve loose.

The latter flung a curse at the vanishing horseman, rose unsteadily to his feet, and lurched round the corner of the hotel. King Cole confronted him. The old cattleman threw his stepson a contemptuous glance.

"Who's that girl riding off with Jeff Wayne's outfit?" he asked sharply.

"She's Hank Smithers' niece." Steve leered unpleasantly. "Wayne's takin' her off to his ranch." He swore, calling the girl an obscene name. "Wayne won't be so lonesome with her round the ranch," he hiccoughed.

"Get out—you worthless sot!"

Steve stumbled away, cowed by the ferocity in the old man's eyes. Lylah's father stared at the little cavalcade disappearing into the depths of a sandy wash. Black rage and grief distorted the cattleman's face as he turned with suddenly leaden feet to enter the hotel. King Cole knew more—had guessed more—than his daughter dreamed.

CHAPTER XX

A GALLANT CABALLERO

DON RICARDO GONZALEZ meditatively rolled a cigarette between thumb and forefinger, his handsome dark eyes lazily contemplating a thin haze of dust lifting from the unseen floor of the Arroyo los Coyotes.

Something of a dandy, this gay caballero. Silver braid adorned high-peaked sombrero and short plum-coloured jacket. A silver slip-clasp bound the dangling chin-strap of soft braided buckskin, and the same precious metal decorated the wide belt of hand-carved leather buckled round his slim waist. The guns peeping from holsters were inlaid with mother-of-pearl, and the big Mexican spurs fastened to serviceable boots of brown leather were heavily chased with silver.

The don's horse, a magnificent Palomino

stallion, was no less handsomely appointed with silver-mounted saddle and bridle. Horse and man showed tell-tale signs of hard riding under the scorching desert sun. Plum-coloured jacket was powdered with dust, and the satiny coat of the horse streaked with drying sweat.

For all his elegancies there was a hard, capable look about Don Ricardo Gonzalez. His shoulders were broad for so lean a waist, his sleepy-lidded eyes singularly steady. Gaze intent on the approaching plume of dust, he neatly finished and lighted his brown-paper cigarette.

Far to the rear of the dust rising from the arroyo suddenly hovered a second and larger haze, low against the horizon. The Palomino's rider appeared a trifle disconcerted by the more distant indications of approaching horsemen. He frowned, suddenly whirled the Palomino about, and rode behind a thick clump of giant cactus. Here he again alertly watched the approach of the nearer lazily lifting dust.

The thud of hoofs came plainly now to the ears of the concealed Mexican; the sleepy eyes narrowed, fixed, like the eyes of a great cat making ready to pounce upon an unsuspecting victim. Not that Don Ricardo was stalking a victim or an enemy. Quite the reverse; he was expecting a friend, or one whom he hoped came bearing a flag of truce. The appearance of the second dust-haze when there should be no dust had merely raised some doubt in his cautious mind regarding the identity of the still unseen lone horseman down in the sandy floor of the Arroyo los Coyotes. If the newcomer was an enemy—so much the worse for the enemy.

The watcher's slim brown hand tightened over the butt of a six-shooter, then suddenly relaxed. Don Ricardo smiled, showing white teeth under trimly waxed black moustache.

Horse and rider were in plain sight now; and the don knew that Palomino horse, so like his own animal, and knew the brown hawk's face of the rider.

The newcomer's own alert eyes espied the tell-tale hoof-prints left by the Mexican's animal. He halted, scrutinized the tracks, and followed their course to the clump of cactus concealing the Mexican. As Don Gonzalez had done, the lone horseman suddenly whirled the Palomino round, and was lost to view behind another cactus growth.

Don Ricardo's smile widened. *"Bueanas dias,* Señor Wayne! It ees I—your frien', Ricardo."

A moment's silence, then an amused chuckle from the opposite tangle of cactus. "You ol' son-of-gun—hidin' out on me!" His fears of an ambush apparently allayed, the speaker spurred into the clearing between the clumps of cactus.

Don Ricardo's horse swung into view, and the two riders clasped hands. The Mexican smiled broadly, eyeing Jeff's Palomino with critical approval.

"These leetle 'orse—she grow beeg, mooch *grande*, eh, my frien'?"

"Silver King is all horse," agreed Jeff. He regarded the don's own Palomino. "Not much difference between 'em, Ricardo. As like as two peas in a pod."

"El Rey Grande hees papa," laughed Don Ricardo. His glance flickered towards the hovering dust-cloud. "You do not come alone, *señor*? Or ees eet you suspec' you are follow'?"

Jeff stared at the distant riders now visible across the wide wash of the arroyo. "My outfit," he reassured the Mexican. "Told Buck to trail me."

"Eet was understan' you come alone—weeth these Palomino." The Mexican's tone was reproachful. "You no trus' me, *amigo mio*?"

"You sent word by Chuck Wallis that if I would meet you here in the Arroyo los Coyotes you would have news of my stolen cows." Jeff's voice was cold. "Can't blame me for wondering what your game is, Ricardo. How come you know I've lost my trail herd?"

"How I know you lose these cow ees no matter," replied the Mexican. "Eet ees that I know how you find these los' cow, no?" Don Ricardo shrugged his elegant shoulders. "W'at you teenk Don Ricardo Felipe Gonzalez e Alvarez ees, my frien', that you suspec' he plan treek you? Ees eet not true that you once saved my life? But for you, my brave Americano frien', the bones of Don Ricardo Felipe Gonzalez e Alvarez now lie so white in those desert, no? An' w'at 'ave I do in return? Nossing! Only geeve you these Palomino you now ride, an' those baby seester Palomino. My frien' "—Don Ricardo made an expressive gesture—"those leetle 'orse no pay those debt Don Ricardo Felipe Gonzalez e Alvarez owe you."

The Mexican's handsome dark eyes rested fondly upon the tall young American; and he said earnestly, in Spanish, "I owe you my life. . . . My life—and all that I possess—are yours to command, dear friend."

"I believe you, Ricardo," Jeff assured him, in the same language. He was honestly ashamed of his first suspicions. "Now tell me all you know about my cows. And talk in Spanish. We'll get along faster."

Don Ricardo looked hurt. "You no like way I espeak those Eenglees? I espeak those Eenglees ver' fine dandy. I 'ave nize Americano *señorita* my frien'. She tich me espeak those Eenglees."

"You speak English great," applauded Jeff. "All right, Ricardo, what about my cows? Chuck Wallis said your men grabbed him and Pat Hogan in some canyon down here, and when you learned they were from Jeff Wayne's outfit you turned 'em loose with a message for me to meet you here in the Arroyo los Coyotes. Said I was to ride the Palomino, so you'd know I got the message."

"It is true what you say," admitted the Mexican, in his liquid mother-tongue. "I captured your *vaqueros*, not knowing who they were." Don Ricardo smiled reminiscently. "They did not surrender without a fight, these two *hombres*— But to proceed. I learned they were from your outfit—a great surprise. I did not know you were up in this country. I learned, too, that they were trailing certain rustlers who had run off with a big herd of cattle you were bringing up from the Pecos to stock a new ranch."

Don Ricardo made one of his expressive gestures. "Alas! It was news that came too late. Your cattle were already on the way to Sonora in the care of my *vaqueros*."

Jeff gave his friend a wild look. "What kind of funny play is this, Gonzalez?" he exploded. "What you mean—my cows are headin' for Sonora—with your *vaqueros*?" The young cattleman's hand slid down to his gun.

The Mexican's eyes glittered. "Look around you, *señor*," he advised softly. "I lift my hand, so"—Don Ricardo's hand touched the top of his tall sombrero—"and what do you see, *señor*?"

In response to the casual signal some dozen dark-faced men suddenly popped into view from behind various clumps of juniper and cactus. Jeff stared blankly.

"The Señor Wayne sees that Don Ricardo Gonzalez is well protected," purred the Mexican. He glanced again at the nearing dust-cloud, now lifting from the floor of the arroyo. "It will be wise to signal your *vaqueros* to remain at a discreet distance—until we have finished our interesting conversation," he suggested. "In the meantime have no fear. I am here as your friend."

Their eyes clashed; and Jeff sensed the steel under the dandified trappings of this slim young Mexican *hidalgo*. He had met a man as cool, as resolute, as himself; and despite the disturbing news that his stolen cattle were apparently in Don Ricardo's possession he found himself inclined to believe that the Mexican's intentions were friendly.

He looked across the clearing at his nearing riders, now swinging into view from the arroyo. Including Buck, there were seven good fighting men there. A mistake now would mean a bloody shambles, a massacre, for another signal from Gonzalez had sent his *vaqueros* back to the concealment of the bushes. His own riders would be blasted from their saddles before they could fire a shot.

"As a friend, *señor*," repeated Don Ricardo softly. "Please—your men—they must remain at a distance." He smiled, held out a slim hand.

"Come, my friend, I pledge my word on the honour of a Gonzalez e Alvarez that I am here to help you in the sacred name of friendship."

"I'll take that word, Ricardo!"

They clasped hands; and Jeff said, "Things have been happening so fast I'm right jumpy these days. Kind of stood me on my hind-legs, you saying your *vaqueros* were pushing my cows south." He grinned. "I'm taking your word you got good reasons for this play." He lifted both hands high in a signal well known to Buck. The foreman returned an answering signal, and the Flying W riders came to a halt some hundred yards away.

Don Ricardo smiled gratefully. "*Gracias*, my friend." He hesitated, frowned, evidently finding his story difficult. "You ask why your cows are on the way to Sonora. It is very simple. For some months I have been purchasing cattle from a man named Smoke Hawker, who owns, so I am told, an outfit known as the Circle Y."

"Smoke Hawker!" Jeff's face reddened with anger. "So Hawker is El Toro, huh?"

"El Toro?" Don Ricardo's voice was puzzled. "I do not know this El Toro—" Gonzalez paused, his smile suddenly sinister. "Ah, I am stupid! El Toro is Smoke Hawker, with whom I shall shortly settle accounts. To proceed—this Smoke Hawker sent me word weeks ago that he had some three thousand head of cattle he could let me have at a

227

low figure. . . . Claimed he had won them at cards from a fool running a brand known as the Flying W. His own range was over-stocked, and he was satisfied to get his table winnings out of them. This Smoke Hawker, as you probably know, operates a large gaming establishment in Cottonwood Wells." Don Ricardo smiled again. It was not a pleasant smile.

"Seems to me you took his word for things kind of easy," complained Jeff. "You might have guessed you were dealing in rustled cows. You know what this country is up here."

The Mexican laughed. "Perhaps I have not been so careful as I might," he admitted shamelessly. "One does not question too closely at times—when the profits are big." Don Ricardo shrugged. "I paid the price as I had before—and asked no questions. It was none of my affair how Smoke Hawker came by the cattle he sold to me—not until this matter of the Flying W herd." The Mexican's trim black moustache twitched angrily. "It was then very much my affair. Alas, I had no suspicion that the Flying W brand was the mark of my good friend and preserver the Señor Wayne! The money, thirty thousand dollars, was paid over to the *vaqueros* in charge. They went their way, these gringo men, and my *vaqueros* went their way—with the cattle stolen from my friend."

"What kind of looking feller was the man who

turned the cows over to you and took the money?" Jeff asked.

"A big man with an enormous and very black beard," Gonzalez told him. "Black as the wings of Satan."

Jeff's eyes glittered. Tex had described just such a man—the stranger who had visited the camp on the Honda the night of the raid.

Gonzalez shrugged his elegant shoulders. "It would appear, my friend, that I am the loser of thirty thousand dollars—perhaps. Be that as it may, your men, seeking these rustlers, arrived on the scene too late. The black-bearded one and his gringo riders had vanished—with my good money. It was natural for your brave Chuck Wallis and his companion to suspect my honest *vaqueros* of being the rustlers. Unfortunately, or fortunately—I think the latter, as matters have turned out—I am most careful to post watchful eyes. Your brave fellows were espied long before they were aware of our presence. It was simple to effect a surprise capture, but not so simple to convince Chuck Wallis that we were not the actual thieves. However, he consented to act as my messenger to you. It is truly an ill-wind that blows nothing good."

"But my cows, Ricardo," murmured Jeff. "What about 'em, feller? You say you are out thirty thousand dollars—perhaps. What you mean— perhaps? Aimin' to get that money out of me?"

"My friend!" reproached the Mexican. "Do you think so lightly of the honour of Don Ricardo Gonzalez e Alvarez?"

"Thirty thousand dollars is a whacking sum for any man to lose," worried the young ranchman.

"Those monee—eet ees nossing," smiled Don Ricardo, returning to the "Eenglees" taught him by his Americano *señorita*; and in Spanish he added grimly, "I said I have an account to settle with the Señor Smoke Hawker, also known as El Toro the rustler."

"I'll be talking to Smoke Hawker myself," growled Jeff. He held out his hand to the other. "Ricardo—I'm shaking hands with a Mexican gentleman—*el caballero grande!*"

Gonzalez flushed under the warm brown of his smooth cheeks.

"*Muchos gracias.* This is for me the happy moment."

They gripped hands and Gonzalez gestured towards a rim of low hills lying some two miles to the south-west. "Your cattle are all there, held in a blind canyon by the *vaqueros* left to guard them. Come, explain to your men that all is well, and we will finish this business."

With a signal to his unseen warriors he swung the Palomino round and rode towards the distant ridge.

Jeff waited a few moments, while from hollow and crevice and gully presently rode Don Ricardo's dark-skinned *vaqueros*, hastening after their chief. At his signal his own men rode up, with hard faces, alert, suspicious. Buck's grin was sheepish.

"Like to have knocked me out of my saddle when I saw them fellers pop up like an Apache war-party," he confessed.

"That's Gonzalez and his outfit," Jeff told them. His wide smile told them something else. Curly Stivens let out a delighted yip.

"Found the cows, huh, boss!" he exulted. "Look at that grin on his face, fellers!"

Buck Saunders spoke gruffly in an attempt to cover his emotions. That an entire trail herd had been snatched from under his nose had sorely vexed the veteran foreman.

"That right, Jeff?"

"Sure is right, Buck. Gonzalez is holdin' 'em back in those hills yonder."

"Let's go get 'em!" The foreman beamed at the grinning faces. "Come on, fellers—let's go get our cows!"

"Can yuh beat it?" marvelled Chuck Wallis, riding neck and neck with Jeff. "Reckon that Mexican is one white man, huh, Jeff?"

Jeff eyed the slim young rider fondly. He had a high regard for the cool-eyed, capable Chuck. The latter's persistence in clinging to the trail of the rustlers had saved him from ruin. "Chuck," he announced, "you can pick out fifty head for your own self any time you've a mind to start a herd. . . . And that goes for Pat Hogan."

"Shucks!" grinned Chuck. "Reckon I'll let Johnny pick 'em out for a weddin'-present. Johnny—he's got him a bride to look out for now."

"I've already told Johnny to pick him out fifty cows and slap his iron on 'em when he gets in from honeymoonin'," Jeff informed him.

The blond Curly Stivens sighed sentimentally. "Sure picked one queen, Johnny did," he declared. "Lucky I didn't see Nellie before that cowboy got his rope on her."

"We're going pardners, Johnny and me," announced Buck Saunders proudly. "I got me a few cows, and soon as Jeff is all settled in the Basin Johnny and me aims to put the Circle N outfit on the map. N means Nellie," he explained. "Johnny and me figgered it out after the wedding."

"Plenty of room, Buck," Jeff said. "Johnny and you and Nellie can stay right on with us at the old ranch-house long as you want."

The romantic Curly heaved another sigh. "Sure was a pretty weddin'," he reminisced. "Nellie looked awful sweet kneelin' there by Johnny in front of Padre Juan, and us and them Injuns all standin' round watchin' 'em get hitched."

From the gap in the hills came the bawling of restless cattle, a deep-throated melody that banished the romance of Johnny and Nellie from the thoughts of Johnny's salty comrades. They grinned, burst into the shrill yip of their clan, and went drumming up the parched brown slope.

The great trail herd got slowly under way for the fifty-mile journey to Crater Basin, the Flying W outfit now augmented by ten of Don Ricardo's *vaqueros*, and accompanied by the latter's pack-train, bearing supplies.

Jeff watched them go with a swelling heart. A Power more mighty than the evil men did had saved him from disaster. He glanced at Don Ricardo, too moved for words.

There was an understanding look in the young Mexican's eyes. He smiled, said softly in Spanish: "Ah, you are thinking, 'Yes, there is a good God after all,' eh, my friend?" Don Ricardo nodded. "It is true."

"And loyalty," thought the owner of the Flying W, thinking of Chuck Wallis and his uncomplaining comrades; "and friends," thinking of the gay young Sonoran. "You have paid your debt, Ricardo," he said aloud.

Don Ricardo gestured grandly. "My friend, one can never repay such a debt. One can acquire new herds, but he cannot acquire a second life in this world."

"My poor hospitality is yours at any time," invited Jeff. "Will you ride with us, Ricardo?"

The young Mexican shook his head. "A matter

of business in Cottonwood Wells," he explained. His smile was suddenly bleak. "A little account to settle with the Señor Smoke Hawker," he reminded Jeff.

"If you'll wait you'll have company," suggested the young cattleman. "Hawker maybe won't be so easy to talk to now his gang is back in town."

The Sonoran gestured carelessly. "Eet ver' easy," he purred. "Those Smoke Hawker—he will joomp through my 'oop like dog, so." Don Ricardo snapped his fingers contemptuously.

"Looks like we'll soon have El Toro dancing on air," grinned Jeff. "That's the next job of work the Flying W aims to look into. You think Smoke Hawker is this rustling rattlesnake, Ricardo?"

"If he is not El Toro he is close to him," guessed the Mexican. He shrugged. "*Si*, if he is not El Toro, he will know the *hombre* hiding behind that name."

"Had me suspecting old King Cole," confessed Jeff. "Looked like a frame-up to keep me off KC-Bar range."

Gonzalez darted him a sharp look; anger, amusement, struggled for mastery.

"You seem surprised?" Jeff's tone was puzzled.

The Mexican laughed. "I am amuse' you suspec' the Señor Don King. Don King no stoop so low you t'eenk. No, my frien'—you ver' wrong to suspec' heem." He eyed the tall cattleman shrewdly. "You 'ave meet those leetle *señorita*, no?"

Jeff nodded, his face reddening under the probing gaze. Don Ricardo drew himself up proudly.

"Those *señorita* ees my cosin," he said surprisingly.

Jeff gave him an incredulous look. The Mexican smiled at his astonishment.

"Ees my name no Ricardo Felipe Gonzalez e Alvarez? My mother was an Alvarez—she seester to Carmela Alvarez, who marry weeth Señor Don King Cole." Gonzalez laughed merrily. "So—those Lylah my cosin, no?"

"Never guessed it," chuckled Jeff, his heart warming more than ever to the young Sonoran. He was aware of the Mexican custom of appending a woman's maiden name to her married one, sometimes to the confusion of historians. A noteworthy instance is the great Spanish explorer Juan Hernandez e Cabrillo, whose memorable voyage up an unknown coast gave California to a King of Spain. It is by his mother's maiden name of Cabrillo that posterity hails this intrepid adventurer.

"You like those cosin, no?" laughed Don Ricardo inquisitively. "She ver' loavely, no? You 'ave meet my cosin?"

"I—yes—I've met her," Jeff stammered. "She—she is very beautiful—"

"Her mother, Carmela Alvarez, was the most beautiful girl in all Mexico," declared Don

235

Ricardo, in his native tongue. He straightened in his saddle, and eyed the six swarthy riders clustered in the gap. "*Adios*, my friend. This has been a happy day for Don Ricardo Gonzalez e Alvarez." He saluted his friend gaily. "I go now to collect a debt from Smoke Hawker."

"Ricardo!" Jeff's voice was pleading. "I'm riding to Cottonwood Wells with you—if you'll wait till we get those cows into Crater Basin."

Gonzalez hesitated. "You fear for my life—that you wish to guard me?" The Mexican's smile was scornful. "I am too smart for Smoke Hawker," he assured the cattleman.

"Not worryin' about you handling Hawker," protested Jeff. "My idea is that we do the job proper . . . clean out that nest of rustlers for keeps. You wait a few days, Ricardo. . . . We'll have one big time together in that rustlers' roost."

Don Ricardo's dark eyes sparkled. He laughed softly.

"You win, my friend. I accept your invitation to visit the Flying W ranch. In the meantime I shall send Manuel to gather news of the Señor Hawker. Manuel has friends in Cottonwood Wells.

The two friends rode down the long slope, followed by the *vaqueros*.

CHAPTER XXI
LYLAH

LYLAH was already awake when Petra Lopez came in with her coffee; she had been awake for hours, watching the dawn creep through the open casement windows, pale fingers that slowly deepened to the shining yellow of the golden glow blooming against the grey *patio* walls. She had slept miserably, she told the soft-footed Mexican woman who had been nurse and companion to her since infancy.

"I don't know what's the matter with me," she complained. "I just can't sleep! I'll be a nervous wreck if this keeps up."

Petra admitted she was puzzled. Knowing nothing of Jeff Wayne, she could not suggest that the *señorita* possibly was in love. It was absurd to lay the blame on love when, as Petra well knew, there were no visible suitors. Petra reflected sadly that life on the KC-Bar ranch was vastly different from what it had been in the old days on the great Alvarez *hacienda*, when gallant caballeros without number twanged guitars underneath the casement windows of the lovely Alvarez *señoritas*.

"It is dull for you here," she pointed out. "There is nothing to quicken the pulse. If you do not go away you will become a discontented, ailing old woman." Petra nodded wisely. "You must go where there is life—handsome young *caballeros* who know how to make love—"

"What nonsense!" Lylah shrugged her bare shoulders. "It's an idea, though—my going away," she added, in a musing tone. "But I'd want to go a long, long way. I'm tired of Santa Fé—Dallas! I'd like to go to Paris. That's where I'd like to go."

The old nurse eyed her suspiciously, mystified by the lovely colour that waved into the girl's cheeks. If she could have thought of a single possible man Petra would have quickly diagnosed the cause of Lylah's sleepless nights. But where could there be such a man? Not one of the cowboys, surely! So rough, so uncouth, so lacking in the grand manner of the gallant *caballeros* of her own Sonora. Not for such as they had blossomed her precious flower. There was one man—Sladen, the huge foreman. Petra had caught his eyes following the girl on more than one occasion. But such a brute of a gringo! Petra shook her head and turned away to order the steaming hot water to be brought for the *señorita*'s bath. She must ask Chaco to keep eyes and ears open. There was a mystery here—some secret her *señorita* was keeping locked away in her heart.

"You must get up from that bed," she scolded, opening the bathroom door for a glance at the beautiful porcelain tub the *señor* had brought at

238

great expense all the way from Santa Fé. "I will send Manuelo with the hot water, and you will bathe and dress quickly. The *señor* does not like to breakfast alone. When you do not breakfast with the *señor* he grumbles like one of his great bulls."

Lylah slid from under the covers and drew on a silken wrap, her gaze resting distastefully on the shining porcelain tub peeping through the open door of the bathroom.

"Let him grumble," she said, in a rebellious tone. "Let him roar like a dozen bulls. And, Petra, I am not going to take a horrid hot bath in the old tub."

Petra gave her a shocked look. "How strangely you behave!" she wondered. "And now that I come to think of it, you have not been yourself since returning from Cottonwood Wells, these days past. It is the same with the *señor.* He is like a bear with a sore head." The old woman eyed the girl shrewdly. "Something happened at Cottonwood Wells . . . something *muy malo.*"

Lylah stared down at her shapely little feet. It was quite true about her father, she reflected. He had scarcely spoken to her since that dreadful visit to hateful Cottonwood Wells. And whenever she was with him she was conscious of his searching, probing eyes, as though he were reading her own torturing thoughts.

She had not mentioned the name of Jeff Wayne to King Cole, nor had he spoken of their new neighbour in Crater Basin. And yet he knew she had met Jeff—knew of her presence in the Flying W ranch-house that afternoon. What, then, was the reason for King Cole's avoidance of the subject? And now this fierce, smouldering anger that possessed him.

Lylah looked at the waiting Petra, saw the mounting anxiety in the latter's face. She shrugged slim, bare shoulders.

"I'm going to swim in the Pool," she announced. "Perhaps a cold plunge will put some life into me. Tell Chaco I'm going over now."

The woman hesitated. "To bathe in the Pool will make you late—" she began. Lylah cut her short.

"Do as I say!"

Petra hurriedly retreated. "The *señorita* was the image of her beautiful mother," she reflected, but there was something else there had not been in the gentle Carmela. There were occasions when the fierce, imperious nature of King Cole cropped out in Carmela's daughter.

Since early childhood, when Chaco had taught her to swim, Lylah had loved the Pool, as it was called, a quiet haven where the rushing waters of Beaver Creek were caught and held by massive granite blocks. Because she loved the crystal-clear depths the place had long been hers exclusively. Jutting granite cliffs screened it from eyes upsteam and downstream, and on either bank grew great trees and clustering shrubs that made of it a bower. It was an unwritten law that the Pool was sacred to Lylah. None dare approach save at the peril of quick death at the hands of Chaco, whose custom it was to stand guard at such times his mistress bathed there.

Lylah slipped into the *patio*. She was wrapped in a long cloak, and carried a towel. A path, shaded by ancient olive-trees, led her to the Pool. She knew without looking that the Yaqui followed a few paces behind.

Pausing where the path disappeared between two tree-bowered boulders, the girl glanced over her shoulder, threw Chaco the customary smile that acknowledged his presence, and was lost in the green woodland depths.

Chaco leisurely sought the boulder from which for years his hawk's eyes had kept vigilant watch. In the distance, riding from the corrals, was the giant KC-Bar foreman. The Yaqui scowled, and fingered the big knife in the belt girding his naked, lean waist. Unerring instinct had long since warned Chaco that Bart Sladen was one who would bear watching.

Early morning sunlight showered the green leaves, falling in a golden spray across the glittering surface of the big pool. Lylah reached the wide, flat ledge that overhung the water, like a platform. A rustic bench was built into one end of the ledge, where shade fell from an overhanging branch. Lylah sat down for a few moments, gaze idling on her sylvan surroundings. A great trout leaped high, sank back with a splash. Lylah smiled faintly. That big trout was an old friend. Suddenly eager for the water, she stood up, let the long cloak slip, and stood poised on the edge of the stone platform, slim arms outstretched, palms touching.

One moment she was a woodland nymph, praying to the sun-god, the next a flashing white arrow that entered the water with scarcely a ripple. Down, down into the jade depths curved the slim, white body; and suddenly she broke water, laughing-eyed, and shaking her dark curls. The water was wonderful, she told herself, not too chill, like sparkling champagne. She felt immeasurably cheered.

For half an hour she lazily and luxuriously swam back and forth across the sunlit water, until she was suddenly aware that she was ravenous for breakfast. She climbed up to the ledge. Sun and air came warmly to her, filling her with a sense of well-being. She stood there, gave herself to the sun's embrace; and suddenly, for the first time in all the years at the Pool, she was conscious of eyes watching her.

For a second Lylah stood frozen with terror, then in a frenzy of haste she seized the long cloak, and, wrapped in its folds, fled like a fawn down the woodland path.

Chaco was waiting patiently at his post. He looked at her sharply as she panted up.

"Chaco!" She addressed him breathlessly, in Spanish. "Chaco—you have been here all the time? You have not been away?"

"Chaco here all time, my *señorita*," the Yaqui assured her. He stirred uneasily. "Something has alarmed my *señorita*? A bear—"

Lylah smiled faintly. "Yes—perhaps a bear—some beast—"

She hurried past him. The Indian's frowning gaze followed the slim, cloak-wrapped figure. All was not well. Something had frightened the *señorita*. Chaco's worried frown twisted into a menacing scowl; he jerked the big knife from his belt, and sped up the woodland path that led to the bowered pool.

Lylah reached her room. She had had a silly attack of imagination, she scolded herself. Something was decidedly wrong with her—sleepless nights were wrecking her nerves.

By the time she was dressed she was laughing at herself. Nobody would dare to spy on her. The risk was too great. Her father, old Chaco, a score of others, would not hesitate to shoot down such an offender—only Chaco would not shoot; he would use that terrible knife.

In a calmer mood she sought the breakfast-table in a sun-warmed wing of the *patio*.

King Cole had lingered, obviously waiting for her. She kissed him.

"I'm hungry," she announced. "The water was

heavenly—like champagne." She babbled on, uneasily aware of his keen eyes.

"Petra tells mc you don't sleep. She is worried—" King Cole hesitated. "Noticed it myself—that you are kind of upset—since our trip to Cottonwood Wells."

Lylah shuddered. "I hope never to see that awful place again," she declared. She sat down, and a Mexican servant glided in with a plate of toast and poached eggs.

"You ain't answered my question. What ails you?"

"It's—it's Steve—he's drinking so terribly," Lylah said desperately. "I—I suppose he hasn't come home yet?"

Her father's shaggy brows drew down in a scowl. "Steve's a worthless pup," he complained. "I'm talking to him plenty when he gets in. I'm through with him if he ain't careful." Cole shrugged. "Steve's gone to the bad . . . he's plumb low. Glad he ain't real blood-kin to us. Sure made one mistake when I adopted him and gave him the use of my name. His mother would have it that way."

Lylah's brief hope that she had turned the subject from herself was blasted by the old man's next words.

"You ain't worrying about a coyote like Steve."

She pretended not to hear, bent absorbedly over her poached eggs.

"What's the latest about the new town?" she wanted to know, with a great show of interest. "Is the railroad coming in by Beaver Creek now we've signed those right-of-way papers?"

"It's that young feller over in Crater Basin you're all upset about," charged her father. "You needn't put me off talking about Steve or the railroad."

She gave him a startled look. "You have never spoken of—of—" Lylah faltered.

"I'm telling you right now that he ain't no good," said King Cole. His voice was suddenly harsh. "Another mistake I made—letting Jefferson Wayne's son horn in on my range."

"What—what has he done?" Lylah's voice was shaky.

"Done plenty." Her father himself now sought to evade. "Come roarin' into Simmons' office and accuses me of rustlin' his cows. Takes Bart Sladen's guns from him and lines us up agin the wall."

"Oh!" said Lylah faintly. Instinctively her heart leaped out in sympathy to the young owner of the Flying W ranch. No matter what else he might be, Jeff Wayne had courage.

"You mean—his cattle have been stolen?" she asked her father.

"The whole dang trail herd," grunted Cole. "I warned him to watch out for those cows . . . told him El Toro would be after 'em."

245

Lylah felt stunned, heart-sick. She was through with Jeff Wayne—despised him—but she could take no joy in the thought of his ruin, this blasting of the plans he had nursed so many years. She gave her father a strange look. Jeff Wayne must have had good reason to accuse the KC-Bar. Had King Cole after all been playing a cruel and ruthless game? Had his offer of friendship—his fair words—been a wicked plot to destroy utterly the son of the man murdered on his own doorstep twenty years ago?

"Was—was it true—this accusation?" Lylah asked the question almost fiercely.

Cole stared at her indignantly; and Lylah saw the truth in his eyes.

"That was foolish of me," she hastened to apologize repentantly. She forced an indignation of her own. "The idea! Jeff Wayne accusing you of being a rustler!" In a lower voice she added: "I'll tell him what I think of him—if I ever meet him again."

"So you've met him, huh!" Cole spoke softly, his smile faintly derisive.

"You know well enough that I've met Jeff Wayne!" flared the girl. "You know all there is to know about my meeting him—almost." The memory of those terrible moments in Lobo Canyon rushed back to her. Her father did not know of those moments.

"Maybe I do . . . maybe I know a lot more'n you think." His keen eyes were probing again.

"You don't know he saved my life!"

"No," admitted her father, suddenly rigid. "Wasn't knowing Jeff saved your life."

She related the story of the plucky longhorn cow and the wolf, the meeting with Jeff Wayne, those moments when Jeff plucked her from the jaws of death and bore her in his arms into the valley of Crater Basin.

"I was terrified when Brazos said you and the boys were coming. . . . I ran into the house."

"What you go and hide in Jeff's house for?" he asked gruffly. "No call for you to be scared of the KC-Bar."

"I wasn't afraid for myself." Lylah coloured. "I was afraid you'd be angry. . . . I'd always thought you hated the Waynes, and thought you would kill Jeff if you found me there with him." Lylah smiled faintly. "You see, after what had happened in the canyon we felt that we were—well—friends. We talked a lot about things—his father's death and his plan to come back to the range when he was a man." Lylah shivered. "And when Jeff said the Flying W was back to stay in spite of King Cole and the devil I was terribly afraid. . . . I knew it meant more killings."

"So you was afraid I'd kill Jeff, huh! What was it to you if Jeff was killed. Jeff wasn't nothin' to you."

Lylah avoided his gaze. "He saved my life, didn't he?" she reminded him.

247

"That the only reason?"

Again that faintly derisive smile. Lylah caught his expression, and interpreted it correctly. She stared at him, her face suddenly pale.

"No!" she told him vehemently. "Why do you torture me? You know that I—" Her mouth quivered, and she rose swiftly from her chair.

"My baby, my Carmela's baby." The old man's voice was inexpressibly tender. "Come to me, my dear." He was on his feet, arms reaching out to her. "Yes—I know you love Jeff Wayne. My eyes are sharp."

"When did you guess?" she asked him tearfully. She clung to him, pressed hot cheeks against his coat. King Cole stroked the shining blue-black hair gently.

"Your eyes told me when I got in that night. You were so demure, so innocent—so happy."

Lylah suddenly pushed away from him. "It's all over! I don't care a snap of my finger for Jeff Wayne!" The tragic look in her eyes contradicted her. She forced a laugh. "It was just a silly romantic notion." Her laugh came again, scornfully. "The cattle king's daughter marries the handsome son of his old enemy . . . ends a lifelong feud . . . and we all live happily ever after—"

The curious expression in King Cole's keen blue eyes halted her; she drew a sharp breath.

"It's all over, I tell you!" Her voice was defiant. "Let's talk about something interesting—Europe, for instance. I'd love a trip to Paris! I was telling Petra this morning." Lylah tucked an arm through his. "I've lost my appetite for breakfast. Let's sit down on the bench and talk about a trip to Paris. We will have to think up a chaperone."

They sat on a rustic bench under a trellised bougainvillaea. King Cole said quietly: "No sense pulling wool over your dad's eyes, girl. This thing ain't done with yet. I reckon you ain't loved a man before, and now that you do it ain't in you to stop loving him like you'd turn off a water-tap."

She was silent, rigid, hands in her lap tightly clasped. Cole tugged thoughtfully at his drooping grizzled moustache.

"You kind of thought Jeff was feelin' the same way?" he finally asked quietly.

She nodded. "I—was sure of it," she answered, in a faint little voice. "Up there—on Sentinel Peak. I could feel what he was thinking. . . . A girl knows—when a man really cares—"

"Sentinel Peak! What were you doing up there?" he interrupted.

Lylah told him about the Winding Stair. King Cole grunted surprise.

"Was wonderin' how you made it back to the ranch so quick. Huh! . . . So you come up through a hole in the mountain? And you and Jeff go out on the bluff and look down into Crater Basin and somethin' tells you that Jeff loves you—"

249

Lylah looked at him suspiciously. "You're making fun of me," she charged, suddenly furious.

"Just tryin' to figger things out," he said mildly. "Just tryin' to figger why you claim you ain't loving Jeff no more, and lying awake nights and moping round all broken-hearted."

"He—he disappointed me," Lylah told her father, unhappily. "I didn't think he was that sort of man."

"What sort of man?" barked the old man. "Don't hold back agin the rope so, girl. I'm your dad—"

Lylah reluctantly told him what she had witnessed in the upper corridor of the Great Western Hotel. King Cole sat very still, staring across the *patio*, a fierce, implacable gleam in his blue eyes.

"Took a woman into the room with him, huh?"

Lylah winced. "If anybody had told me I would have said it was a lie," she said drearily. "But I saw them—with my own eyes."

"I'll tell you something else." King Cole's voice was harsh. "Jeff Wayne took this woman back to his ranch with him. Saw 'em riding off together, and so did Steve. He's got her over in Crater Basin right this minute."

"Let's not discuss it any more," she begged. "I told you it was all over." She forced a scornful laugh. "I've been a perfect little fool—thinking I was in love at a moment's notice just because a man saved my life." The self-applied lash seemed to please her; she sat up proudly. "No business of mine how many women Jeff Wayne keeps at his ranch!"

The implacable look in her father's eyes told her that he thought differently.

"I say it is all over and done with!" she cried desperately.

"Not for him," said King Cole, in a grim voice. "There was nothing I wouldn't have done for Jeff Wayne if he'd been decent. Nothing of mine he couldn't have had for the asking." The old cattleman shook his head sorrowfully. "You can pack your trunks," he told the girl. "You're taking that trip to Paris, and when you come back to the KC-Bar—there won't be any Flying W over in Crater Basin."

She flung him an agonized look; she could have screamed. Her father's voice rasped on, implacable, relentless:

"Passed it by when he insulted me—accused me of stealing his cows—but no man can make my girl love him—and then go flauntin' a cheap woman in her face—and get away with it."

"You leave Jeff Wayne alone!"

Lylah flung the words at him.

King Cole looked at his white-faced daughter with fierce, moody eyes. "That's the worst of it," he groaned. "You still love the feller. . . . He's got to pay plenty—for hurtin' you."

The girl sprang to her feet, flung him a stricken look, and fled into the house, to the seclusion of her room.

King Cole's deadly resentment appalled Lylah. She had done it now! Killed Jeff Wayne as surely as if she had pushed him over the cliff above the falls. There was no mercy in her implacable old father when hate was in him.

She shivered. Her love for Jeff Wayne had sentenced him to death. No matter what he had done to her, she loved him—always would love him. Lylah closed her eyes, recalled those moments when he bore her to safety in his strong arms. She had known then that she loved him— that he would love her. Those minutes on the bluffs under grey Sentinel Peak, overlooking vast Crater Basin, had told her he loved her; she had felt the force of it sweeping him.

Distracted, she paced the room like a young tigress. There must be a way out . . . there must be a way to save Jeff, she told herself fiercely again and again. A sudden thought halted her restless feet. This woman she had seen with Jeff—this woman he had carried off to his ranch in Crater Basin—there might be an explanation!

Lylah seized on the thought hungrily. They were judging Jeff without a hearing—jumping to cruel conclusions. Come to think of it, the girl had seemed rather decent, an innocent, a shy young face . . . not the face of a hardened creature.

Hardly aware of what she was doing, Lylah hurriedly changed into her riding-clothes, and went swiftly out to the stables.

Bart Sladen emerged from the small adobe building he used for his foreman's office. She deigned him a mechanical smile, and would have passed on; but was surprised to find him towering in front of her.

"Been wantin' to see yuh." He smiled. "Ridin' any place in partic'lar?"

Lylah said she hadn't the least idea. "Just going for a ride," she answered him.

"Come along with me," invited the foreman. "Was headin' for Willow Camp myself. Got a bunch of weaners there I want to look over for ticks."

"I'm in a bad humour," Lylah explained. "You'd be hating me before we were half-way to Willow Camp." She shook her head. "No—I want to be alone."

The big foreman grinned. "Hatin' yuh is the last thing I'd be doin'," he protested. "Fact is, Lylah"—she raised her brows at his use of her name—"there's something I want to tell yuh— something personal—"

"I'm sure I can't imagine anything personal we have to talk about," she said, a trifle coldly.

Lylah had never liked the big KC-Bar foreman; in fact, could scarcely endure him. His heavy, mask-like features, his bright, restless, beady eyes, had always been repulsive to her. She often wondered why her father tolerated him. There was something repellently savage and brutal about the man, despite his oily, suave demeanour. No doubt he was highly capable, else he would not be foreman of the great KC-Bar ranch. She forced a polite smile.

"Sorry. . . . Hope you will find the weaners doing nicely."

To her surprise Sladen continued to bar her path. She looked at him, vaguely uneasy, with growing indignation. The man seemed suddenly huge, colossal, quite terrifying.

"What I'm wantin' to tell yuh is that I'm figgerin' on bossing an outfit of my own right soon," he said, watching her closely. "Been thinking a heap about yuh, Lylah—" There was a curious smirk on his broad, swarthy face. "Never seen a gal so purty as you. Been thinkin' your dad 'ud be right tickled to have me for a son-in-law. I think a heap of yuh. Your dad—he's gettin' awful old—needs a man that knows cows like I do. Can't depend on Steve to run the KC-Bar right. Steve's plumb useless." He smirked again. "What yuh say, Lylah? Your dad 'ud be awful pleased to see us get hitched."

Lylah stared at him, too dumbstruck for words. There was something unclean in that odious smirk on Sladen's face, something—Lylah shrank with sudden loathing.

"Sladen"—her tone was furious—"were you near my swimming-pool this morning?"

The flicker in his eyes, that widening smirk, told the girl her shot had hit the mark.

"Get out of my way!" she blazed.

She brushed past him, cheeks flaming, unutterable contempt in her eyes.

The smirk was gone from Sladen's face; the mask lowered. Brutal rage contorted the dark features; beady eyes glittered venomously. With something like a snarl he swung quickly into his office.

There was nobody in the stable to saddle a horse for her. Lylah pulled down her saddle from its peg and threw it on the bay mare that had replaced her drowned Chiquita. Her fingers trembled; she had difficulty in lacing the cinch. Her one thought was to get away—into the high hills, where the air was clean. She led the mare outside, and climbed into the saddle.

Sladen, slyly watching from his office window, saw her ride away at a gallop and turn into the trail that wound up Beaver Canyon, the trail to Burro Mesa—and Sentinel Peak.

An ugly gleam crept into the man's beady eyes as he watched from his window. Some thought apparently hugely elated him.

CHAPTER XXII
ACCUSED!

THE passing days had wrought a subtle change in Crater Basin, an intangible difference not readily apparent to the eye. One felt, without understanding, that something epic had taken place, something vast in potential promise.

The explanation that came to Jeff was amazingly simple—fundamental. The vast valley no longer lay in its primitive isolation. Where so recently had reigned the awesome hush of the silent places now was heard the bawling of cattle, the thunderous challenge of great range bulls—the voice of man, busy with the thousand and one tasks of home-making. For Johnny Wales, now healed of his wound, had arrived with his pretty bride. The sleeping wilderness had awakened with a vengeance.

Perhaps more than anything else the presence of a young woman wrought mysterious alchemy with life at the Flying W. To these clean-minded, womanless young riders of the range the pretty, blonde Nellie was the high-priestess, the sacred symbol of *home.* Theirs was the chivalrous homage due to all good women from the galloping knights of cowland. Even the older Barbecue Thompson, autocrat of the kitchen, and the grizzled, cynical old Brazos were not immune from the softening influence of Johnny's pretty and friendly bride.

Barbecue spent arduous hours putting a polish on the rusty kitchen stove, and otherwise beautifying his particular domain. No longer did he slam the dishes on the table with gruff warning of "Yuh kin take it, or yuh kin leave it." Beaming benevolence was now the fat cook's keynote—when within sight or hearing of Mrs Johnny. No withering salvos from his lips at the sudden demand for clean towels, nor did he sneer at the much smoothing down of wet hair and the new fashion of a daily shave.

And Brazos, hard-bitten veteran of the range-lands, was no less the paragon of kindly benevolence. Cannily aware of a young wife's weakness, Brazos won Mrs Johnny's heart with long tales of her husband's prowess. Johnny would have been amazed had he heard some of the epics of his past. Like all born weavers of tales, Brazos made shameless use of a picturesque imagination.

Perhaps more than any of them was Jeff himself aware of the subtle change. He was achingly conscious of vague longings—an emptiness in his life. He found himself envisioning the presence of another young woman in the old ranch-house his efforts had rehabilitated from the unkind years; a girl with shining blue-black hair and eyes of golden brown. He wanted to see her again; knew that the day would come when he must see her again if that gnawing emptiness was to be satisfied. Barbecue had slyly brought up the subject of the Stetson hat still hanging on the wall in Jeff's room.

"Mebbe I'd best mosey over to the KC-Bar with that thar hat, boss," he suggested. "Don't seem perlite keepin' her Stetson this way."

"You leave that Stetson alone," warned the boss of the Flying W irritably. "When I'm needing your advice I'll ask you."

"Like to have bit my head off," the cook complained to his crony.

Brazos shook his head. "Somethin' on Jeff's mind," he opined. "He don't act natcheral. Ain't been himself since he got in with them cows . . . and that's two days ago."

"It's love," declared the rotund cook solemnly. "Jeff's awful bad in love, and don't seem to know it." Barbecue heaved a deep sigh.

Jeff had a reason for delaying his visit to the KC-Bar. Serious business was in the offing, an affair in which his friend Gonzalez was to play an important and necessary *rôle*. He was waiting word from the debonair Sonoran, who had bade Crater Basin *adios* the previous evening and departed with his *vaqueros* in quest of information from certain of his countrymen in Cottonwood Wells.

Don Ricardo's disclosures concerning his dealings with Smoke Hawker proved that the latter was a member of a well-organized gang of cattle-thieves. It was even possible that the saloon man was himself the elusive El Toro. Jeff thought not, however, agreeing with Gonzalez that Hawker's activities were confined to the marketing of the stolen stock. Hawker was a key that would unlock the mystery, and Jeff was resolved to possess that key. Through Hawker he would strip the mask from the man whose sinister brain sought to destroy the Flying W. That the trail might yet lead to the KC-Bar rather appalled Jeff. He still had his doubts regarding King Cole; the secrecy maintained by El Toro was, in Jeff's opinion, highly suspicious. He was not entirely convinced of the old cattle baron's innocence. It was not beyond the bounds of plausibility for the ingenious King Cole to play the *rôle* of a mythical El Toro in an attempt to crush an unwanted rival. Until this troublesome aspect of the affair was settled Jeff was reluctant to face King Cole's daughter again. Lylah could have only hate for the man who exposed her father as a hirer of thieves and killers. And soon the mystery would no longer be a mystery. Smoke Hawker was the key to the enigma—and the next twenty-four hours would see Smoke Hawker in his hands.

Engrossed with his thoughts, Jeff was suddenly aware that he was riding across the tule-covered marsh—the deep boom of the falls in his ears. He had set out from the corrals with a brief tour of inspection in mind.

Smiling faintly, he reined the roan and stared at the great silvery plume hanging down the sheer side of the cliff, to lose its feathery tip in clouds of misting spray. Urge to see Lylah had unwittingly governed his bridle-rein—brought him to the Winding Stair.

The thought of her set his heart hammering; and, still under the sway of that same compelling desire, he rode on through the tules and into the cave behind the veiling mist. . . .

Lylah was too angry to notice that she had turned into the Beaver Creek Canyon trail. She rode at a steady pace, following the twisting gorge through the Burro Mountains. It was not until she reached the rugged uplands of Burro Mesa and saw the slim minarets of towering Sentinel Peak that she realized blind, overpowering impulse had guided her.

She reined in the mare in some dismay. The Winding Stair! The great ledge overhanging Crater Basin Falls—Jeff Wayne!

Her face pale, she stared at the lofty grey crags that marked the place where Jeff and she had stood and gazed across the great valley of Crater Basin. Lylah's breath quickened; she knew that she should turn back, send the mare scampering down the trail—instead she rode forward across the mesa, drawn by an invisible force she was powerless to resist.

The roar of the falls came faintly to her ears, and another occasional note that puzzled her—the challenging bellow of a range bull, the bawling of cattle. What were cattle doing in Jeff's valley? Jeff had no cattle! The trail herd had been stolen, so her father had told her only that morning. Lylah rode on with mounting curiosity.

Other ears had marked the bawling of cattle in Crater Basin. Steve Cole, red-eyed from his prolonged debauch in Cottonwood Wells, reined in his sweat-lathered horse with a surprised oath.

Cows in Crater Basin! He listened intently. No mistaking that sound. Steve climbed from his saddle, concealed his horse behind a huge boulder, and crept warily towards the cliff's edge.

A definite purpose had brought Steve Cole to the rugged mesa overlooking Crater Basin. Some-where in the valley was the girl Jeff Wayne had stolen from him. Steve had other plans for Hank Smithers' pretty niece, plans that Jeff had thwarted. Steve knew it was hopeless to attempt to enter the valley by way of West Pass or the Gap. Both were too well guarded. But one could look down in the valley from the surrounding high cliffs. It was in Steve's mind that after a careful estimate of the surrounding topography he could post certain expert marksmen at the most likely points—hired killers, who would crouch ambushed in the crags until a day came when Jeff Wayne's bullet-riddled body would be found lying below the cliffs.

The thought brought an ugly gleam to Steve's bloodshot eyes as he crawled towards the cliff. The sound of shod hoofs somewhere behind him brought the man to a sudden standstill. Instinctively he flattened down behind a scrubby juniper-bush, peered stealthily. A dazed expression came to his eyes. The rider was his stepsister.

Steve watched fiercely. What was Lylah doing in the vicinity of Crater Basin? Suspicion mounted in his drink-disordered brain. Lylah was here to meet Jeff Wayne—a secret tryst. He had been right that afternoon in believing the girl was hidden in Jeff Wayne's house. It was plain that one woman was not enough for Jeff Wayne. A malignant grin distorted the face of Lylah's stepbrother. Here was a new angle. No need to post his killers on the cliffs. He had only to wait where he lay crouched behind the junipers, and Jeff Wayne was delivered into his hands.

Unconscious of the gloating eyes watching her, Lylah left her mare and went slowly towards the great ledge overhanging the falls. The hill sloped steeply, following the narrow chasm down which rushed the water that was the source of the falls. The descent took her from Steve's sight. He rose and followed stealthily, careful to keep the

262

boulders between them. He came in view of the overhanging ledge above the falls, and halted with a smothered oath of surprise. . . .

Lylah stared unbelievingly at the tall, straight figure standing on the wide ledge overlooking the valley. As if drawn by the intensity of her gaze, the man looked round. She poised for flight, heard his startled exclamation of her name; she found she could not move—her limbs refused to obey her will.

Helplessly she waited, face white, eyes scornful.

Jeff, after a momentary paralysis, came swiftly towards her, a glad light in his grey eyes.

"You—of all people!" he exclaimed. "Wasn't expecting to see you." His expression altered. "Why—what's wrong." He smiled uneasily. "You don't seem pleased to see me."

"No!" she said, in a low, tense voice. "You are quite right. I am not pleased to see you. In fact, I had hoped never to see you again."

Jeff looked at her dumbly.

"Why should a self-respecting girl wish to see you?" Voice and eyes withered him. "You are not the man I thought you were, Mr Wayne." The colour was back in her cheeks now. "I know everything. There is nothing you can say to me." She turned away abruptly.

Jeff came to life; a quick stride placed him in front of her. Lylah eyed him haughtily.

"You don't leave until you explain what you

said." Jeff's voice shook with repressed anger. "Just what is this all about?"

"Need I tell you?" Her eyes flashed disdain.

"I'll say you need!" said Jeff furiously.

Lylah was suddenly pale again. The hurt expression in his face tortured her. "I—I saw you take that—that girl into your room!" she gasped. "Oh, why do you force me even to speak of it!"

Jeff's expression was bewildered.

"Oh, I saw you!" she cried. "I saw you with her in the hotel! And then you carried her off to your ranch. You can't deny it! Father saw her ride away with you. She's down there now!" Lylah gestured towards the valley. "Oh, I think you are just too low!"

Enlightenment dawned in his eyes. He looked at her curiously, nodded his head. "Yes—reckon you saw me all right," he admitted quietly.

"You don't deny it, then!" Lylah cried furiously. Her voice broke. "Oh, Jeff! How could you!"

"No, I ain't denying what you saw," he said, in the same quiet voice. "I'm just denying what you thought about what you saw." He smiled gravely at her incredulous look. "That was Johnny's girl, and that was Johnny's room you saw us go into. Johnny was sick, and Nellie was nursing him."

"But you—you carried her off with you—"

Jeff's eyes twinkled. "Sure I did . . . took Johnny along with her, and inside of an hour Padre Juan was saying the marriage words over 'em."

He related briefly the incidents of Johnny's romance. Lylah's knees felt oddly weak; her mouth quivered; she wanted to abase herself—go on her knees to him and beg his forgiveness. She could only gaze at him with stricken eyes. Jeff sensed her remorse.

"Nothing to worry about," he assured her. "Don't blame you."

"You'll forgive?" she asked, in a faint little voice.

Jeff grinned. "Tickles me to death to know you care enough to be—to be—" He stammered, and gave her a scared look.

It was Lylah's turn to take command of things. She smiled demurely. "Yes? To be—what?" She spoke softly, dark eyes tender under their veiling lashes.

"To be jealous," said Jeff, suddenly bold.

The dark lashes lifted, and what Jeff saw in those golden-brown eyes started that old hammering of his heart.

"Yes, I was so jealous—so jealous—I could have died—"

She was in his arms now, and what Jeff said to her and what she said to Jeff does not really matter. The same things have been said so many times—will continue to be said as long as the human race is human.

Steve's voice, husky with hate, pulled them apart. Unnoticed by the engrossed couple, he had quietly stalked them. His unshaven face, showing the marks of carousing nights, was twisted with vicious rage. A gun was in his hand.

"What's your game, feller? Makin' love to my sister—kissing her—" Steve raised the gun threateningly. "Had ought to kill yuh like a yellow coyote."

"You're drunk!" Lylah's eyes sparkled angrily. "Go away from here, Steve Cole! You mind your own business!"

Steve gave her a sneering glance. "I'm on to yuh, missie. Yuh're nothin' but a hussy . . . meetin' your lover up here on the sly."

"Careful what you say, Cole." Jeff's voice was deadly. "This is no affair of yours."

Steve laughed unpleasantly. "Foxy, ain't yuh, Wayne? Reckon Lylah's going to be right peeved when she hears about you and Hank Smithers' little blonde niece. Got sick of Nellie awful quick, didn't yuh, feller. Or ain't one woman at a time enough for yuh?"

Steve's bombshell proved to be a dud. He had expected Lylah's eyes to fill with horror and indignation. Nothing of the kind happened. Steve's jaw sagged. They were laughing at him.

"Think I'm a liar, do yuh?" he blustered. "You can ask the old man. He saw that hussy ride off with this feller."

"Listen, mister," rasped Jeff. "If Johnny Wales hears you calling his wife names he'll sure take you apart."

"Meanin' what?" demanded Steve, his fuddled brain unable to comprehend just what had gone amiss with his plans to crush this budding romance.

"Meaning that the young lady you are so disturbed about is Mrs Johnny Wales," explained Lylah cuttingly. "I know all about Nellie; and now that you understand the situation perhaps you will kindly be on your way," she added, in a biting tone.

Steve scowled, unwilling to concede victory to this man who had twice humiliated him, taken his gun—beaten him with bare fists.

"Not leavin' yuh here alone with him. Ain't proper—you here alone with this feller," he said sullenly.

"You're too drunk to know what you're talking about," Lylah told him contemptuously.

She changed her tactics, spoke in a coaxing voice. "Oh, Steve, please be nice! Don't spoil things for me when I'm so happy." She looked at Jeff, blushed. "I'll tell you a secret . . . I'm going to marry Mr Wayne."

"Like hell you are!" snarled her stepbrother. He glared at Jeff, lifted his gun. "Get movin', feller. I'm warning yuh to keep away from my sister after this. There'll be orders out to plug yuh on sight if yuh come ramblin' round this range."

"Oh, you're impossible!" stormed the distressed girl.

"Just what have you got against me, Cole?" asked Jeff quietly. "You heard what Lylah's father said the other day—that our outfits were to be friends."

"He wasn't figgerin' on yuh hornin' in on the fam'ly," sneered Steve. "Yuh sure figger wrong, feller, if you aims to get a stranglehold on the KC-Bar by marryin' Lylah. I got something to say about that." He gestured savagely. "Told yuh to get goin', didn't I, mister?"

Jeff and the girl looked at each other helplessly. Both realized that further argument could only feed Steve's drunken anger. Jeff was reasonably certain that he could drop Steve if it came to gunplay. Such a termination of the affair was unthinkable. He could not ruthlessly slay Lylah's stepbrother in front of her eyes. It would be a sorry deed for the day that had brought her to his arms. Lylah read his troubled thoughts, and smiled faintly.

"Perhaps it is best for you to go, dear," she said gently. Her voice faltered. "I'll—I'll not forget." She gave Jeff a wonderful look—a look he knew she intended he carry away with him. The vicious-eyed, drunken Steve, the menacing gun, were things of no consequence; she wanted him to go with the memory of those unforgettable moments quickening his heart. His eyes answered her, told her that he understood.

Steve's gaze followed him longingly. But for

Lylah's presence he would unhesitatingly have emptied his gun into the young cattleman's broad back. The girl sensed the murderous desire, watched him closely, ready to clutch the threatening gun-arm.

The tall figure vanished. Lylah drew a sigh of relief, and eyed her stepbrother contemptuously.

"You coward!" Her voice was bitter. "You would have shot him in the back—if you had dared."

Steve leered, and holstered his gun. "I'm tellin' yuh now, missie—Jeff Wayne ain't livin' long enough to marry yuh—"

Steve's grin froze into a mask of ghastly fear; he snarled an oath, reached for the holstered gun, staggered, and fell forward on his face. And from the distant boulders rolled the crashing report of a six-shooter.

Lylah screamed.

A shout answered her, Jeff's voice; she heard the quick beat of his boots on the rocks. He came running up, breathless, was at her side and staring with startled eyes at the limp form crumpled at her feet.

Like one in a dream, Lylah saw that he held a gun in his hand. She gazed at it, terrible fear, horror, creeping over her face.

Dumbly she watched while Jeff bent over the still form of her stepbrother. After a brief moment he straightened up.

"Still breathing," he announced. His gaze swept the wild terrain, came back to her, caught her questioning, horrified look. Slowly the horror was reflected in his own face.

"You don't think that I—fired that shot?" he demanded almost roughly.

"Who—who else would have—" She faltered, glanced at the gun in his hand.

Jeff eyed her gloomily. The question was not unnatural, even from Lylah. He could not deny that the finger of suspicion readily pointed straight at himself.

The sound of approaching hoof-beats cut short his dismayed reflections. Four riders clattered up, and Jeff recognized the KC-Bar's giant foreman, Bart Sladen.

They drew rein, stared silently for a moment at the sprawled form of Steve Cole. Suddenly the foreman's gun was pointing at Jeff.

"Get the skunk, boys."

Sladen's voice was ominous; and, looking at him, Jeff was disturbed by the cold malignance in the man's eyes.

"You've figgered this wrong, Sladen." Jeff's voice was mild. "Wasn't my gun that did this job." He stared at the weapon in his hand. "Pulled it when I heard the shot . . . thought some *hombre* was trying to plug me."

"We seen yuh, mister," came the curt answer. "Two of us seen yuh shoot young Cole. No argument about it. You done this killing, Wayne."

Speechless, the young cattleman suffered them to remove his guns, tie his hands. One of the cowboys examined the gun taken from his hand, ejected an empty shell. Sladen smiled grimly.

"Save that shell, Panamint. That's evidence."

Jeff shrugged. No use explaining that he had shot a rattler coming up the Winding Stair. He could take them to the Winding Stair and show them the dead snake—he chose to preserve the secret of the Winding Stair. The absurd accusation that they had witnessed the shooting of Steve Cole chilled him. These men were determined to have his life . . . had themselves slain King Cole's stepson for the sole purpose of pinning the crime upon himself. Intuitively he knew that back of this new mystery was the deeper mystery of El Toro; and it appeared that the answer was—the KC-Bar.

Jeff looked miserably at the girl. Lylah was bending over the limp body on the ground, weeping softly.

"For Steve," he wondered bitterly, "or is she weeping for Jeff Wayne?"

CHAPTER XXIII
ADIOS

KING COLE had small regard for the son of the widow he had married in his reckless youth. Steve had long since forfeited his stepfather's affection. It was not grief, then, that filled the old cattleman's heart and deepened the furrows in his harsh face as he listened to the tale unfolded by his foreman. There was no occasion for sorrow in the news that an assassin's bullet bade fair to terminate Steve's vicious and useless life.

King Cole's emotions were directed entirely at Jeff Wayne. He was righteously indignant. Not because it was Steve who was shot, but because it was Jeff who had done the shooting. He had overlooked Jeff's insult to himself—he could not overlook the flaunting of another woman in his daughter's face—this wanton shooting of her stepbrother. Steve was a worthless sot, but the manner of his passing at the hands of this man was a direct affront to the KC-Bar.

"If Steve dies Jeff Wayne hangs," he promised Sladen.

"Steve ain't got a chance," Sladen prophesied. "Doc Mosby says that slug tore him to pieces. Lucky the doc was here on account of Chico's broke leg. Not that a hundred docs can do a thing

272

for Steve now." The foreman was sorrowful. "Just kind of makes me feel a heap better to know we're doin' all that can be done," he added.

"Shot him in the back, huh?" raged the old cowman.

"Never give Steve a chance. Me an' Panamint—we was combin' those draws for strays—seen Wayne sneakin' through them big boulders . . . had his gun out . . . we couldn't see nothin' of Steve or Lylah from where we was or we'd have jumped Wayne before he pulled off the shootin'." Sladen growled an oath. "Oh, we seen him all right! Found the empty shell in his gun." He drew the brass shell from a pocket and handed it to his chief. "Same as he uses in those guns he carries."

"He'll swing for it," repeated the old man grimly. "Keep a good watch on him. Don't want him makin' a break." With a curt nod of dismissal Cole walked slowly into the *patio*, and halted as his daughter suddenly confronted him. She was very pale.

"I—I heard you!" she gasped. "I can't bear it! You—you musn't—"

"Jeff Wayne ain't worth your tears," King Cole said harshly.

"Steve would have killed him—if I hadn't been there," she told him. "Steve would have shot Jeff in the back—when he left us—only he was afraid of me."

Her father eyed her curiously. "How come you

273

were up there?" he wanted to know. "You been meeting Jeff Wayne on the sly?"

"Never!" she denied vehemently. "I just happened to ride in that direction . . . Jeff was there. He was as surprised as I."

"And Steve trailed you, huh? Wanted to see what you were up to." He motioned the girl to the bougainvillæa-bowered bench, and sat by her. "Tell me all you know about it, honey," he said gently. "Maybe there's things about this business I ain't heard right."

"I don't think Steve followed me," Lylah told him musingly. "I think Steve was already there—to spy on things down in the valley. You see, he thought Jeff had taken that girl into the Basin, and went there to spy—or something. I've been thinking about it a lot—"

She saw resentment darken the old man's face at the reference to the girl. "We were terribly wrong about the girl," she added quickly. "Jeff told me all about her."

King Cole's shaggy brows lifted sceptically. "Reckon he's right good at explaining things," he commented dryly.

"We had no right jumping at conclusions," Lylah declared sorrowfully. She related the story of Nellie's romantic wedding. King Cole seemed dazed.

"Maybe we did bark up the wrong tree," he admitted uneasily. His face darkened again. "But he can't explain away his shooting Steve from ambush—"

The girl shuddered, and gave him a piteous look. "He—he could only deny it," she said simply.

"Two witnesses—and you there when it was done," he reminded her curtly. The old man gave her a sharp glance. "Don't hear you saying Jeff didn't do that shooting."

"Only that—that it is impossible for Jeff to commit a murder—and that was murder, if Steve dies," Lylah said, in a low, tense voice. "I know everything—the evidence, the witnesses—convict Jeff, but I can never believe he shot Steve. Not after what had happened—"

"What you mean, girl? After what happened?" King Cole's voice was puzzled.

"Jeff asked me to marry him. I—I said I would—"

The old man stared at her, thunder-struck. The situation was becoming more complicated than he thought.

"Steve came up with a gun . . . he was quite drunk. . . . I thought he would kill Jeff then and there. He said, Steve said, that he'd seen us. He talked dreadfully to Jeff . . . said he would kill Jeff on sight if he didn't keep away from me." Lylah's voice was bitter. "He tried to tell me all that nonsense about the girl, only I shut him up."

King Cole's voice was very gentle. "You love him, honey? You love Jeff Wayne?"

She gave her father a look. He nodded. Words could not have told him more.

"I told Jeff to leave us," she went on. "Steve was getting more and more ugly—and threatening." Her voice broke. "Jeff left us—and then, when I was telling Steve what I thought of him, he seemed to see somebody—the killer, I suppose. Steve looked terribly frightened, and tried to reach for his gun just as he fell at my feet. The shot sounded quite near," she added. "I think Steve recognized who it was . . . he looked horribly scared."

"Sladen wouldn't lie about that shooting," mused the cowman. "Sladen ain't got reason to frame Jeff." King Cole shook his head. "If Sladen claims he saw Jeff shoot Steve there's no question about it."

"If Steve could talk—oh, if only Steve could tell us whom he saw shooting at him!" wailed the girl.

"And Panamint backs him up," muttered the old man. He shook his head distressfully. "If it 'ud been in fair fight I maybe could see my way to fix things up. But it was a low-down killing—if Steve dies." King Cole snorted, rose to his feet. "I'm goin' in to talk to Doc Mosby. Maybe he can do something to give Steve a chance to talk. Reckon it was Jeff he saw, though." Lylah's father stamped away, frowning, and muttering to himself.

The girl's slim body drooped. She had told her father the truth. She could not force her heart to

276

believe Jeff guilty of a cowardly killing. Cold reason declared he was guilty—something that was bigger than reason cried out that it was not so.

A soft padding of feet drew her attention. Lylah looked up. Chaco was crossing the *patio*, coming to speak to her. She saw that the Yaqui's usually stolid face showed signs of deep agitation; there was a curious red glow in his sombre eyes as he spoke in the tongue of her mother.

"*Señorita*—it is bad for the young Señor Wayne. The men are making such angry talk. It is planned to take the young *señor* from the *rancho cuartel* and hang him."

Lylah's dark eyes widened; she uttered an anguished cry.

"The Señor Sladen goes among the men . . . his talk makes them very angry with our young *señor*. Sladen tells them that Steve must be avenged— that our young *señor* must die quickly—before Don King can have time to change his mind."

Chaco paused, staring fixedly at his white-faced mistress. "My *señorita*, why is it that Sladen desires the death of our young *señor* in such haste, before it is known if Señor Steve will live—or die?"

Lylah's golden-brown eyes dilated; the Yaqui's question was like a spark, touching off a train of powder, sending little explosions of frantic thought through her brain, explosions that all flared redly into one word—WHY?

She repeated the word aloud, fiercely. "Why?" Why was Sladen inflaming the KC-Bar men to immediate action? Why was he so anxious to make certain of Jeff Wayne's death?

The Yaqui spoke softly: "The *señorita* does not know why Sladen seeks the life of the man she loves?"

The girl gave him a startled look.

"You—know, Chaco, that I love him? How is it you know I love the Señor Wayne?"

"Chaco knows the little *señorita* has always loved him—as he loves her." The old Indian's eyes glistened. "Chaco always know when his little *señorita*'s heart is glad—and when it is troubled."

Lylah's eyes were misty of a sudden.

"Chaco, you're a dear," she told him. Her lips quivered.

The Yaqui's eyes gleamed for a moment, then he said quietly: "Sladen wishes the death of the Señor Wayne because he hates him. Sladen is jealous of the young *señor*."

Lylah was conscious of a horrid sensation inside of her, as though a slimy hand, Sladen's hand, was clutching her heart. Chaco's words had flashed a picture before her—the scene near the corrals that morning—Bart Sladen, huge, colossal, confronting her, barring her path, smirking as he asked King Cole's daughter to marry him.

So much had happened since that absurd proposal for her hand . . . it had quite gone from her mind. Chaco's words brought it all back. And suddenly Lylah knew why Bart Sladen was stirring up the men to a hasty lynching. She knew, too, whose gun fired the bullet from ambush. She questioned the Yaqui further.

"Why do you say such a thing, Chaco? Why do you say Señor Sladen is—is jealous?" Her tongue stumbled at the word. "Sladen—jealous!" she thought furiously. "How dare the brute think he has that right!"

The Yaqui was showing her something that lay in the open palm of his brown hand. She gave it a puzzled glance, saw that it was an ornament, a concha, about the size of a fifty-cent piece, a silver concha, popular with cowboys as adornment for their leather chaps.

"What about it?" she asked.

"It is something I find," muttered the Yaqui. "It tell me why the Señor Sladen want to kill your *señor*."

"I don't understand you at all," she complained. "What has that silver button got to do with Sladen and Mr Wayne?"

She read a curious look of shame in the faithful eyes. "It is not well that I tell the *señorita*," muttered the Indian. "Soon I will give the concha back to the man who lost it." Chaco's fingers caressed the handle of the big knife in his belt.

Lylah was silent, downcast. There was no need to question the Yaqui further. Chaco had found that silver concha somewhere in the vicinity of her swimming-pool. Sladen had lost it there that morning. She understood now why Chaco suspected the big foreman of sinister designs.

She rose from the bench, and, telling the Indian to await her return, went swiftly into the house. Petra was in the hall, her arms full of supplies from the medicine closet, a worried, harried look on her comely dark face.

The girl halted her. "How is he? How is Steve?" she asked.

The woman shrugged plump shoulders. "It is in God's hands," she replied solemnly. She shrugged again. "I think that the wise God does not desire that he shall live. Also that funny little doctor man says he cannot live."

Petra would have moved on down the hall. Lylah grasped her arm.

"Does the doctor say how long he can last?"

"Not long," Petra informed her. "It is Don King's wish that Steve have strength to talk before death takes him. The little doctor is doing what he can with stimulants to give the Señor Steve the strength to talk."

Petra hurried away importantly, conscious of a certain amazement at the grief in the girl's face. She had not supposed the Señor Steve's demise would greatly grieve Lylah. Petra herself was positive that such an event would be a blessing to the Cole family.

Lylah returned thoughtfully to the bench in the *patio*. A plan was forming in her mind; a desperate plan, but the situation was desperate. Jeff's life, she realized, depended upon her own cool and resourceful action. Jeff had saved her life. She was resolved to save his. Any moment might see her father's hard-eyed cowboys exacting swift justice on the man Sladen accused of a cowardly shooting. Or Steve might die—and her stern father remain unswerving in his decision to hang the supposed murderer. Perhaps King Cole would have that satisfaction at a later date, but the man he would hang would be Bart Sladen.

Lylah was confident now that the crafty foreman had purposely shot Steve down for the single purpose of pinning the crime upon a man he hated. She was to learn later that her deductions were only partly correct. There was another and more urgent reason animating the KC-Bar foreman's sinister activities.

Lylah addressed the waiting Yaqui sharply: "Chaco, do you think you can get Diablo into the olive-orchard without anybody seeing you?"

The Indian nodded briefly, a sudden exultant gleam in his eyes. Diablo was King Cole's great black stallion.

"Hurry, then," she commanded, "and stay with

Diablo until—" Her look told him what was in her mind.

"It is done," the Indian muttered. He hesitated, fingering his big knife. "*Señorita*, there is one guarding the door—the man Panamint—"

Lylah shook her head. "No! There must be no more killings!"

The Yaqui shrugged his powerful naked shoulders and glided away on noiseless feet. Lylah gazed after him, her mind busy with the problem of the man guarding the door of the *cuartel*. Another thought dismayed her. The key? Even if she got rid of Panamint she was helpless without the key!

A thought struck her, and she went swiftly into the house, to the deserted office, where a search brought to light a second key to the door of the *rancho cuartel*. There were dozens of keys in the drawer of her father's desk, among them the one she wanted, plainly marked with a tag. Lylah seized it, and hurried from the room.

There was an ominous silence outside the *patio* walls. Lylah knew it for the fateful hush before the storm. Somewhere, not far distant, the KC-Bar men were foregathered in grim assembly to discuss the fate of the man locked behind the adobe walls of the *rancho cuartel*. Intuition told her their meeting-place would be the long bunkhouse, which, fortunately for her plan, was well out of sight of the small adobe building sometimes used as a gaol. Everything now depended upon her success in reaching the *cuartel* undetected.

A prayer on her lips, her heart in her mouth, Lylah sauntered across the yard towards the vineyard, where the great spreading vines grew high on their frame supports. She felt more secure now, and went swiftly in the direction of the *cuartel*, which stood midway between the house stables and the olive-orchard, ancient, gnarled trees that formed an impenetrable barrier to the eye once one was embraced by their spreading grey-green branches. She prayed that Chaco would not fail her—that he would have Diablo waiting there.

She came in sight of the squat little building. It was not a squat little building to Lylah. It was a mighty fortress, and the cowboy sitting on his haunches in front of the door was a monster dragon with a thousand eyes.

The girl halted, eyeing the man despairingly. She knew there was only one way to dispose of the guard—had known it all the time. The sight of that hard-faced, capable-looking man shook her confidence. An order from her would mean nothing to Panamint. He took his orders from Bart Sladen; also he was the man who had corroborated the foreman's assertion regarding the shooting of Steve. Lylah's presence in the neighbourhood could not fail to arouse his suspicions, and put him on the alert.

The girl pondered, suddenly removed her small six-shooter from its holster, and thrust the weapon inside her blouse.

Panamint got to his feet, grinning, as she sauntered up, a grin that did not cover the hard suspicious gleam in his eyes.

She saw the quick glance at the vacant holster, saw his tension relax. Lylah smiled at him.

"Father is furious at *him*." She nodded at the *cuartel* door. "Father says he's going to hang him if Steve dies."

Panamint shrugged. "The boys is awful peevish 'bout that shootin'," he declared. "No tellin' what they'll be up to—even if Steve don't hand in his checks." The cowboy's grin was sinister. "Yes, ma'am, sure would hate to be standin' in Wayne's boots."

"I don't blame the boys one bit!" she forced herself to speak indignantly, trying to keep the tremble out of her voice. "Oh!" She stared down at the handkerchief that had slipped from her fingers.

Panamint grinned, gallantly stooped to retrieve the dainty wisp; Lylah's hand flashed inside her blouse.

"Stay as you are," she said, in a low, fierce voice. The little gun was pressing hard against the cowboy's ribs. "Mind what I say—or sure as I'm King Cole's daughter I'll pull the trigger, Panamint."

Panamint was in no hurry to die—not just yet;

he held the stooping posture, one hand closed over the little handkerchief lying in the dust. Like the majority of the KC-Bar riders, the cowboy wore two guns. Lylah plucked them from their holsters and tossed them near the door.

"Now you stand up, and be careful with those hands."

He obeyed, and at her second command faced the *cuartel* door, and pressed it tightly with his body, hands held high above his head. Lylah kept the gun hard against his spine, reached past him, and inserted the key in the lock. A quick twist, a push with her foot, and the door swung open. She spoke again, and Panamint lurched across the threshold; she followed at his heels and swung the door shut.

Jeff was sitting on the earthen floor, arms tied behind his back, ankles bound. The sight of him left her limp for a moment. She held on to herself, spoke curtly to Panamint.

"Untie him."

The cowboy sullenly obeyed.

Jeff struggled stiffly to his feet, and seized the ropes. Lylah watched, relief in her eyes.

"Better hang him, too," she suggested coolly.

Jeff made a good job of it. Panamint was going to have a sore mouth for days to come. The Flying W man straightened up from the task, and looked at the girl questioningly. As yet he had not spoken a word.

"Sladen is working up the men to come and hang you," she told him. Her lips quivered. "I—I had to do something—"

"Even if I did shoot Steve?"

"I never really thought you did," she confessed. "You couldn't—" She broke off, listening intently. "We can't stop to talk now. Quick—Chaco has a horse for you in the olive-orchard. I'll show you." She opened the door cautiously, peered into the yard, and beckoned him to follow. In a moment they were outside. Lylah turned the key in the padlock.

"The guns," she said, "Panamint's guns."

Jeff was already reaching for the captured weapons. He holstered them, and hastened after the girl as she fled round the building.

Chaco was waiting in the olive-orchard with the big black stallion. The Yaqui's swarthy seamed face broke into a thousand wrinkles of delight as the two ran up. Jeff threw him a cheerful grin, and, turning quickly, gathered the girl in his arms. Lylah smiled gloriously up at him.

"Jeff!" she half sobbed. "Oh, Jeff! . . . ride fast . . . and remember—I love you!" She clung to him, gave him her lips. "*Adios*! go with God!"

Spreading grey-green olive-branches hid horse and rider from their eyes. Lylah staggered towards the old Yaqui, reached blindly for his outstretched hand, and clung to him. She was feeling queer; her knees seemed to have no strength in them.

Chaco's hand tensed over hers.

"*Señorita*—they come!"

Booted feet were clattering across the yard. The girl's heart stood still. There was something appalling in the sound of those treading feet; one sensed stern decision reached—implacable resolve to execute that decision. They came with a grim lack of words. One heard only that sinister trampling of boots.

There was a hush; a key scraped in the rusty lock; Lylah could picture the amazement, the dismay, the mounting fury in the fierce eyes peering into the gloomy cell.

A shout broke the stunned silence; cries, oaths, Sladen's stentorian voice yelling commands. Boots went clumping on the run as infuriated men made a rush for horses. Riders surged past, and were lost from sight behind spreading olive-branches. Others were scattering to cover all possible trails.

Chaco grinned at the girl.

"Diablo fast," he reassured her. "No horse catch that Diablo. Soon our young *señor* be at Winding Stair."

The thought comforted Lylah. The Winding Stair was a secret that would baffle Sladen and his riders.

Above the thudding of hoofs dying away in the distance rose the harsh voice of King Cole. Lylah's courage revived. She was not afraid now to be seen by Sladen. The foreman would be furious at the part she had played; she desired her father's presence at the first encounter with the man. King Cole might be angry with her for freeing Jeff Wayne, but she was not in fear of her father. And soon he would learn the truth—would be glad she had thwarted the terrible purpose of these misled men. Lylah had no proof yet that could convince King Cole that Sladen was the cowardly assassin who had shot Steve. She was fiercely resolved to deliver that proof—would force a confession from Panamint. Chaco would know a way to make Panamint talk. . . . Chaco was an Indian—a Yaqui.

She hurried round the corner of the *cuartel*, the Indian at her heels. King Cole was striding rapidly towards Sladen, waiting in front of the gaol door. Lylah saw that her father was in a bristling rage. She halted, scornful of Panamint's malevolent glance.

The cowboy stood slightly behind the big foreman, rubbing his chafed wrists. The others had disappeared in futile chase of the man they had sought to hang.

"Sladen!"

The old cattleman's voice was ominous.

"Steve's done passed out—"

The foreman shrugged his shoulders. "Dead, huh? And she goes an' turns the killer loose!" He flung an ugly look at the girl. "The boys'll pick him up before he gets far. Won't bother none to bring him back this time."

"You can leave Jeff Wayne out of this business," rasped Cole. There was an Arctic light in the old man's blue eyes. "Sladen, before Steve died, he did some talkin'—"

The foreman started visibly. "Talked, huh?" His voice was suddenly tense, smoky eyes watchful. "Well, what-all did Steve tell yuh?"

"Said you did that shootin', feller. He saw you pullin the trigger—"

"Steve was ravin'—out of his haid," derided Sladen. He darted a glance at Panamint, upon whose hard face was a shocked, frightened expression. "Plumb out of his haid," repeated the foreman.

"That ain't all Steve told me, Sladen!"

King Cole fairly spat the words.

"Steve told me a lot more about your doin's, Sladen. No wonder you aimed to shut his mouth—"

Anger, indignation, had dulled the old cowman's usual caution. The dying Steve had made grave charges against the KC-Bar's trusted foreman, charges that King Cole considered far more heinous than the shooting of his worthless stepson. King Cole should never have confronted Sladen so recklessly.

"He might," thought Lylah frantically, "at least have carried a gun!"

For scarcely were the words off the old cattle-man's tongue when Sladen's gun was covering him; a swift gesture to the recently disarmed Panamint, and the latter had acquired Sladen's second weapon, was holding Lylah and the Yaqui at bay.

King Cole's face worked convulsively. Undaunted by the menacing gun, he loosed his fury.

"You're fired!" he barked. "I'm firin' you here and now, you low-down—"

"Don't say it!" snarled his ex-foreman. The man's heavy face was a mask of hate. "I'll drop yuh in your tracks!"

Cole subsided, affected more by the sheer terror in his daughter's face than by the threat.

Sladen motioned to the open door of the *cuartel.* "In there—the three of yuh! Panamint, if that Injun goes for his knife start your gun smokin'."

Lylah's look implored her father to comply. She was desperately afraid of Sladen now. There was no telling what the man might do next. She wanted to get away from those eyes of his. Sladen might suddenly change his mind—might pull the trigger.

The thought that shrivelled her with fear was now searing King Cole, restoring his old-time coolness and self-control. Bitter invective, threats, would only further inflame the evil in this man— add to his daughter's peril.

Shaking his head sorrowfully, the veteran cowman followed Lylah and the Yaqui into the gloom of the *cuartel*. The heavy door slammed shut; the key rasped in the big padlock. And presently the hard drumming of hoofs told them that Sladen and his henchman were gone.

CHAPTER XXIV

A MIDNIGHT ROUND-UP

BUSINESS was brisk in the Longhorn Bar. Lean-flanked riders from the Cimarron rubbed shoulders with burly bullwhackers from the Santa Fé trail, and grizzled desert prospectors swapped their lore with bearded miners from the silver-veined peaks of Colorado. Trim cavalrymen from the Reservation, and border desperadoes; swarthy traders from south of the Rio Grande—gaunt boomers from Oklahoma; the clink of bottles sliding across the bar to clamouring, thirsty ones, the tinkle of glass. Cold-eyed gamblers, shuffling their cards—girls in flimsy gay raiment.

Smoke Hawker's smile was complacent as he turned from the peep-hole through which he was wont to keep a secret eye on the activities in the big dance-hall. The night promised a rich harvest in silver and gold. Hawker's yellow eyes glinted greedily; his gaze went to a square mat of buffalo-hide under his desk chair; his smile widened, appeared to stretch the brown parchment-like skin of his thin, sharp face to bursting-point.

A glance at the door leading into the dance-hall told him that the bolt was in its socket; the other door, leading directly to the rear of the building, he always kept locked. None used it save certain ones who desired to come and go in secret. It was a stout door, held secure by a massive bar. Between this door and the corner was a single window, set with iron bars and covered with a dark curtain. The night was warm, and the window was open to admit the cooling breeze from the desert. The dark curtain gently stirred, as to the touch of fingers.

Hawker's gaze came back to the buffalo mat. With two swift movements he pushed the chair back and slid the mat aside, disclosing a square trap-door in the floor.

Again the man's questioning glance swept doors and window, rested fleetingly on the gently stirring curtain. Apparently satisfied, he knelt on the floor and pulled the trap open. Underneath was a cavity about two feet deep and three feet square, partially filled with a number of small, bulging canvas sacks. Hawker eyed them gloatingly.

Had he glanced again that moment at the barred window he would have noticed the curtain behaving strangely. Instead of gently stirring to the night wind it moved stealthily in a definite direction until a tiny opening lay between its fringe and the casement. A pair of eyes suddenly peered into the room, fixed exultantly upon the man kneeling at the secret treasure vault.

With a startled jerk Hawker looked round at the bar-room door. Somebody was knocking for admittance.

The saloon man swiftly and noiselessly lowered the trap and replaced buffalo mat and chair as before. The rap on the door was repeated; Hawker strode across the floor and slid the bolt back.

"What's up?" he demanded testily as his visitor slipped into the room. He closed the door and shot the bolt.

The town marshal's hard eyes swept the room suspiciously. The curtain stirred faintly to the night air; Stiles frowned, strode over, closed the window.

"What's the idea—shutting out the air?" complained Hawker sourly.

"Never can tell who might get a notion to eavesdrop on us," Stiles muttered. He seemed uneasy. "Big crowd in town to-night. No tellin' but Jeff Wayne's got fellers staked out watchin' things here."

"Seems to me the Flying W outfit has left you jumpy as a cat," sneered the saloon man.

"Jeff Wayne ain't losin' that bunch o' cows this easy," grumbled the marshal. "Cottonwood Wells ain't seen the last of them Flying W fellers." Stiles frowned worriedly. "Ed Burger found Pascoe down in the rim-rock . . . shot between the eyes."

"So much the better for us," Smoke Hawker told him indifferently. "Pascoe was an old Frying-pan man, Wayne's old outfit. If they'd got him alive Pascoe might have squealed to save his own neck. Pascoe knew too much, and so did Sinful Smith. Lucky break for us Smith got plugged when he pulled that gunplay from the balcony." He paused, eyeing his gunman keenly. "Where's Ed now?" he asked abruptly.

Stiles jerked his head towards the dance-hall door. "Out there, likkerin' up some. Says he's got to see yuh pronto . . . and, believe me, Ed's sure got hot news for yuh."

"Send him in," grunted the saloon man. "Maybe you should stay out there . . . keep an eye peeled for trouble—seein' you're so nervous about Jeff Wayne." Hawker's yellow eyes sneered at the marshal. "Not that you've scared me with your old woman's talk of what Jeff Wayne can do to us. Now Ed Burger and the boys are all back in town it would suit me fine to have that Flying W outfit drop in again." The saloon man's smile was sinister.

Stiles rapped out a sullen oath. "You wait till yuh hear what Ed's got on his mind," he said tartly. "Maybe yuh won't feel so good." With which parting shot the marshal unlocked the door and stamped resentfully out.

Hawker stared thoughtfully at the closed door. Despite his own cool self-confidence, the marshal's very apparent anxiety disturbed him. Stiles was not easily frightened.

The door opened quietly, this time without the formality of a knock. Buck Saunders would have recognized the newcomer as the burly, black-bearded stranger who had visited the chuck-wagon the night of the raid. He gave Hawker a brief nod, and slumped into a chair.

"Stiles says you got bad news, Ed." Hawker eyed his visitor questioningly.

Burger shrugged his powerful shoulders. "Ain't so sure it's bad news," he said, in a baffled tone. "It's sure all-fired queer news. Yuh'll rec'lect I told yuh I'd left Solvang to trail Gonzalez after we turned the cows over to him. Well, yesterday, Jeff Wayne's outfit overtook Gonzalez other side of the Arroyo los Coyotes. Solvang says it looked like Gonzalez was expectin' Wayne to meet him there . . . said Gonzalez was holdin' the herd in one of them blind canyons more'n two days."

Hawker muttered a startled oath, and stared incredulously at the burly rustler. It was plain that the latter's story shocked him.

"Don't seem reasonable . . . Gonzalez givin' up those cows. Not after handin' us that thirty thousand," worried Burger.

"Something's gone wrong!" The saloon man's voice was hoarse with fear; the yellow eyes glanced furtively at the buffalo mat under the chair. "Gonzalez has framed us!" Hawker swore venomously. "Hell is like to break loose if Gonzalez an' Wayne have got together on this business."

Burger stirred uneasily. "Ain't figgered it out at all," he muttered. "What's Gonzalez get out of a deal with Wayne? Wayne ain't payin' him no money to get his cows back. Unless Gonzalez gets his thirty thousand dollars he's one big loser on the play."

Smoke Hawker's tawny eyes sneered at him. "You're dumb . . . or you'd see what's back of it."

The black-bearded man gave him an ugly look. "Got it all figgered out, huh? Well—I'm listenin'—"

"King Cole," said Hawker softly. "You're forgettin' King Cole."

Burger started violently in his chair, and swore a savage oath.

"I get yuh!" He rolled dismayed eyes. "It's a deal with the ol' man!" he gasped.

"King Cole 'ud hand over more'n thirty thousand dollars for El Toro's hide," Hawker went on. "That's one thing Gonzalez can get his money back on, eh, Burger?"

"Gonzalez don't know about El Toro for sartain," argued the black-bearded man.

"He knows enough to make a mighty close guess—enough to swing you and me and a dozen others," said the saloon man hoarsely. His glance flickered at the buffalo mat. "Wasn't worryin' much about Wayne," he added, "but King Cole's a different proposition."

Burger nodded, his face pasty above the black beard. "Ain't stayin' here to swing!" he exclaimed, with an oath. He sprang from the chair. "Hawker, you hand over my share of the loot. I'm high-tailin' to some place a long ways from here." Terror was in the rustler's eyes. "Like as not there'll be half a hundred gun-shootin' cowboys ridin' in before sun-up!"

The saloon man was suddenly watchful. "Run if you want to run," he said indifferently. "Ain't leaving myself." He shrugged high, thin shoulders. "Reckon we're getting too excited over this business."

"You can stay an' hang if yuh want," growled Burger sulkily. "Me—I'm leavin', an' leavin' now. You hand over that coin, Smoke Hawker."

"Ain't got the coin here," Hawker told him smoothly. "Already sent it out of town. Got to thinkin' of the big crowd we'd have in to-night, and figgered to be safe."

Burger glared suspiciously. "Yuh're lyin'. You ain't had a chance to send that coin outer town." The burly rustler's voice was suddenly threatening. "I'm on to yuh, feller. You aim to have me high-tail it outer town an' then grab my share of the loot for your own self."

The saloon man shrugged indifferently. "No sense getting ugly. You can run away and lose out on the play, or you can stay with the rest of us, and we split when the show's over."

"I'm takin' my share right now!" snarled the other man furiously. His gun menaced the saloon man.

"Help yourself," sneered Hawker, undisturbed. "Take your share, if you can find it. Only it ain't here—and that's the truth."

Muttering oaths, the rustler hastily ransacked desk drawers, and searched a cupboard and a small closet. Hawker watched with faintly derisive eyes.

"Seems like yuh're right," Burger muttered, in a disappointed voice. He flung a murderous look at his companion, and holstered his gun. "Who's that knockin' on the door?" he added apprehensively.

"Stiles," reassured Hawker. "Let him in, Ed."

Burger unlocked and opened the door. The town marshal stepped inside quickly. His hard face wore a baffled look.

"Gonzalez is here," he told them, in a wondering voice. "Just rode into town . . . an' he's come along." Stiles jerked his head at the door. "Out there now at the bar. Says he wants to see you, Smoke."

There was a stupefied silence; the saloon man and Burger exchanged astonished looks; and Hawker said in a dazed voice:

"You say Gonzalez wants to see me?"

Stiles shrugged. "You heard me," he growled. "He's alone . . . you say the feller is alone?" Burger's eyes glittered. "I'd say we got this Gonzalez where he can do some explainin'," he told them, with a sinister smile. "Me—I'm plumb curious about him turnin' them cows over to Wayne."

The three men eyed the dance-hall door reflectively. Hawker asked curiously:

"Gonzalez actin' natural?"

"Acts like he allus has," answered the marshal. "Cool an' smilin'—friendly enough, I'd call him."

Hawker seemed relieved; he smiled, nodding at the others. "Burger's talking sense," he said. "We sure got Gonzalez where he can do a heap of explaining."

"I'll send him in to yuh." The marshal turned to the door. The saloon man stopped him, glanced at Burger. "I'll talk to Gonzalez alone," he told them. "Ed, you wait in the bar . . . help Stiles keep an eye on things. Reckon Stiles better be out front, where he can watch the street." Hawker paused, frowning thoughtfully. "Listen," he went on. "If I come out to the bar with Gonzalez and buy him a drink you fellers will know I want you to grab him when he walks out. Do it right . . . not too close to our place. Don't want folks getting curious."

They nodded, and waited for him to finish. Hawker grinned.

"If Gonzalez comes out of here alone you'll

know there's nothing wrong," he went on. "Got it straight, boys?" He repeated his instructions.

The marshal shrugged impatiently. "We got yuh the first time," he grumbled. "If Gonzalez and you come out to the bar and you buy him a drink it's the tip-off for me an' Ed to grab him before he slopes outer town. If he comes out of here alone it means thar's nothin' for us to worry about, and we just let the jasper ramble."

The door closed behind them. Hawker resumed his chair, and rolled a cigarette with meticulous care, tawny eyes fastened on the door. Some thought apparently amused him; he laughed soundlessly, shot a glance at the buffalo mat under his feet. The door swung open quietly, revealing the elegant person of Don Ricardo Gonzalez on the threshold.

The Mexican paused, trim black moustache lifted above glistening white teeth in a smile that held a hint of mockery, it seemed to the saloon man. He stiffened in his chair. The next instant Gonzalez was inside the room and closing the door. Hawker heard the bolt click home. He scowled, uncomfortably aware of chills playing up and down his spine.

"No need to lock the door," he said tartly.

Gonzalez smiled. "Eet ees ver' eemportan' these theeng I 'ave to tell you, Señor Smoke Hawker," he blandly explained. He drew a chair from the wall. "You permeet, *señor*—"

Hawker nodded. "Sure—sit down, Ricardo. What's on your mind?"

"*Gracias.*" Gonzalez deliberately rolled a cigarette, gaze fastened on the saloon man's mask-like face. "My mind—eet ees mooch trouble, *señor*, *muy malo.*" The Mexican shook his handsome head sadly. "You 'ave deceive me, my frien'." He touched a match to his cigarette, exhaled a cloud of blue smoke.

"You're talking riddles, Gonzalez." Hawker's eyes were suddenly apprehensive; his hand moved stealthily towards the loosened button of his black frock-coat. "How come you figger I deceived yuh?"

Gonzalez started a gesture with the hand holding the cigarette; it slipped from his fingers, struck his knee in falling. Muttering annoyance, the Mexican brushed at the burning tobacco—and when his hand came up it clasped the butt of a long-barrelled six-shooter.

"Señor Hawker mus' plees take ees 'and away from those leetle gun under ees coat," he purred.

For a fleeting moment the saloon man's tawny eyes clashed with the long black orbs of Don Ricardo, then reluctantly his long white hand sank slowly down to his knees.

"*Gracias.*" The Mexican inclined his head. "You no like w'at I say, eh, *señor?*"

"You guessed right the first time, Gonzalez," snarled the saloon man. "What's the play, feller?" He shot a furtive glance at the door.

"The *señor* mus' keep ees voice ver' low," warned Don Ricardo sternly. He tapped the gun lying across his knee. "You make too mooch noise you ver' dead *hombre*." The Mexican's face was no longer bland, nor his voice friendly. His eyes glittered; his voice came low, deadly. "You no ween those cow at cards . . . you steal those cow from Señor Wayne." Gonzalez paused significantly. "Señor Wayne ees my frien'. Long time ago he save my life. I fight ees fight like my own."

Surprise crept into Smoke Hawker's eyes. His guess that King Cole was mixed up in this affair was not the answer. Gonzalez went on:

"W'en I learn' w'at 'appen I send word queek to Señor Wayne. I geeve back those cow you steal from heem, *si, señor*." Don Ricardo's smile was mocking. "So my frien' . . . you mus' geeve me back my thirty thousand pesos."

Hawker suddenly smiled. "Sure thing, Ricardo," he agreed affably. "We can fix it up if that's the way you feel about it." He shrugged. "Thought you knew all the time the cows I been selling you was stolen stuff. If you hadn't found out that Wayne owned these Flying W cows there wouldn't have been a peep out of you."

"My pesos," reminded the Mexican, frowning. "We talk about my pesos, *señor*."

"Sure," repeated the saloon man. "You stick round till morning, Ricardo. Sent that money over to Abilene yesterday. To-morrow you and me can ride over there, and I'll fix it up with you."

"Maybe—before those morning—Don Ricardo Gonzalez mooch dead *hombre*, no?" slyly insinuated the Mexican. His smile mocked the other, and was suddenly a menacing glare. "You beeg liar, *señor!*" He gestured the man to stand up.

Hawker sullenly obeyed, lifting his hands above his head.

"We now go to those door," purred Gonzalez. He indicated the rear door, by the barred window, and pressed his gun against Hawker's spine. The latter winced, walked stiffly in the desired direction. "Now you keep those hand on wall," purred the voice in his ear.

Hawker obeyed. Gonzalez reached out his free hand and slipped the bar; the door swung open. Hawker's face went ghastly pale. The man standing there was Jeff Wayne of the Flying W.

He came in swiftly, followed by Tex Malley, Curly Stivens, and three of Don Ricardo's *vaqueros*. These last, at a curt nod from Gonzalez, immediately fell upon the hapless saloon man, thrust a gag in his mouth, and tied his arms behind his back.

The Flying W men watched the proceeding in grim silence, eyes hard, lips unsmiling. Gonzalez alone appeared amused. He threw Hawker a mocking smile, went to the buffalo mat, and uncovered the trap in the floor.

Jeff spoke. "All right, Curly—you take this jasper to the horses."

The blond cowboy's .45 dug into the prisoner's back. "Move your laigs, feller."

With a last despairing glance at Gonzalez piling bags of gold into the arms of his grinning *vaqueros* Smoke Hawker stumbled out into the darkness, Curly's gun prodding him on.

"About time we was hearing from Chuck and Slinger," Tex muttered to Jeff.

"We'll give 'em five minutes," Jeff decided. His gaze went to the bar-room door. "Somebody knocking!" he added, in a whisper.

Gonzalez drew back from the rifled *cache*. "*Vamose*," he whispered to the *vaqueros*.

Bearing the heavy bags of pesos, the three men stealthily followed Hawker and Curly into the darkness. Gonzalez hurriedly replaced buffalo mat and chair. The knock came again. The Mexican's eyes questioned Jeff, and the latter silently crept to the door, motioning the others to follow. Tex Malley's glance espied the peep-hole. He placed an eye to the opening, stared for a moment, and looked excitedly at Jeff.

"It's the black-bearded jasper," he whispered. "The feller that come to the chuck-wagon the night the cows was rustled."

The knock was repeated, an impatient double

tattoo; a gruff, grumbling voice reached them faintly above the clamorous hubbub of the dance-hall. Don Ricardo's eyes glittered.

"*Si*," he told his companions, in a low whisper. "Those *hombre* ess Burger. Those Burger breeng those cows to me."

"We'll take him along with the others," muttered Jeff. He grinned at Tex. There was a look of unholy joy in the cowboy's eyes. The memory of the black-bearded stranger was a thorn in Tex Malley's heart.

"Let me in, Smoke. It's Burger," came the complaining growl from the other side of the door. "Gotta see yuh quick. Looks like there's some funny play bein' pulled off. Cain't find Stiles nowhere . . . ain't seen him since he went out to watch things in the street."

The three men looked at each other. Tex grinned.

"Looks like Chuck and Slinger ain't lost no time," he exulted.

Jeff nodded, pressed against the wall, gun in hand. Tex took the other side of the door, which suddenly swung in as Gonzalez slid the bolt back. Burger lurched into the room, and swiftly the door closed behind him. Two guns pressed hard against the rustler's sides; he froze in his tracks, a pained expression in his eyes. Slowly he lifted his hands. A quick movement of the Mexican's hands removed the black-bearded one's pair of six-guns, and in another minute Tex and Gonzalez were hurrying their bound and gagged prisoner into the darkness beyond the rear door.

Jeff thoughtfully contemplated Hawker's observation hole in the wall. It was obvious that the tiny opening served a double purpose. No doubt the guns of Hawker and his hired killers had more than once poured sudden death through that loophole.

Ordinarily a small picture, hung from a nail, concealed it from view. The picture was on the floor, leaning against the wall. Jeff replaced it on the nail. Eyes could peer in, as well as out.

A similar small picture hung on the other side of the door; Jeff tilted it slightly, smiling grimly as he saw a second loophole. He foresaw the usefulness of these little loopholes. As yet he must await word from Chuck Wallis before staging the final act of the little drama he had written round the town of Cottonwood Wells. And from what Burger had inadvertently let slip about the mysterious absence of the town marshal Jeff surmised that Chuck and Slinger had not been idle these past minutes. . . .

Solvang's startling news that Jeff Wayne had recovered the stolen herd from Gonzalez had aroused deep misgivings in the mind of the town marshal. The unlooked-for arrival of the debonair Mexican but served to strengthen his fears. Stiles distrusted all Mexicans on principle, and

Gonzalez in particular. The man's cool insolence invariably irked him; he yearned much for the opportunity to eliminate the gay young Sonoran.

Signalling the lean, dust-covered Solvang, the town marshal made his way out to the street. Solvang gave him a surly look as he came clattering up.

"Seems like I earned me a rest," he complained bitterly. "What yuh want, Stiles?"

"You gotta help me watch things on the street," the marshal told him. "Yuh was tellin' me yuh worked for the ol' Frying-pan down on the Pecos when Wayne was foreman of the outfit."

"Pascoe an' me both," grunted Solvang. He swore. "Burger was tellin' me he found ol' Pascoe lyin' out on the rimrock."

"Sure did," growled the marshal. "Reckon yuh plumb hanker to get yuh a Flying W scalp for killin' your friend, huh, Solvang?"

"Yuh're readin' my mind like a book, feller." Solvang added a fierce imprecation.

"Maybe yuh'll get your wish," Stiles told him. "Solvang, yuh know these Flying W fellers on sight—most of 'em were Frying-pan men before Jeff Wayne brought 'em up here." The marshal paused, staring intently up the dark street in the direction of the Great Western Hotel. A tall, bent-shouldered figure suddenly hurried from the doorway, dimly lighted by a kerosene lamp. "Wonder what Hank's all excited about," he muttered. Keeping his gaze on the approaching hotel man, the marshal picked up the threads of conversation. "What I mean is for yuh to keep a watch out here. . . . If yuh spot a Flying W man yuh'll know what to do. Lots of strangers in to-night . . . might be some Flying W men among 'em for all we know."

Hank Smithers evidently espied the marshal in front of the Longhorn; he broke into a shambling run. The marshal and Solvang eyed him sharply, and saw that the hotel man was in the throes of mingled excitement and fear. Stiles rasped out a curt question.

"What's goin' on? A killin'?"

"It's that feller . . . he's come back!" stuttered Smithers. "That feller Doc Mosby was 'tendin' for blood-poisonin'. He's back, awful sick, an' wants the doc—"

The marshal's eyes glittered. "Yuh mean that Flying W feller?" he demanded eagerly, "that Johnny Wales *hombre*?"

The hotel man nodded. "Yuh told me to tip yuh off if any of them fellers come in again," he said, more calmly. "Yuh want to get him, Stiles?" He grinned. "I didn't tell him the doc wasn't in town. Doc Mosby's over at the KC-Bar," he added.

"Reckon Solvang an' me can give him all the doctorin' he needs," snarled the marshal. He grinned at the rustler. "Huh, Solvang?" He winked humorously at Hank Smithers. "All right, Hank.

You go on back and tell this jasper the doc's comin' pronto."

The hotel man grinned uncertainly, and went shambling up the street towards the hotel. The marshal and Solvang waited a few moments, then followed, walking in the road to deaden the sound of their approach.

A lone cow-pony stood with drooping head at the hitch-rail in front of the hotel. The marshal paused for a brief scrutiny of the brand, nodded in satisfaction.

"Flying W iron all right," he grunted to his companion.

The two men drew their guns and stepped cautiously across the creaky floor-boards of the porch. Stiles nodded to his companion, and leaped through the door, Solvang close on his heels. The expectant grins on their hard faces froze into masks of horror.

Hank Smithers had spoken the truth, but not the entire truth, when he told the marshal Johnny Wales was back. Johnny was back with a vengeance—a healthy .45 in each hand, a cheerful grin on his good-looking face; and crouched on either side of the door were the cold-eyed, deadly Slinger Downs and the nonchalant Chuck Wallis.

Three pairs of six-guns menacing him were too much for the town marshal, a coward at heart. His own weapon fell from limp fingers; his hands went up.

Of sterner stuff was the hard-eyed Solvang. Snarling an oath, the rustler's gun flashed up—the roar of two .45's rattled the windows; Solvang staggered, gun slipped from nerveless fingers, and the rustler's lifeless body slid gently down against the wall—lay in a huddle on the floor.

Slinger blew the smoke from hot gun-barrel. "Never did like Solvang," he said coolly. He stared at the cowering marshal. "Wish it had been you," he told his old enemy.

Chuck Wallis took a hasty glance at the dark street. The bark of the .45's was not apt to attract much attention in Cottonwood Wells; it was already close to midnight, the saloons and dance-halls making uproarious noise of their own. Chuck was reasonably certain that the exchange of shots between Slinger and the dead Solvang had passed unnoticed. He motioned to Hank Smithers.

"Get goin', Hank. Meet us round back of the hotel. That bronc we brought yuh is plumb gentle," he added.

The hotel man nodded, and glanced vindictively at the dazed town marshal.

"This mangy dog-hole has seen the last of me, Stiles," he chuckled. "And the last of you, maybe." He strode out to the drooping cow-pony, a curious look of elation in his weary eyes.

A few moments later five horsemen rode out of the shadows behind the Great Western Hotel and melted into the darkness across the street. One of the riders was the dejected town marshal, shorn of his weapons, and securely bound. And among those escorting him was Hank Smithers, ex-resident of Cottonwood Wells, now bound for Crater Basin, where Johnny's pretty bride was waiting to welcome her uncle to his new home. . . .

A gentle rap on the outer door warned Jeff that Chuck had arrived. He opened the door, and the cowboy slipped into the room.

"Everything hunkydory," he told Jeff jubilantly. "That fool marshal walked right into the trap nice as apple-pie. Turned him over to Gonzalez and his *vaqueros*." Chuck Wallis beamed. "Maybe we ain't rounded up El Toro, but, we sure got three of his gang hog-tied proper. Looks like we'll have a real hangin' when we get round to it." Chuck's expression grew contemptuous. "And if I know a skunk I'm bettin' Stiles will come clean with El Toro's name before he swings."

"Where's the rest of our fellers?" Jeff wanted to know.

"Waiting down at the end of the street . . . all of 'em 'cept Johnny. Buck sent him along with Gonzalez . . . said Johnny was a bridegroom, and couldn't take chances catchin' a bullet." Chuck laughed softly. "Johnny was awful peevish."

"Don't want to start things too soon," ruminated Jeff. "Want to give Gonzalez time to get a good leg on the way."

"Gonzalez is ridin' fast," Chuck assured him. "He's all of two miles away by now. Needn't wait on him if you're ready to set her off."

Jeff nodded assent, and they went silently across the floor to the door leading into the dance-hall. Jeff indicated the two loopholes.

"You take the two on your side . . . I'll 'tend to the others," he whispered.

Swiftly they removed the two small pictures and peered into the long room, sighting their guns at the big kerosene lamps swinging from the ceiling. And with the roar of their .45's two of the big lamps danced to the impact of heavy bullets, became nests of mounting flame that licked hungrily at the inflammable ceiling. Two more shots belched through the loopholes; the remaining lamps went the way of the others. Startled cries now shattered the stunned silence that had followed the first salvo from their guns. Pandemonium broke loose in the Longhorn, screams and yells—a mad rush for the street. Jeff and Chuck raced for the rear door in a wild dash for their horses. From the distance came the sound of drumming hoofs, the wild, yipping war-cry of the Flying W outfit.

Led by Buck Saunders, the yelling cowboys swept down the street, guns spitting yellow flashes. The demoralized mob surging from the Longhorn wavered, then scattered like chaff before the whirlwind charge of Jeff Wayne's fighting men.

As suddenly as they had come they were gone, in a cloud of dust that sifted through a darkness now driven back by leaping, crackling flames from the doomed dance-hall. . . .

From a distant hill-top the Flying W outfit gazed back at the red glow against the night horizon.

"She's burnin' purty," said a satisfied voice. "Won't be much left of that onery rustlers' roost when that fire gets done."

"Cottonwood Wells will sure keep hands off the Flying W after this," grunted Slinger Downs.

"Looks like the hotel's smokin' up!" exclaimed Buck Saunders.

"Your eyes ain't lyin', Buck," drawled Chuck's soft voice. "Johnny's new uncle-in-law kind of wanted to see how good she'd burn. Sure flames up some, that old dump."

Chuck Wallis glanced at Hank Smithers. There was a look of supreme contentment in the eyes of Nellie's uncle as he watched the distant flames.

CHAPTER XXV

CHACO SETTLES AN ACCOUNT

THE flames winked and rolled against the dark horizon. Sladen reined his horse with an oath. The meaning of that red glare was shockingly clear to him.

Dismay shook Sladen to his boot-heels. Chin

thrust tensely forward, he gazed in silence at the angry sky. The sight of the burning town appalled him. He swung from the trail, and pushed into the south as fast as the darkness and the rough country would permit.

The night was no blacker than Sladen's mood as he spurred his horse towards the Honda. Oaths frothed from his lips. He had thought to strike a triple blow when he shot Steve Cole. Steve knew too much about certain matters . . . his drunken tongue made him a menace. To silence that tongue for ever, and at the same time place the crime on Jeff Wayne, had seemed a stroke of genius. The love scene he had witnessed in the shadows of Sentinel Peak had fanned into killing hate the already keen dislike and fear he felt for the young Flying W man. He was afraid of Jeff Wayne. The latter's elimination would soon have been a necessity. Sladen spat a savage curse into the night. But for Doc Mosby Steve Cole would not have had those few damning conscious moments . . . Steve's mouth would have been closed for ever, Jeff Wayne swung from a KC-Bar tree—that hoity-toity girl weeping for a dead lover.

Sladen's thoughts lingered regretfully with the girl. She was a pretty piece. He had been strongly tempted to carry her off with him, which would have been folly. The most important thing in life at this time for Bart Sladen was to put many miles between himself and the blasting wrath of King Cole. He wished now that he had put a bullet into the old man instead of locking him with the others inside the *cuartel*. KC-Bar riders, returning from the chase after Jeff Wayne, would have soon released the prisoners from the *cuartel*—were no doubt now hot on his own trail. He wondered if Panamint would make good his escape into Mexico. Panamint had flatly refused to ride to Cottonwood Wells with him, had left him at Beaver Fork, and headed for the Rio Grande. Sladen wished now that he had taken the cowboy's advice . . . but he had hated to leave all that money for Smoke Hawker to pocket.

The late moon pushed over the horizon, filtering pale light through the darkness; and presently Sladen was following the tree-lined course of Honda Creek, pushing easterly towards the desert, where its waters would seek cool underground channels deep below the sun-scorched sands.

Soon the horse was splashing across the shallows of Buffalo Crossing. Sladen let the thirsty animal drink, his gaze idling across to the opposite bank. Suddenly he stiffened. Shadows—spooky, dark shapes—seemed to sway under the limbs of a big cottonwood tree growing near the water's edge.

A chill ran down Sladen's spine.

It was the tricky moonlight! He was losing his nerve—needed a stiff drink.

Sladen suddenly was sure that it was not the

tricky moonlight deceiving his eyes. Those spooky swaying things dangling under the cottonwood were men—or had been—

He savagely dragged his horse's head from the water, and sent the animal plunging across the shallows and up the bank.

For long, quaking moments Sladen stared with shocked eyes at the three dead men dangling from the tree. The night wind swayed the branches gently, and the three bodies kept up a weird jigging motion—literally dancing on air.

Sladen forced himself to draw near. The blood drained from his face. He knew those men—the long, skeleton frame, the death's-head face, of Smoke Hawker, the massive shoulders, the coarse black beard, of Burger, the burly town marshal of Cottonwood Wells.

The ex-foreman of the KC-Bar was sweating. He had the answer now to those red flames against the night sky. Jeff Wayne had struck this lightning and ruthless blow. Hawker, Burger, Stiles, dangling there from that tree—three dead men— bore silent and terrible testimony to the long arm of the Flying W. The game was up. . . . A greater danger than the wrath of old King Cole now lay like a shadow of death across his path. . . .

Two hours later Sladen was pushing steadily across the wind-swept dunes of the Sinks. The dawn came up, and soon a molten sun in a sky of brass. He drove his horse mercilessly, the fear of death dogging his heels. He had one big canteen, freshly filled before leaving the Honda. If luck held he should make Coyote Springs before his water gave out. The following dawn would put the desert behind him—a grim, vast barrier between himself and any possible pursuit. He was reasonably certain that the inhospitable sand-dunes would discourage even Jeff Wayne. Only a man in desperate plight would dare the perils of these treacherous shifting sands.

It was soon apparent that luck was not to be on Sladen's side. The horizon took on a pale yellow haze, little dust-devils crawled and whisked in front of him; and suddenly the sandstorm drove down in a withering, blinding blast that blotted out land and sky.

No horse would face that stinging onslaught; there was nothing Sladen could do but wait. He swung from the saddle and crouched against his horse, seeking the protection of the animal's body from the flying sand.

He grew conscious of a strange sound—a curious whispering note—the song of the desert dunes as they crawled across the desert floor.

Sladen knew those shifting sands could soon cover the unfortunate man lying in their path. He had heard tales of men and horses trapped in these crawling dunes, and found later, when some new storm sent the restless sand slithering from their bones.

He seemed to be breathing, chewing sand. Sand sifted into his hair, stung eyes and face, covered him with a thick, yellow mask, choked him, aroused a maddening thirst. He was reluctant to draw on his scanty water-supply, hoping against hope the storm would soon subside.

The slow hours dragged on. Sladen felt himself slipping into a coma. He must have water at any cost. Shielding his inflamed, smarting eyes with one hand, he fumbled for the canteen tied to the saddle. The horse, patient so long, stirred nervously, took a sudden stride forward. The unexpected movement threw the man off his balance; with a choking cry of fury he sprawled into a sand-drift.

Sladen struggled to his feet, uttered a frightened scream as he saw the vague bulk of his horse growing indistinct behind the whirling veil of sand. Shouting imprecations, he went groping blindly in pursuit. Before he had taken ten steps he knew the chase was hopeless. His horse was gone—the precious water—

Sladen knew then that he was lost. Soon his legs would refuse to hold him up—the whispering, rustling sand would come crawling over his prostrate body. And some day, perhaps years later, some desert wayfarer would chance upon his bleaching bones.

Muttering incoherently, the half-crazed man stumbled blindly on. . . .

Sladen stirred, groaned weakly. Something was pressing against his mouth, something cool, wet, was trickling between his cracked, blistered lips. He opened his inflamed, red eyes; a man was kneeling by his side, holding a canteen to his mouth. He drank greedily, and the canteen was suddenly withdrawn. Presently he was allowed another and longer pull at the canteen.

Sladen felt suddenly wonderfully refreshed. He sat up, stared under swollen eyelids at his benefactor. The face was vaguely familiar; and suddenly Sladen saw that the man squatting near him was Chaco. Instinctively his hand sought and clasped the butt of his six-shooter. But perhaps the Yaqui had come in peace. Else why the life-giving draughts of water?

He took another pull at the canteen. Every moment found him conscious of returning strength. He had his guns . . . a few more moments and he would not fear a dozen Yaquis like Chaco . . . a half-naked Indian, whose only weapon was a knife. Sladen took another long drink, lowered the canteen, and grinned at the impassive face watching him.

The Yaqui suddenly spoke. "The *señor* glad Chaco come, no?" Chaco's voice was the satisfied purr of a great cat.

Sladen eyed him uneasily; he did not care for the gleam in the Yaqui's sombre eyes.

"What yuh want, Chaco?"

319

Sladen's hand was working stealthily to free his gun.

The Yaqui opened a brown palm, displayed a silver concha.

"The *señor* lose heem near the *señorita*'s pool, no? Chaco find heem—breeng to the *señor*—"

For a moment Sladen stared fixedly at the silver ornament lying in the brown palm, then slowly he glanced sideways at his leather chaps, saw the place from which a concha had been torn. He had not noticed his loss before. A look of fear crept into his eyes. Chaco knew how he had come to lose that silver button.

The Indian was speaking again. "Ah, the *señor* understan' . . . and now Chaco geeve heem concha back to the *señor*—"

A flip of the open palm sent the silver ornament stinging against Sladen's face. And with the movement Chaco was on his feet, his long knife gleaming in his other hand.

Sladen choked out an oath, flung up his gun, and pulled the trigger; screamed again as the hammer clicked harmlessly, a scream that died in a choking gurgle as the big knife flashed from the Yaqui's hand. . . .

Jeff Wayne halted the roan and stared sombrely at the limp body of King Cole's late foreman. His glance went to the Yaqui, stolidly wiping the blade of his knife in the sand.

Jeff was a little vexed that he had arrived too

late to take Sladen alive. He had wanted to see Bart Sladen dangling from the cottonwood-tree by the side of Smoke Hawker and the others. He did not blame the Yaqui. Sladen had pulled his gun on Chaco, who had been forced to use his knife in self-defence. Jeff had seen the whole affair while spurring to the scene. He would never know, though, nor would anyone know, the real reason why the Yaqui had saved Sladen's life only to slay him.

Jeff's gaze swept across the bleak desert wastes to the riders scattered along the horizon. One of those horsemen was old King Cole, relentlessly clinging to the trail of his recreant foreman.

Jeff smiled grimly, flung a last careless look at the dead Sladen, and swung the roan towards the oncoming riders. He knew the restless desert sands would soon cover that lifeless body—he knew that El Toro would no more ride the rustler's trail.

CHAPTER XXVI

A DATE FOR PADRE JUAN

THE longhorn cow raised her head from the yellowing buffalo-grass and stared suspiciously at two riders approaching leisurely across the sandy floor of Lobo Wash. Apparently deciding the newcomers meant no harm to her or her white-faced calf, the cow presently resumed her contented browsing. The intruders drew rein under a huge cottonwood-tree.

Lylah espied the grazing longhorn, laughed softly, reminiscently.

"There's that little cow and her bald-faced calf!" she exclaimed. "It doesn't seem possible it is only two weeks since the day you shot that wolf!"

"The wonderful day we met," murmured Jeff. He smiled teasingly. "And how King Cole's lovely daughter did hate the impudent young stranger from the Pecos!"

"She did not!" denied King Cole's daughter indignantly. Lylah leaned towards her companion. "I'm going to tell you a secret, Jeff darling. . . . When you raced with Death for my life I knew in those moments that I loved you—would always love you—" Lylah's lips were very close to his. "When did you first know you loved me?"

"Not quite so soon," Jeff said honestly. "Not until we rode with Chaco to the Winding Stair. I didn't want you to leave me . . . and suddenly I knew I loved you."

Their faces were very close now, and presently Lylah, flushed, starry-eyed, straightened in her saddle.

"There," she sighed. "I always wanted to come back here to this spot where we first saw each other—and have you kiss me."

Jeff chuckled. "A pleasure to oblige," he assured her. He grew serious. "What's the latest news about the new town?" he wanted to know.

"The railroad is coming through," Lylah told him. "The thriving Western town of Cole Mesa is an assured fact. Hank Smithers is to open the first hotel," she added, "and darling Doc Mosby will put up his M.D. shingle." She frowned thoughtfully. "We should have a church . . . yes, we must have a little church."

"We'll fix it up with Padre Juan," decided Jeff. He smiled at her. "Padre Juan has promised to ride over to the KC-Bar a week to-day. I told him there was to be a wedding. Padre Juan is right good at marryin' folks," he added, in a contented voice.

Lylah blushed, reached out a hand, and clasped his. "I can scarcely believe it," she whispered. "Can you, Jeff?"

The Palominos pressed shoulder to shoulder; and Jeff's arm went round the girl's slim waist.

"Ricardo'll be there," he said presently. "It's going to be a mighty nice weddin'."

"And Buck and Curly and Slinger and Chuck Wallis, and dear old Brazos and Barbecue—oh, and all of them will be there—at our wedding!" chanted Lylah.

"Buck Saunders'll make a great foreman for the KC-Bar," Jeff prophesied. He laughed softly. "You should have seen Chuck Wallis's face when I told him he was the new foreman of the Flying W."

"Chuck Wallis is a nice boy," she asserted.

"All of 'em are nice boys," declared Jeff. "They don't come finer—and they're all our friends."

Dust-clouds lifted lazily against the southern horizon, tell-tale banners of a great trail herd's march. Jeff smiled contentedly. Old man Perry of the Frying-pan was ahead of time in sending the promised five thousand cows. The girl read his thoughts.

"Yes," she told him softly, "the Flying W is back to stay."

Her gaze followed the longhorn cow, now walking briskly down the strip of mesa, evidently seeking to rejoin the family herd. Close on her heels trotted the sturdy white-faced calf. She was a staunch fighter too, that little longhorn range mother.

Arthur Henry Gooden recalled that "I was still a babe in arms when my parents took me from Manchester, England, to South Africa for a four-year stay in Port Elizabeth, then back to England for a brief time, and finally the journey that made me a Californian. Reaching the San Joaquin Valley in those days meant work from sunup to sundown. Always plenty for a boy to do. But there were compensations—my rifle, my shot-gun, my horse. By the time I was ten I was master of all three and the hunting was good." Gooden began his career as a Western writer working in Hollywood beginning in 1919. *The Fox* (Universal, 1921) was the first feature film based on one of his screenplays and starred Harry Carey. For what remained of the decade, Gooden worked in the writing department at Universal, turning out scenarios for two-reelers and feature films as well as serials like *The Lawless Men* (Universal, 1927) based on Frank Spearman's popular character, railroad detective Whispering Smith. In the early 1930s Gooden left Hollywood to live in a stone cabin in the foothills of the San Jacinto, overlooking the sand dunes of the Colorado Desert. The life he led there was primitive: no electricity, no gasoline, no telephones, but he had his typewriter and began writing Western novels, beginning with *Cross Knife Ranch*, first published by Harrap in London in 1933. In fact, although he would eventually have various American publishers, the British editions of his novels continued to be published by Harrap until 1951. *Smoke Tree Range* (Kinsey, 1936), one of his finest stories, was brought to the screen by cowboy star Buck Jones in 1937, Gooden's only screen credit during that decade. Gooden had a distinguished prose style and was always able to evoke the Western terrain and animal life vividly as well as authentically address the psychology of many of his complex characters with the sophistication of a master storyteller.

Center Point Large Print
600 Brooks Road / PO Box 1
Thorndike ME 04986-0001 USA

(207) 568-3717

US & Canada:
1 800 929-9108
www.centerpointlargeprint.com